The heat of the explosion caressed
Henry's face, seeming to wrap around
him in its hot embrace.

There was only a bright light before him, one so powerful it blocked out everything else.

Try as he might, he couldn't remain conscious, and though he fought with every ounce of his iron will to stay awake, he slipped into a dark oblivion, one he wondered if he would ever awaken from.

ANTHONY GIANGREGORIO

DEAD WATER

DEAD INCURSION

BOOK 12

WHAT HAS COME BEFORE

Many years ago, a deadly bacterial outbreak escaped a lab to infect the lower atmosphere across America, unleashing an undead plague on the world.

With rain clouds filled with a killer bacterium, to venture outside in the rain was tantamount to suicide.

To get caught in the rain and exposed to the bacteria would be instant death. But that wasn't the end. Once dead, the host body would rise again, becoming an undead ghoul, wanting nothing more than to feed on the flesh of the living.

Time passed, and eventually the bacteria burned off in the atmosphere. But mankind still wasn't safe. The virus then mutated inside the host, and to be bitten by one of the living dead was a death sentence. Sickness followed by a painful death, only to return as one of the undead.

The United States was torn asunder; civilization collapsing like a house of cards in the weeks after the dead began to walk.

But mankind survived, eking out a dreary existence, always keeping one eye open for the attacking dead.

At least, that is until suddenly, for no known reason after years of existing, the walking dead collapsed and the threat was over.

But though the dead are gone, the world is still a very dangerous place, fraught with peril.

Gone are cell phones, the internet, restaurants, and shopping malls; now all lost relics of a culture slowly fading into history.

In this new apocalyptic world, a man follows the rules of the gun, where the strong are always right and the weak are usually dead. Major cities are nothing but blackened husks, nothing but giant tombs filled with the rotting corpses of the fallen dead.

Across America, towns have become small municipalities with makeshift walls protecting them from attackers. Strangers are not welcome and are either shot on sight or made to move on, that is, if they are not exploited by the rulers of the towns.

Through the destruction of what once was walks a man, crushing death beneath his steel-tipped boots. Before, he was an ordinary man, living a quiet life with a wife and a career, but the rules have changed and, so too, has he adapted, becoming a warrior of death who wields a gun with an iron fist, but shows mercy and wisdom when it is needed.

His name is Henry Watson, and with his fellow companions, Mary, Jimmy, Cindy and Sue by his side, he travels across a blighted landscape, searching for someplace where he and his friends can lay their heads down in safety.

Though life is fleeting, each breath means the possibility of one more day of survival, and a better future for all.

Chapter 1

Henry couldn't believe this was the end.

After so many years of battle, struggling to survive against the walking dead, only to end up perishing deep underground; it just wasn't right.

Glancing to his left, Sue stood firmly; legs spread apart, her .22 in her hands, firing at the attacking spider droids. Near her were the others, Jimmy, Cindy and Mary, each firing as fast as they could pull the triggers to their guns. The noise in the small confines was deafening, the air filled with the stink of cordite.

But underlying that din was the continuous clickety-clacks of the spider droids metal legs on the cement floor.

Only moments ago Henry had realized fighting back was a hopeless endeavor. Trapped by the droids, the first in the assault line even now jumping into the air at the companions, its pincers ready to tear and rend the soft flesh of the humans, the only thing left any of them could do was die, though he knew each of them would go down fighting, no matter how lost their cause was.

The security droids had come at the group only minutes ago, the droids' thirst for blood almost a tangible thing from the instant they arrived. Their emotionless red eyes seemed to glow with mechanical intelligence, and so far, all the companions had thrown at the gleaming silver machines had been for naught. Bullets only bounced off the shining carapaces, and though the impacts slowed them down, it did little to stop the killer sec machines.

Deep below ground inside Area 51, Henry had hoped the underground bunker would be the groups' salvation, after barely escaping the clutches of the brutal biker gang named the Skullfuckers, the chapter President Vincent out for far more than blood if he managed to capture the companions.

A desperate race had occurred, the companions managing to stay one step ahead of the murderous biker gang.

They had almost been caught by the gang upon reaching Area 51, but by sheer luck and some basic knowledge of government redoubts from a past exploit, the friends had found the hidden entrance and entered the bunker, only a moment before being caught by Vincent and his cronies.

A wounded Jimmy had quickly been brought to the Medical Bay to be given much-needed antibiotics to protect his gunshot wound from turning gangrenous. But no sooner did Jimmy receive the drugs than a wave of shining silver spider droids had appeared, attacking en masse.

Once more the companions had to run for their lives, dashing through the underground bunker, the sec droids nipping at their heels. They had almost made it, too, if not for hitting a dead end.

The end was only seconds away, and there was nothing Henry or any of the others could do but die valiantly.

As the first of the two dozen charging spider droids came soaring through the air at the companions, and Henry was bringing his arm forward to toss the last grenade, suddenly a retractable armor-plated bulkhead dropped down from the ceiling, moving faster than anyone could have imagined, cutting the humans off from the attacking spider droids. When the panel seated into the floor with a loud metallic clang, the passageway actually shook for a split-second from the sheer weight of the panel.

The first spider droid moving in the air ended up bouncing off the panel like a tennis ball, and it rebounded back into the other aerial droids behind it, all of them falling in a heap at the foot of the panel, legs kicking back and forth, pincers snapping on empty air. Undaunted, they quickly righted themselves and began to scratch and scrape at the blast-proof panel, which was far too thick, the metal made of sterner stuff than the exit door they had eaten through as if it had only been cardboard.

Scrabbling like dogs wanting to go out for a walk, they kept trying to cut into the panel, but no matter how much they tried, they barely made a mark on the smooth surface. Not knowing how to give up, their programming not allowing it, they continued to scratch and cut at the panel, and would not stop until their power cells finally ran down—whenever that might be.

On the opposite side of the panel, the five humans stopped firing in shock and surprise, a few stray bullets hitting the panel and ricocheting off into the ceiling. Henry pulled his throw of the grenade at the last instant, realizing the way was blocked, and quickly shoved the pin back into the orb before letting go of the handle. With a sigh of relief, he slid it back into a pocket for safe-keeping.

For a moment there wasn't a sound inside the corridor, and even the droids couldn't be heard on the opposite side of the thick panel. Ears ringing from the constant gunfire, each of them turned to look at one another, everyone confused as to why they were still alive—not that they weren't relieved of course.

It was just that it happened so fast it was too much to process.

Jimmy was the one to sum it up finally. "Uh, what the fuck just happened? We're not dead."

There was a soft whirring and the camera in the ceiling swiveled to look down at the group, Henry spotting it first. "Looks like someone's watching us right now. Maybe that's who dropped that panel and saved us—or trapped us, depending on how you look at it."

All eyes turned to take in the camera, which glared back at them emotionally. Jimmy, being Jimmy, flipped off the camera, then flashed everyone a wise-ass grin as he shot out the camera from the wall so they couldn't be monitored anymore. The report of the shotgun was deafening in the small space. A few pellets that didn't lodge in the ceiling buzzed around the room before losing momentum and dropping to the floor.

"Oh nice one, Jimmy!" Mary yelled, angry as hell. "Way to endear whoever's watching us. Did it even cross your mind that if they raise that panel again we're all dead?"

Jimmy opened his mouth to reply, then closed it, as he pondered Mary's muted words through his ringing ears. Finally, he said, "Ah, no, not really. Shit, sorry, I guess I shouldn't have done that."

"No, you shouldn't have," Henry shouted, his voice controlled though he was also angry, the yelling more to allow himself to hear his voice over the ringing in his ears. It was like he was living inside a church tower, the ringing was so bad. He walked around the small space they occupied, searching for any weaknesses and finding none. "But it's done now so let's see what happens next." Now that he knew about dropping bulkheads, he realized that the dead end wasn't really a dead end. The wall they'd come up against when retreating from the spider droids was just another bulkhead panel, not a true wall. He told the others as much.

Jimmy moved up to close to Henry so he could yell into his ear. "Then, old man, why don't you use that grenade and blow the other section away and we can escape."

Henry shook his head. "No simple explosives are gonna take out those panels, Jimmy. Even if we wanted to try it, the concussion when the grenade goes off, and us with no where to go for shelter, would probably kill us."

"Huh, good point, well, it was worth a shot." He moved over to the left-hand wall and slid down it, stretching out his wounded leg. "I'm gonna sit down for a bit if we're hanging around for a while. My leg's killing me. When you gave me that antibiotic shot, a painkiller would have been nice, too."

"Yeah, sorry, you're right," Henry agreed. "I'm sure we could have found some aspirin or Motrin or something."

Sue went over to Jimmy while reaching into her pocket. "Here, Jimmy, I have some aspirin." She handed him the small white bottle.

"Awesome, Sue, you're fantastic." He swallowed four pills dry, wincing as he choked them down. He tossed her the bottle and she pocketed it once more.

"So what do we do now?" Mary asked as she looked around the small space like a caged animal. The others did the same, feeling the tension of their capture by some unknown person or persons. They all knew in any given situation, the first few moments of a trap being sprung were the best chance of escape, but there was nothing they could do at the moment.

Everyone was tense, walking a razor's edge, knowing they were trapped like rats in a cage. Jimmy made a comment and Mary yelled at him again, then Cindy jumped between them, defending Jimmy from Mary. Sue tried to get everyone to get along, and finally Henry yelled at the top of his voice, "Enough already! All of you stop fighting with each other. It's not accomplishing anything!" He glared at each of them. "Whoever trapped us here's got us dead to rights. All we can do is be ready for what comes next."

"Like the panel going up and the robots coming at us again?" Jimmy asked.

Henry shook his head adamantly. "No way, Jimmy, if whoever has us wanted us dead like that, they didn't need to drop the panel. No, they have something else in mind."

"You got that right, sonny," a voice said from a hidden speaker somewhere in the ceiling. The voice was distorted and it was difficult to tell whether it was a man or woman, young or old, though the voice using the word 'sonny' gave everyone the feeling the owner was older than all of them.

A small four-inch panel slid open on the ceiling in the far corner, and another camera dropped down.

Jimmy got up, aiming his shotgun at the new camera as well, finger in the trigger, but the voice quickly snapped out, "You shoot that camera, sonny, and you're all dead. I'll let the gas in there and you'll all be picking daisies come morning." There was a dry cackle, unmistakable even with the distortion. "Or maybe I'll just let those droids in to finish ya off. Now all of you drop your guns and knives. Do it now or you're all dead! The game's over and I win. Simon says I win, so you have to drop your guns. Do it now!"

With no other option, Henry placed his Glock and panga on the floor, the grenade as well, as the camera operator would have seen him with it moments ago. The others followed him, disarming one at a time.

"What did we get ourselves into here?" Mary asked, referring to them coming to the installation. From the second they'd stepped foot inside the complex they'd been fighting for their lives. No one responded; there was no need.

"That's good, that's real good," the voice said, satisfied. "Put your hands on your heads, too."

With no choice in the matter, the group followed instructions.

For a full minute, there was no response from the hidden speaker, and Henry was beginning to get worried. But then the panel that had been at their backs, not the one holding off the spider droids, slid upwards into the ceiling, a hiss of compressed air filling the space as the bulkhead retracted.

No one moved, not knowing if they should or not, and not wanting to push their luck, at least not before knowing who they were up against.

"Okay, you get to live a little longer. The Leader says you may keep breathin'. You should know if there had been any sign of aggression you would've gotten the gas."

"That's good to know," Henry said. "Can we put our hands down now?"

"Huh? What? No, I mean yes, yes, okay. Sure, okay, yes, you can lower your hands." There was the briefest pause. "But don't touch your weapons!" There was a pause, "Are any of you rotters? Any of you bit?"

"What do you mean? I don't understand." Henry looked at the others, but no one seemed to know either.

But then Sue offered, "I think he's asking if we're deaders, Henry. You know, zombies."

"Deaders?" Henry shook his head. Did the voice not know the undead plague was over? Well, whether he did or not, Henry wasn't about to tell him. Information was power, and perhaps if the voice from the hidden speaker didn't know the walking dead had been destroyed, it could come in handy at a later date. So he simply replied, "No, none of us our rotters, we're all healthy."

"That one has a wound. He wasn't bit?"

Henry looked at Jimmy, who shrugged. "No, he was shot. I got the bullet out, which was why we went to the Medical Bay, to get some antibiotics."

"Yes, the Leader saw you there, saw you wake up the clickers."

"Clickers?" Cindy asked, curious.

"The spider bots; the security droids for this complex," the crackly voice explained. "They run on their own, can't be turned off. The Leader's tried but it can't be done."

"Mean little bastards," Henry said. "Thanks for saving us from them."

There was no response for a full two minutes this time, and Henry was beginning to wonder if the speaker had halted the conversation, but then the voice said, "The Leader wants to know how you got into this place. This place is fortified, security and all that. No one should be able to get in here without B-10 clearance. You people don't look like you have that."

"We don't," Henry replied.

"Then how the blazes did you get in here?"

"That's a long story," Mary said, speaking up.

"The Leader has time. All the time in the world and then a little more. With rotters topside there's nothing much to do anymore."

Jimmy opened his mouth to say something in reply but Henry glared at him, assuming it was about the end of the walking dead. The look on his face told the younger man to be quiet. Jimmy understood and halted his speech.

"You have the code to gain access topside. You got to have it or else no other way to get in here. No one else has ever come, you see. Not since the rotters first came around here topside. This place was sealed up tight, tighter than a nun's pussy, by golly. No alarms went off either, so you got in here all legal-like. Unless you used the transfer station, but no one has ever come here that way. So you must have come from topside. The bots found you but they'll go after anyone who don't know about them. Damn things, killed three of my friends. Almost got me too, but I was too fast for them. Closed off that section of the complex, trapped them there. Not get me. The Leader is safe, will always be safe. 'Bots, rotters, nothing will ever hurt the Leader." As fast as the rambling had begun it ceased, silence once more descending over the group of five.

Henry glanced at Mary and Cindy, each returning his gaze with the same seriousness on their faces. They were in a bad situation once more. The crackly voice, whether male or female, though it felt like it was male, was crazy, there was no doubt about it. Whether they liked it or not, they were totally in the owner of that voice's power. Whoever ran the complex would have access to all kinds of weapons, whether it be the gas they'd been threatened with or who knew what else. Or if the hidden voice wanted to, all it needed to do was open the other panel and let the spider droids back at them. The companions were at the hidden voice's complete mercy, and when that person was nuts, it wasn't a very good feeling.

Mary looked at Henry and then up at the speaker, wanting to talk. He nodded for her to go ahead.

"Yes, we have the code to gain access into this complex. We found it on a map taken from some cannies. We think they got it from someone else, probably someone who came from here. We were being chased by a biker gang and we came here hoping to escape them."

A cackle of laughter came from the hidden speaker. "So you didn't know what you were coming to. Took a chance and came here."

"Yes," Henry said. "That's right. We come in peace. We're good people. We don't hurt anyone unless they're trying to do us harm first."

"You don't mean the Leader no harm?"

Sue took a step forward, as if it mattered. "No, we come in friendship. Please believe us, we're decent people just trying to stay alive. We could really use your help."

The hidden speaker went silent. One minute passed, two minutes, then three. The tension inside the small space was palpable, everyone ready to explode into action even if it was just to break the anticipation of what was coming next. None of them were any good at waiting for the other shoe to drop.

Jimmy stood up, going to Henry so he could whisper into an ear. "We need to run for it, old man. This guy's bat shit crazy. We need to make a break for it."

"Oh really? And where are we running to exactly? We have those security droids on one side and falling panels on the other. Even if we got past the one he just raised, there's sure to be more."

"Well," Jimmy replied. "We can't just sit here and wait for the axe to come down either." He moved away, leaning against the wall to rest his leg, arms crossed over his chest, angry at his help-lessness. The corridor was wide open before them, but he also knew Henry had a point. Though the way looked clear, it was far from safe to use.

Mary moved close to join the conversation, Sue and Cindy listening as well.

"Who do you think he is? That is if it is a 'he.' And who's this Leader he talked about? Maybe a commander or someone of this base?"

"Could be. But I don't think so. I think it's a man, too. Don't know why, just do. Sounds old as hell, too—and like Jimmy said, bat shit crazy."

With no response from the hidden voice, they busied themselves by gathering their weapons and gear bags and placing them in a neat pile, making sure they were ready if needed. Then everyone sat down and waited, knowing there was really nothing they could do, and their fates were in the hands of someone else. Everyone wanted to sleep, for they'd been on the run non-stop for more than a day, but it wasn't possible. They needed to be ready for whatever came next.

Every now and then, when no one was speaking, they heard the faintest of scratching from the opposite side of the panel, where the spider droids were no doubt there, still trying to gain access to the humans beyond.

When it was around the fifteen minute mark, and everyone was sitting silently, waiting for news, the hidden speaker crackled to life once more.

"The Leader has decided your fate. Yes, indeed, your fates have been contemplated but good. For now, you've been given a reprieve. For you see, only those who have no hate in their heart may enter this place, may seek salvation. But I'm still not convinced you all can be trusted, not yet, so do as I say and you can continue to live."

"Uhm, thanks?" Henry said, not too sure that was what he should say.

"Are you all hungry?"

"Hell yes, we're hungry," Jimmy said quickly, rubbing his stomach. "I feel like I haven't eaten in years."

"Then you may break your fast. Leave your weapons where they lay. You won't need them down here under the Leader's protection. On this side of the complex the bots can't get you. Walk down the hallway and take the first right you get to, then follow it till you see the cafeteria. There you may eat what you like from the freezers. But clean up after yourselves. The Leader keeps a clean complex and will be watching you at all times."

With Henry leading the way, the group set off down the hallway, the weapons staying on the floor where they left them. None of them liked going deeper into the base unarmed; they all basically felt naked and vulnerable. But with no other choice, they did as they were told.

Every so often they went by another camera, which remained immobile to their passing. They walked for over twenty minutes, and Henry reckoned they had walked more than half a mile before finally coming to another panel, which blocked off access to what lay beyond. A sign on the wall in the shape of an arrow pointed past the panel, the word CAFETERIA on it.

Everyone stared at the panel before them.

Jimmy tapped it with his knuckles, hearing the same echo, telling of the density of the other ones. He shrugged. "Was worth a try."

They waited for a full five minutes but nothing happened. Unease took over once more, everyone wondering what was going to happen next, and not liking that they had no control over it.

Finally, Henry stepped over to the closest security camera, glared up at it and said, "What the hell are you waiting for? Open the door. Look, I'm starting to get a little tired of this. We told you we're friendly. We put down our weapons and left them behind us. What more do you want from us? Either kill us or trust us, but do something for Christ's sake! There must be enough people down here to outnumber us, so we want to see this Leader of yours face to face."

He stared at the camera, waiting, wondering if he would hear the hiss of gas filling the corridor any second, or the clicking of the spider droids, the Leader calling Henry's bluff, but instead more dry cackling came from another hidden speaker.

"You got some balls on you, sonny. I'll give you that. The Leader is impressed. Very well, go, eat, enjoy." The panel slid up, retracting into the ceiling, the hydraulics hissing once more. "The Leader will see you later."

With the passage now open, the five friends continued onward, only walking a few yards before entering the cafeteria itself. Behind them, the panel slid down once more, locking them inside the cafeteria.

Entering the large space, the main thing they all took in was the normalcy of it all. Looking like a cafeteria from a hospital or a college, the floor clean, the soft hum of appliances, such as refrigerator and freezers, it all seemed far too normal from what they were used to.

As everyone spread out, with the exception of Jimmy, who sat down immediately, wanting to rest his leg, they soon found a fully stocked freezer, filled with freeze-dried steaks and vegetables, as well as pies and cakes. A vending machine had candy still in it, though the candy was years out of date, and when Henry went to a glass display case, he was shocked to see Coke and Pepsi cans inside. Taking a few cans, he carried them to the others as they all joined Jimmy at a long table. He handed them out, and a moment later there was the sound of cans opening, that particular sound they knew so well as the seal was popped and the air inside escaped. Everyone drank the warm soda fast, as if they needed to before the can dissolved from their hands and they realized it was all a dream.

Sue was the first to get up, and she went to the back of the cafeteria, pulling out a few different meats and veggies from a freezer. "You all have never seen me in the kitchen. I'm going to cook us up a feast."

"You need any help?" Mary asked.

"No, dear, I'm actually looking forward to this. I'm going to tune out everything and just focus on cooking. It'll be a nice change."

"Okay," Cindy called, "but if you want help, just ask."

"You just relax and look after your man, Cindy, and let me take care of fixing the meal."

"That reminds me," Henry said, looking to Jimmy. "We need to check that bandage." He spotted a First Aid kit on a far wall. "Mary, would you go get that?"

"Sure."

Jimmy stretched out his leg, but Henry shook his head. "Nope. Drop 'em sport, so I can get at it easily."

Reluctantly, Jimmy did as ordered, Mary holding back a grin as she handed Henry the First Aid kit. One pant leg was torn, ripped and covered in drying blood from where Henry had cut into the material to get at the wound earlier. Jimmy was in sore need of a new pair of pants.

Jimmy glared at Mary. "Can we have some privacy, please?"

She smiled, unable to hold it back. "I think I'll go help Sue, even if she says she doesn't want it." She walked away, leaving Henry with Jimmy and Cindy.

Henry peeled away the bandage, then wiped up the dried blood, checking the wound for infection. "So far so good, Jimmy. Hopefully, that's the Cipro fighting off any infection, though it's too early to tell for sure. You know, when I took out that bullet, it wasn't the most sanitary of operations."

Jimmy winced as Henry began wrapping the wound with a new layer of fresh gauze. "Hey, old man, that's me. I'm like Superman when it comes to fighting off diseases."

"Sure you are," Henry patronized. "Just try and stay off it for a few days and I think you'll be good as new in a week or so."

"I'll do my best, but I can't speak for everyone that's always trying to kill me—along with the rest of you guys."

Cindy chuckled at that, smiling as she watched Henry and Jimmy together. It never ceased to amaze her how the two interacted. Like father and son, though she knew never to use that analogy around either of them. The two men were so similar sometimes she wondered if Henry wasn't really the younger man's father, for he sure acted like it.

"Yeah, good point," Henry said.

Jimmy pulled up his tattered pants, then sat down again, stretching the wounded leg out. Henry washed up in a porcelain sink mounted to the wall, wanting to get the blood off his hands, both new and old. The liquid soap in the dispenser was too thick to come out, the moisture having dried to a cement-like consistency after years of being inside the container. Still, he did the best he could.

Soon, the scent of cooking meat filled the cafeteria, causing everyone's stomachs to begin rumbling, and mouths to salivate.

When Sue finally carried out a large pan filled to the top with steak and chicken, and Mary followed with a large pan of steamed vegetables, it was like they had all died and gone to food heaven.

Placing the food on the table, both women looked down proudly. Then Sue raised a finger to halt everyone, and said, "One more thing, don't touch anything." She ran off, back into the kitchen.

"Well, hurry up," Jimmy yelled. "I'm starving over here!"

Sue returned a few seconds later, holding plastic silverware and Styrofoam plates. "It's not good for the environment but then I think the environment is the least of our problems nowadays." She handed them out, each of the group taking the stuff with a nod and a smile.

"Okay, dig in," Sue said and just like that, everything that had happened to the five friends thus far was forgotten, their attention solely focused on eating.

For the next thirty minutes they ate, and talked and laughed, simply enjoying being alive and together. Though Henry constantly let his eyes scan the large space for signs of danger, by the time he was finished eating, he was getting a little lazy in that department, and all he wanted to do was sleep.

All eyes were heavy, and it took all their effort could to stay awake.

Sue made coffee, and though slightly stale, the caffeine helped to wake them up, if only barely.

A full hour had passed from the moment Sue carried out the food, and as they sat around the table, sleepily despite the coffee, the crackly voice they had come to know began speaking again. "Okay, you've eaten. Now it's time to meet the Leader."

Henry and the others all sat straight up as the blast panel that had closed behind them upon entering the cafeteria began to slowly retract into the ceiling, exposing what lay beyond.

Henry was the first to stand up when he saw what was on the far side of the panel, and he scratched his head in surprise. "Well, I'll be. I don't believe it."

Chapter 2

Major Ishmael Varakov stirred in his bedroll, his eyes cracking slightly so he could take in his surroundings. For a brief moment he forgot where he was, but as his mind focused, it all came crashing back to him.

He was still at the radar installation in Alaska, along with his men, after crossing the Bering Strait from Russia, in the hope of invading America. His small army of forty men was the scouting party, to test the defenses of the United States now that the walking dead were no more. But so far there had been no resistance, only a few pathetic villages that his men had ransacked, taken whatever they wanted, and leaving the rest for the wolves. Behind his small army, lay nothing but spilled blood, death and destruction.

The night before there had been an attack by a band of snipers, but even this paltry excuse for an ambush was quickly put down. A female prisoner was taken hostage, and her screams as the men had raped and tortured her, had gone long into the night, until finally ceasing altogether. An Asian man was also captured, but the man had given up nothing, so Varakov had ordered him killed and the body discarded like trash.

Late that night a powerful storm had descended over the area, the wind howling, the temperature dropping.

By the next morning the storm still hadn't let up, so he had given orders to remain within the warm buildings until it passed.

That was two days ago, and as he opened his eyes on the third morning of his forced stay, he listened for the sounds of the blowing wind over the snoring of Streltsy — his second-in-command — and the few other men sharing the room with him.

Nothing. All was silent outside the walls.

Rising, he stretched and yawned before going to the door, and carefully bracing himself, lest the wind force it out of his hands, he opened the door a crack.

Bright sunshine filtered in, blinding him with its brilliance as it reflected off the pristine snow. Feeling the need to empty his bladder, he stepped outside into the snowdrift that had accumulated against the building almost up to his knees.

It was a beautiful day. The sky was a deep blue, only a few stray clouds drifting overhead, and those thin and wispy. The sun felt good on his face, though the temperature was still below freezing. With steam billowing from his nose as he breathed, he went to the side of the building and urinated.

There were no signs of the corpses of the Asian man and the boy who'd been shot in the doorway—the latter being one of his men who had been hit by one of the snipers at the beginning of the attack. Both bodies had been dumped in the snow days ago. Not even a few scraps of bloody clothing remained under the new layer of ice and snow.

The wolves had taken care of that he figured. On the first night the beasts had crept into camp under the cover of darkness, and had fed on the two bodies while the corpses were still warm, and later, had returned to drag the frozen bodies away to feed on them at their leisure. Varakov had been told this by the guards who walked the perimeter, making sure no other attacks would occur.

Having spotted the wolves the first time, the guards had tried to scare them away, but all they'd received in response was a rising of hackles and low growls. The guards had retreated, not wanting to tangle with the ferocious killers, especially not over worthless dead bodies. Even their firearms gave them very little comfort against the hungry beasts of the wild.

The wolves were always with him, Varakov surmised with pride, as if the animals sensed that wherever the major went, slaughtered corpses would be left in his wake.

Since the sniper attack there had been no more incidents, other than a fight that had broken out between two of the men over rations. One man had accused the other of stealing rations, while the other said it was the first man who had been doing the stealing.

Varakov had come to the building of the altercation, Streltsy and five more armed soldiers behind him, not that he needed them. He felt confident in his authority to have gone there alone, but Streltsy would not take no for an answer, so in the end, Varakov had let the men accompany him.

"What is this about?" Varakov had demanded of the room, and of the two men who'd been placed on their knees before him.

The Quartermaster stepped forward from the crowd of other soldiers gathered around the two accused men. He quickly explained what the men were accused of.

Varakov looked down at both soldiers kneeling before him as he took in what he was told. "Well, what do you two have to say for yourselves?"

The first man spoke up first. "I did not steal anything, Comrade Major, I swear." He pointed to the man beside him. "It was Uri who did it, and now he tries to make me his scapegoat."

"Is this true, Uri?"

"It is a lie, Comrade Major," Uri said quickly, holding his chin high in the air. "I am no thief, and even if I was, I would not risk punishment for a few extra scraps of meat. He lies, too scared to take responsibility for his actions. I promise you, Comrade Major, if it had been me, I would be man enough to tell you."

"I see." Before the second man had time to register what happened next, Varakov pulled his sidearm and shot him in the face, the 9mm round hitting the soldier in the left eye. The soldiers standing behind the kneeling man jumped backwards in shock when the dead man's brains splattered across their legs and waists. The body fell over, blood leaking from the massive head wound to pool on the floor, the eye destroyed, a gaping hole left in the bullet's wake.

Uri watched his partner die, and turned to look up at Varakov. "Thank you for believing me, Comrade Major."

"Who says I do?" Moving calmly, as if his next action was no more than a casual gesture, Varakov shot Uri in the face as well, killing the man instantly, the execution a replay of the first soldier's, another pool of red covering the floor.

No one spoke inside the room, the soldiers shocked to see both men slaughtered like cattle. Though hard men all, witnessing the brutal deaths of two of their own was still a sobering deal.

Major Ishmael Varakov looked at his men as they returned his gaze. "The matter is settled. To me, they were both guilty. If not for stealing then for a lack of loyalty." He holstered his Makarov PM. "Let that be a lesson to the rest of you." His gaze fell on the Quartermaster. "Keep the men in line, or else next time it will be you with an extra hole in the head. Do you understand me?"

The Quartermaster swallowed hard and nodded. "Yes, Comrade Major, of course, sir." He looked ill, and no doubt wondered if he might end up dead in the next few seconds, despite the warning.

Turning, Varakov exited the building, Streltsy and the men with him following. As they crossed the ground covered in fresh snowfall to return to their own barracks, Streltsy moved up beside Varakov and asked, "Comrade Major, we have already lost too many men on this excursion. To me, killing one would have sufficed. I must ask if it was truly necessary to kill both of them."

Varakov stopped walking, his breath pluming out before him with each exhale. He made sure the soldiers following them were out of earshot. "Comrade Streltsy, the men are not just soldiers, they are murderers and rapists, and some even worse. Remember, they were taken from the gulag. Give these men a second chance and they will use that chance to knife you in the back. They only understand one thing. The fist."

"Ah, I see. Forgive me, Comrade Major. I should have known better than to question your decision."

Varakov began walking again, Streltsy also. "No, Comrade Streltsy, do not think that way. I need a second who will question me if he believes I am mistaken. I do not need a 'yes' man, I need someone I can trust." He stopped walking and placed a hand on Streltsy's shoulder, his fingers gripping the man tightly, but not so tight to cause discomfort. "That man is you. We are far from our home, my friend. We only have each other to watch our backs." He released Streltsy, but not before squeezing one more time for assurance.

"Thank you, Comrade Major. I will not let you down."

"See that you do not." When they reached the building Varakov quickly opened the door to enter, wanting to get out of the cold. "Pass the word to the other men. After a quick morning meal, we break camp and begin moving once more. Anchorage, and the spoils of war it will provide, awaits us." He didn't wait for a reply from Streltsy, knowing there was no need. Stepping inside, the heat of the fire striking him in the face, the warmth a welcome respite after being outside, he closed the door on his second-in-command.

Chapter 3

"You gotta be fucking kidding me," Jimmy said in disbelief, as he turned in his chair to see what Henry was already looking at.

The others quickly followed, until everyone was staring at the entrance to the cafeteria and what stood in the doorway, all with surprised expressions on their faces. Sue moved closer to Henry, taking his arm in hers, wanting to be close to him for whatever went down next.

Though the moment was about as tense as it could get, Henry still felt himself noticing how her right breast pressed up against his arm. How he felt the softness of her body pressing into his side, and could detect the scent of her hair, which was from a bottle of shampoo she traveled with.

In the entrance to the cafeteria, stood a hunched-over, single old man, holding a gun pointed at the group. On each hip he wore a sidearm, and two bandoliers filled with an assortment of different caliber ammunition criss-crossed his chest, making him look like an extra from a war movie. The weapons seemed to weigh him down a bit too much, as if a child was playing dress up with his father's armaments. He wore a threadbare janitorial uniform, instead of what Henry would have expected, such as a military uniform, although there was a collection of military insignia pinned to the right side of the chest, all clustered together messily, as if that same child was also playing dress-up with his daddy's medals, too.

But what was also so surprising was that the man was alone. Henry had expected when their hosts finally showed themselves, that it would be a compliment of armed security guards, uniformed men covered from head to toe in riot gear, holding state-of-the-art weapons.

Not one lone janitor.

It was hard to discern the man's true age by just looking at him. He was so hunched over and bent that he might have been sixty or even ninety. His hair was bone white and hung across his shoulders in stray clumps, as did the long beard hanging almost to his belt buckle. Around the mouth, the beard was stained yellow from nicotine, and bits of food from past meals still clung to wisps of hair.

With so much hair covering his face, the features of the man were hard to see, but embedded within the stray strands, a pointed nose, thin lips and deep-set blue eyes could be detected within the creases of flesh. He stood no more than five feet two inches tall and couldn't have weighed more than one hundred and fifty pounds soaking wet. There was a deformation to the left shoulder, which caused him to look like a hunchback due to his posture.

"That's an HK submachine gun he's holding," Henry said softly so the others could hear.

"How do you know that?" Jimmy asked.

"I was flipping through a gun magazine I'd found one time, and I remember seeing that gun, that's all."

"Oh yeah?"

"Yeah," Henry replied. "Seems guns are our lives now, I do my best to read up whenever possible. That gun impressed me." He paused for a moment, recalling what he'd read. "If I'm right, that's an M-5. When fully loaded it weighs around seven pounds. Not too good for distance, but within twenty feet, like we are now, that gun would rip us to shreds before we could scream."

"Thanks for the info, old man, I feel so much better now that I know what kind of gun is gonna kill me at any second."

"Welcome to Area 51. I am the Leader of this complex," the old man said. "Did you speak the truth when you said you come in peace?"

Henry felt confused at the appearance of the old man. Where were the scientists and military personnel that would have been living on the base? Could it be true there was no one left but this one old dotard?

Henry took a step away from the table, his hands out where the man could see them. He felt naked without his weapons, and thinking back to where his Glock and panga lay in the passageway somewhere inside the complex, he felt a longing for them like a child to a security blanket.

The old man took a few steps forward, entering the cafeteria. As he moved closer, Henry was able to get a better look at the man's eyes. The way they darted back and forth meant that he was either nervous or unstable; but Henry also saw that he was alert, the eyes sharp and focused.

Henry stopped after moving a few feet closer. "I told you already we aren't your enemy. We mean you no harm if you feel the same. We were being chased by a group of bikers and we came here out of desperation."

The old man nodded. "Ah yes, the hooligans. The Leader has seen them; they gather around the exit into the complex. They have made camp and are waiting for you to leave here."

Henry filed that bit of information away for later use. Instead, he asked, "So, are we okay to stay here for a while? At least until either the bikers leave or we come up with a way to deal with them. That is, unless there's another way out of here." He figured there had to be more than one entrance/exit to and from the base.

The old man shook his head. "Only one way in or out now. There were three others before but those ways were destroyed years ago to keep the rotters from getting inside." He hesitated and added lower than before, "Or keep 'em from getting out." He seemed to think back. "But no more rotters anymore. Nope. They all died." Then he came back to the present. "What are your names?"

"I'm Henry Watson, and this is Jimmy Cooper. The young woman with the dark hair is Mary Roberts and beside her is Cindy Jansen." He gestured to Sue. "This is Sue Anders."

The old man seemed to pause when Sue was introduced, his gaze lingering on her for so long that Henry could see Sue become uncomfortable. Finally, Henry cleared his throat to get the old man's attention. "What's your name, friend?"

"My name is Adam, and I'm the Leader of this place. I am the law here, so if you cross me, I make the punishment and the punishment is always death."

"Good to know," Henry said, not letting the threat get to him. He quickly glanced at the others, especially Jimmy, to make sure they didn't respond in a way that would upset the old man. If the old coot had wanted them dead, heaven knew he'd had countless times to make it so.

"So, where's everybody else that lives here?" Jimmy asked.

"Did you eat well?" Adam asked, ignoring Jimmy's question.

"Yes," Cindy said, speaking up. "Thank you. Sue made us a meal. It was wonderful."

"We haven't had meat like that in a long time," Mary added. "Usually it seems like we're eating out of expired cans of food or MRE's."

Adam cackled, his voice cracking. "Well, dearie, there's enough food to last your entire lifetime down here. Hell, two lifetimes!"

Henry took a step closer, Adam swinging his M-5 towards Henry's stomach. Henry raised his hands and stopped moving. "Our weapons. When do we get them back?"

"All in good time, sonny, all in good time. I need to make sure your heart is contrite, that you have no violence in your souls." He looked at his feet for a moment, as if thinking. "This is unprecedented, you see. No one new has ever come down here before. Never. Not even by the transfer station."

That was the second time the old man had used that term and it had now piqued Henry's curiosity. If it was a way for people to arrive, then perhaps it could be a way to leave when the time came, one that would have them exiting far away from Vincent and his cronies. If the opportunity came to search the complex, he would make sure to see if he could find this 'transfer station,' whatever it was.

Adam stepped fully inside the cafeteria. Turning around slightly, he aimed a small black box at the opening, and the heavy panel dropped down from the ceiling. Henry watched, figuring the box was some sort of remote control when Adam wasn't in the control room that operated the complex's defenses.

Adam moved around the table the companions were at until he was standing at the head of it, all eyes watching him warily. The geriatric was a wild card, and from past experiences, the group knew not to take chances with wild cards, but they also weren't in a position to do anything at the moment but wait.

Jimmy leaned in close to Henry, as the older warrior rejoined the group at the table. "We can take this old coot easy," he whispered. "There's five of us and one of him, for Christ's sake."

"No," Henry responded, his voice a whisper. "He could kill half of us before we take him down with that room sweeper. Leave it, we'll bide our time for now and see how this plays out."

"I think it's a mistake," Jimmy replied.

"Duly noted, now shut up about it."

Adam was busy picking from the food left on the table.

"Help yourself," Sue said. "We're all finished anyway and it's really all your food anyway."

"Don't mind if I do," Adam cackled. He sat down and pulled the entire platter towards him, digging into a bloody steak with his left hand, using his teeth to tear chunks from the meat. His right hand placed the M-5 on the table, but his hand never left the weapon, a statement that he was still on guard and wary.

His mouth full of food, the small old man said, while spitting bits of meat onto the table, "When you have been cleared, all of you will be allowed to explore this facility. But only when you have been cleared."

"How long does that take?" Cindy asked.

Adam shrugged, his bony shoulders barely moving. "Don't know. Your faces were scanned and have been inputted into the computer. If no warnings come back, then you aren't terrorists or something like that; then you'll be cleared and your weapons will be returned to you."

"Terrorists?" Mary said in disbelief. "Adam, when was the last time you were outside? You do know what's been going on out there, don't you?"

Adam stopped eating and glared at Mary. "Of course I do, dearie. I'm old, I'm not a fool. Fit as a fiddle. I am, yes, yes, that's right. I'm fit as a fiddle floating down the river. The rotters took over the world. They tried to do it down here, too, but they were stopped." He continued eating, not elaborating. Then he had a coughing fit, and seconds passed with Henry wondering if the old man might die right there of a heart attack, but eventually, he regained his composure. Spittle coated his beard and he wiped it away with the back of a filthy sleeve of his tattered janitorial uniform. On the right chest pocket, the name **Stan** was embroidered, which seemed strange given the old coot said his name was

Adam. Just another mystery of this place, and the old man was added to the collection, Henry figured.

Annoyed at the crazy janitor, Jimmy leaned back in his chair and made a circle with his thumb and forefinger while the old man coughed. He began miming jacking-off, making sure his arm was low and hidden behind the table so that Adam couldn't see the movement. But when he glanced at Mary, he saw her frowning in disproval. Jimmy stopped his action and smiled at her, giving her an apologetic grin; she looked away. "So who died and made you the leader of this place anyway?" Jimmy asked sarcastically when Adam had fully recovered from his coughing fit.

But the old man either didn't get the sarcasm or didn't care. Instead, he gave Jimmy a hard smile that had the younger man cringing. "Why, sonny, everyone did."

Chapter 4

When Adam was finished eating, he directed the companions to leave the cafeteria with him.

"What about cleaning all this up?" Sue asked, the mess of the eaten meal spread out on the table. "The kitchen needs some cleaning too from all the cooking I did."

"Leave it, dearie," Adam said, leering at Sue a little longer than Henry would have preferred. The old man's eyes seemed to hover over Sue's breasts, his eyes caressing her neck and face. "You can come back later if you pass the tests. All of you."

He gestured with the barrel of the M-5 for them to march, then raised the blast panel so everyone could leave the cafeteria.

Henry was in the lead once more, Jimmy hobbling beside Mary and Cindy. They wanted to help him but he'd waved them off, wanting to walk for himself. He was healing fast already, and though sore as hell and with a heavy limp, he could manage on his own.

The group walked for another twenty minutes, Adam barking directions when they were needed. They weaved in and out of corridors, until even the best among them would have been hard-pressed to return to the cafeteria by memory alone. Some hallways had large doors with signs stating they were laboratories, and others were being used as office space. One sign on the wall caught Henry's eye as he passed it. It showed the way to the Armory. He filed that away as someplace he would want to visit if given the opportunity.

Halfway to where Adam was taking them, Henry glanced over his shoulder to Sue, who was last in line, Adam trailing close behind her. The lecherous old coot was staring at Sue's ass as she walked, drool sliding out of the corner of his mouth like a starving man having a dangling turkey leg held before him.

A rise of jealousy filled Henry and he slowed and let the others pass him, until he was even with Sue. Then, taking her by the shoulders, he placed her in front of him, making sure to flash Adam an annoyed look before doing so. If the old coot understood the male posturing, he didn't respond. But he did let out a dry cackle, while wiping his nose on the back of his soiled shirtsleeve.

"What did you do that for?" Sue asked, a little too naïve to understand what was happening.

"No reason," he said flatly.

Eventually, Adam called out for the group to stop walking. Jimmy was the most relieved. Though he'd started out with good spirits, limping but making do, now his leg was paining him terribly, and he desperately wanted to get off it and rest.

Adam aimed his little box at the wall before the group and there was the hiss of hydraulics; the wall began to retract into the ceiling a moment later.

"This place is a maze," Mary said to Cindy.

"I know. I am so lost right now." Cindy looked at Henry. "You think this place is bigger than that one in Colorado?"

Henry shrugged. "Maybe. It's hard to know for sure without seeing the entire blueprints. The maps on the wall probably don't show all of it, only what they want personnel to see."

"Go on inside, go on. This is your new home till you're cleared." Adam gestured for everyone to enter the now exposed entranceway.

Mary and Cindy were first inside, then Jimmy, Sue, and finally Henry, who stopped at the doorway, not looking what was within the room, but only having eyes for Adam. Behind him, Henry could hear the others marveling at something, and they all sounded pleased. He wasn't concerned where Adam had taken them. "So what now?" Henry asked, standing about seven feet from Adam. "We've complied with everything you've asked of us since we came down here."

"Now you rest," Adam said. "When you wake the answers will be supplied. For who lives and who dies, who walks under the sun and who lies before the moon." He began to laugh, before it degenerated into a coughing fit.

Henry considered trying to attack the old man while he was coughing, and he even took a step closer to make his thought reality, but no sooner did he move than the M-5 came up and the barrel went level with Henry's chest. The coughing fit stopped and the eyes of the old man grew clear. He said nothing, just stared at Henry, his finger caressing the trigger of the gun.

"Cant blame a guy for trying," Henry said with what he hoped was a charming grin.

The barrel of the M-5 flicked subtly, like a man nodding, and Henry knew exactly what that slight movement meant. Stepping back, he turned and passed through the doorway, the panel dropping on his heels so he had to step lightly or risk getting hit.

Once more he and the others were locked inside what was basically their prison. But like before in the cafeteria, where though confined they had access to food, now they were locked within a large dormitory.

The dorm was a long room with over fifty beds in it, each section of ten—five beds to a side—having a partition that could be used if the sections needed to be separated. Each bed had a footlocker at the foot of the bed and a tall metal locker at the head, as well as a small metal nightstand. There was a full communal shower, with twenty showerheads, all lined up; sparkling white tile adorned the walls and floor of the bathing area, and there was a large cabinet filled with razors, bars of soap, shaving cream and towels. Latrine facilities were there of course, as well as a small kitchenette in the center of the long room, the cabinets stocked with mostly dry goods such as crackers and trail mix, all sealed in aluminum/Mylar packaging, straight out of an MRE pack, and tins of peanut butter and jelly. Three microwaves lined a counter, and a refrigerator hummed softly, though there was nothing in it to keep cold. One of the best things to find was a small storage room filled with BDUs, white underwear and socks for men and women of all sizes. Though not fancy, it was more than sufficient attire.

Another room off the main one was obviously a rec room. A large flat screen TV was mounted to the wall, and there was a shelf unit filled with DVD and video tapes of popular movies and TV series from a few years ago. At the time the world collapsed, the films would have been recent, but now they were mere remnants of a world long dead.

The air temperature was a comfortable sixty-eight degrees, the circulating system keeping the environment free from dust. Florescent lights hummed in the ceiling, but each section of the dormitory had a control panel to turn off the lights. But even if the main lights were turned off, there were still smaller, red lights mounted to the walls high up near the ceiling, in the corners, which always remained on, bathing the area in a dull red glow.

As Henry walked in, joining the others, who had finished looking around quickly, they all came at him as one, talking and trying to get his attention.

"What do we do now?" Mary asked.

"Are we really going to let that old bastard control us?" Jimmy added.

"We can't just sit here and do nothing," Cindy said.

Henry closed his eyes as he was bombarded with their opinions. Then he took a deep breath to calm himself before opening his eyes and raising his hands with palms outwards, yelling, "All right, enough! I hear you! Give it a rest!"

Everyone stopped talking, but their gazes were still locked on Henry's face.

"Look, I hear you, all of you, but I don't know anything more than you do, and until we get more information, I say we take all this in stride."

"But that guy's fucking off his rocker!" Jimmy yelled. "We can't let him control us like puppets."

"You're partially right, Jimmy, and I want to argue with you about it, but the old guy could have killed us or let us die countless times and he hasn't. The odds are whatever he thinks he's *checking* on us will be fine. How can it not be? There's no more internet for Christ's sake. And I highly doubt whatever database this place has contains anything about us." He moved to a bed and sat down. "Just calm down and stop worrying about the future for once. Look, we're safer in here than anywhere above ground, we've got full bellies, soft beds and showers. I bet there's even hot water." He pointed to the small kitchen and one of the cabinets, its door hanging open, exposing the contents within. "We even have snacks for later."

"So we're supposed to wait around for that old fucker to come back, and if he says we didn't pass, he just kills us?" Jimmy was getting all worked up, his face beet red. He was sitting on a bed to rest his leg.

"I didn't say that," Henry rebutted. "Here's my idea. We set up some sort of alarm so if he comes in here when we're sleeping, we'll know about it. We can also sleep at the farthest end of the room so he has to come all the way inside to reach us."

"That's it?" Jimmy said, being the most vocal, the women simply listening.

"Yes, that's it. If he comes in to kill us, all we can do is fight back." He sighed. "Jimmy, I don't have all the answers. Hell, I wish I did. But the truth is that the old buzzard's got us cold. All we can do is wait and hope for the best."

Jimmy seemed to calm down slightly. If Henry wasn't engaging in the argument, he began to lose some of his steam. "That's a pretty shitty plan, old man, you know that right? It's actually one of the worst you ever came up with."

Henry only smiled. "Yeah, you're probably right."

Forty-five minutes later, the group had broken up slightly as they went to explore their limited resources some more. Cindy and Jimmy went off to a corner of the dorm to prepare to take a shower. Once they were finished, Jimmy would get a new bandage for his gunshot wound and then a fresh pair of BDU's.

Mary walked out of the shower room, steam billowing out behind her. She was wrapped in a large towel, another wrapped around her head to dry her hair. In her hands, she carried some toiletry sundries, such as a razor and a small bottle of shampoo.

Henry and Sue were sitting at a small table in the kitchenette, talking, when Mary walked over to them. Setting the items she carried on the table, she pulled the towel from her hair and began rubbing it dry.

"How was it?" Sue asked, her nose detecting the fresh scent of soap on Mary.

Smiling from ear to ear, a relaxed look on her face, Mary laughed. "How was it? It was amazing! I can't remember the last time I had a shower like that." She barked out a clipped laugh and added, "I even shaved!" She shook her head. "Honestly, it felt so strange to be shaving my legs and stuff, you know? I mean, when we're out there," she pointed upwards, signifying the world above ground, "traveling, trying to survive, the last thing on my mind is having hairy legs. But down here, with no one trying to kill me at the moment, it just seemed like the right thing to do." She laughed again. "I went through three razors to get the job done, too."

Sue laughed with her, knowing the feeling. "I've got a lot of work to do myself," she said and winked at Henry.

Jimmy and Cindy appeared, each holding towels and partially undressed. "Are you finished, Mary?" Cindy asked. "Can we go now?"

"Sure, all done," she said. "There's plenty of hot water left, too." She shook her head again in happiness. "The tank must be huge and there's only the five of us. I bet I could take an hour long shower and the water would never get cold."

Cindy smiled eagerly. "We may put that to the test." With a wave they headed off to wash, Jimmy limping alongside Cindy. "Make sure you clean that wound good, Jimmy," Henry called.

"Don't worry, Henry," Cindy answered. "I'll make sure it's taken care of." There were First Aid kits in each section of the dorm, filled with bandages, antibiotic sprays and other items found in a basic First Aid kit. More than enough to wrap Jimmy's wound once he'd showered.

Once inside the shower area, Cindy stripped off her clothes and jumped right under a hot spray, squealing with delight as the warm water hit her flesh.

Jimmy watched her bounce around under the water and he felt himself getting aroused. He couldn't get out of his clothing fast enough, before he had joined her under the hot stream of the shower head. They didn't need to share, there were more than enough shower heads, but neither gave it a second thought when they only used one.

"Mary was right. This is heaven," Cindy said as she spit out a mouthful of water like a fountain. "I could stay here forever."

"Yeah, I know what you mean," he said as Jimmy began to wash his face and hair, then the rest of his body.

Cindy turned around to face him. Her hair was plastered to her face, water running down her cheeks, across her breasts, to trail down to the junction of her thighs. Jimmy had been at half mast when entering the shower, but seeing Cindy standing there, her nipples perky and hard, her curvaceous body exposed to him like few times before—it seemed they never had the opportunity to fully undress—he felt himself more aroused than any time he could think of in the past.

"Here, let me soap you up," Cindy purred seductively as she took a bar of soap from a small shelf embedded in the wall tile.

"Be my guest," Jimmy said, trying hard not to let his voice shake. Sometimes, when he was alone with his thoughts, he wondered just how he'd been so lucky to have found someone like Cindy. Hell, sometimes he thought the zombie apocalypse had been the best thing to happen to him. Crazy as it sounded, it was true. Before the dead walked, he'd been a lazy, pot-smoking loser, with not much future in doing anything but getting high. But after the apocalypse began, he'd found himself constantly tested, and over time, thanks to being exposed to people like Henry and Mary, and later Cindy, the constant hardships he'd had to endure had changed him, molded him from a lazy slob to a tough, competent human being. Sure, he was still Jimmy Cooper, the wise-ass cracking guy he'd always been. But he was now so much more. He was a better person. He was a better Jimmy Cooper than he could have ever hoped to be, as fucked up as that all sounded.

After all, how messed up did a guy have to be to only become a better person because the world ended?

All this flashed through his mind in a nano-second, but then he had better things to occupy his mind with. Cindy had finished soaping him up, taking careful care to wash his genitals. He was so hard he felt that he could have drilled through solid concrete using just his penis if he'd had to. The term 'diamond cutter' came to mind.

Cindy had Jimmy step under the shower spray so he could rinse off the soap, then she pushed him gently out of the water and against the wall. He squealed like a little girl softly when his back touched the cold tile, but then that changed to a moan of pleasure as Cindy went to her knees before him and engulfed his manhood in her mouth.

He sighed with pleasure, his eyes closed, as she began to slowly move her head back and forth, while one of her hands worked energetically between her thighs. Instantly, the wound in his leg, which was always a dull throb of pain, evaporated as he savored the insane pleasure he was feeling. Suddenly, he opened his eyes and let out a louder grunt, then he felt himself exploding into Cindy's mouth. Surprised at the orgasm, as she hadn't expected him to reach it so fast, she pulled her head back off him, but still used her hand to stroke him dry.

Feeling exhausted, spent, wasted, and sleepy all at the same time, Jimmy slumped against the wall.

Once the waves of pleasure had faded, he realized he'd basically just prematurely ejaculated from his heightened excitement. Now he felt embarrassed. One thing no woman had ever said about him was that he didn't have staying power.

"Oh shit, babe, I'm so sorry. I…I don't know what to say. It was just so amazing, I…" He trailed off, his face red from both his climax and embarrassment.

Cindy stood up and washed her face clean of Jimmy's excitement. Rinsing her mouth out as well, she went to him and kissed him deeply. "It's fine, lover, don't worry about it. It's been a while for both of us and to tell you the truth, I got off too just before you did."

That brought him around to more interesting things than his lack of staying power. "You did, did you?"

She nodded, biting her lip sexily. "Uh-huh. That was just a warm up, something to get out of the way so we don't have to rush." She reached down and grabbed his soft member, gently rubbing it. Already, he could feel a new stirring of passion. "Once we finish in here, and wrap your leg, then we can find a secluded corner and try again. What do you think?"

Jimmy grinned from ear to ear. "I say let's finish up in here as fast as possible."

She nodded and they went back to the business of washing, now that both were relatively satisfied for the time being, though each time Jimmy glanced at her, her full breasts, her tight abdomen, her strong legs and buttocks, he felt himself hurrying to finish.

They completed washing and then shaved all the areas on their bodies that had been ignored for far too long. Jimmy had a good week's growth of hair on his face and it took a lot of grooming with just the razors. Cindy made a joke about him manscaping a little and he laughed at her, but when she had set off to the row of mirrors and sinks, and she was out of sight for a second, he did use a new razor on his scrotum, doing a little shaving where he normally didn't do it. He thought it would be a fun surprise later when she discovered it. Weird though it felt, he did a decent job without cutting himself and bleeding out right there on the shower room floor. Now that would have been an embarrassing way to go, with blood shooting from his balls as he lay on the floor bleeding out.

"You almost done, lover?" she called and poked her head around the corner. The shower room was separated from where the toilets and mirrors were.

"Yup, just about," he called, then turned off the water and wrapped himself in a towel.

With a grin on his face at the fun to come, he hobbled out of the shower room to join Cindy.

A few minutes later, the last two of the group gathered in the shower room to bathe.

Unlike Jimmy and Cindy, Henry and Sue separated at first. Henry wanted to shave before a mirror and use a sink, while Sue wanted a little privacy as well to shave everything she needed to as well as use the toilet, something Henry had done a few minutes before she arrived.

Knowing they had the area to themselves, Henry stripped out of his filthy clothes, and other than his boots and belt, he planned on trading out his worn clothing for a fresh pair of BDU's, underwear and socks.

While Sue hummed to herself in the nearby shower stalls, Henry lathered his face with a can of shaving cream taken from the cabinet. Beside him, were three disposable razors. He didn't know if he would need them all, but he didn't want to have to search for fresh one halfway through the job so he'd stocked up beforehand.

Wiping the mirror clean of the light condensation that had built up on the surface, despite the ventilation system, he stared into his own eyes, taking stock of what he saw before him.

There were a few more wrinkles on his tanned face than he was used to. His dark brown hair had some more streaks of white in it as well. He didn't like the white but Sue said it made him look distinguished. He'd laughed at that. Imagining that when he was blowing some coldheart away, the last thing thought by the slain man would have been how he thought his killer looked 'distinguished.'

Wincing from a tinge of pain as he raised his hand to shave while holding the razor, he swiveled his waist slightly and glanced at the flesh wound on the upper part of his left arm, then moved closer to the mirror to get a better look. The blood was dry and the wound looked like it could use a good cleaning, but was barely more than a very deep scratch.

He turned his back to the mirrors, and though it was awkward, managed to see most of his back between his shoulder blades. There was an ugly welt where the biker chain had struck him, and it looked like it could use a good cleaning, too, but it didn't need stitches.

When both wounds healed, he would have two more scars to add to the dozens he already had. There'd been a time when his body had been devoid of scars, with the exception of something that had happened when he was a child. But since the dead began to walk and every day was a constant battle to survive, he'd picked up more war wounds than he could have counted even if he wanted to.

Turning back around, he had to admire his physique. Where there once had been the classic beer belly of a middle-aged man, now his abdomen was rock hard, ridges of muscle shifting beneath his skin. His arms had never been that flabby, even before the dead walked, but now they were nothing but muscle and sinew, his shoulders broad and powerful.

Any fat he'd once held had either been burned off from exertion or metabolized by his own body when times had been tough and food scarce.

He couldn't resist a slight grin as he took it all in.

"Screw the Atkins diet," he muttered. "Try the apocalypse diet. If you survive, you'll be fitter than ever before."

"You say something?"

He shifted his eyes over his shoulder, using the mirror to see Sue standing a few feet behind him.

She never looked more beautiful. Or more natural.

Sue was wrapped in a towel, her hair draped over one shoulder, still wet. Looking down at her legs, they gleamed under the fluorescent lights, freshly shaven. "Your legs are shaved I see." He couldn't resist adding, "Anywhere else as well, may I ask?"

She chuckled and padded over to him like a cat, standing so close her breath caressed the back of his neck. She kissed his shoulder. "Wouldn't you like to know." She leaned back and looked at his reflection in the mirror. "I'm going to pay for it later, too. When a woman shaves her legs after not doing it for a while, it itches terribly, but I think it'll be worth it."

"I certainly hope so," he joked. "Hell, your leg hair was getting longer than mine!"

She slapped his arm playfully, smiling widely. Then her features took on a look of concern as she examined his wounds. "These need to be cleaned ASAP, mister."

"Okay, just let me finish shaving."

"Fine, I'll be back in a few minutes with something to clean those with and then into the shower with you."

He turned fully as she began to move away. "You gonna join me?"

She stopped walking and with a sly smile opened her towel and flashed him. She was nude of course, her skin freshly scrubbed. His eyes took in her full breasts, her strong, flat stomach, then dropped lower to the juncture of her thighs. There was now a neatly groomed triangle of hair there, also blonde. When she shifted her legs slightly he was presented with just the briefest glimpse of her sex as well. "Of course. I'm dressed for it, after all." Then she covered up and padded out of the room.

With a grin that would not disappear, he got to shaving, wanting to finish as fast as he could to get on with what he hoped would be more than him just getting his wounds clean.

She returned five minutes later, just as he was about done.

"I was talking to Mary for a few minutes; hope you missed me."

"Of course I did," he said, swiping at the last bit of stubborn hair under his chin. He hadn't shaved in a week or so, and even when he'd bathed in the pond at the golf course, something like worrying about facial hair hadn't been relevant.

She took his free hand and gently pulled him towards the showers. "Then come with me."

He tossed the razor into the sink, not worrying about cleaning up. That could be done later, after more important matters were addressed.

Sue carried an assortment of items, such as gauze for his arm, and antibiotic spray for his back. She turned on one of the shower heads and water cascaded down. Then she took off her towel and tossed it onto a hand bar, the end catching it nicely and not falling to the floor.

"Nice toss," he said with a grin.

She nodded. "Get under the water and I'll wash you."

He sniffed an armpit and winced at the odor. "I need it, too. I smell like a cannie's latrine after a feast."

"Nice image," she said, scrunching her nose in disgust.

"It's the truth."

She shoved him under the water. He let out a quick gasp as it hit him. It was cold.

"Whoops, sorry." She quickly adjusted the temperature. Like Mary had said, they could have used the shower for hours and the hot water probably would never have ceased flowing.

As the water warmed up, Henry lowered his shoulders, which had tensed up. "That's better. You trying to freeze me to death?"

"So much for big tough Henry Watson," she jibed. "Let's start at the top and work our way down, all right?"

"Sure, you're the boss."

"Don't you forget it, buster." She lathered up his hair and began to scrub him down. She had to reach up to get to the top of his head, and as she did so, her breasts pushed against his muscular back, soft and yielding. He could feel her erect nipples pushing into him and he found himself getting aroused even more than he already was.

He reached around and grabbed a firm butt cheek, squeezing it playfully.

She slapped his hand away like he'd touched a hot stove. "Nah-ah, not yet. First we clean you, then we play."

But he would not be denied and he spun around so fast she let out a yelp of surprise. He wrapped his arms around her and pulled her in close, practically crushing her to him. She let out a gasp of surprise but she didn't complain.

Their bodies pressed together tightly. He shook his head to get off any soap dripping down his face, then crushed his lips to hers, the two kissing passionately, tongues entwined in a dance of love.

They remained in that position for a full three minutes, while hands roamed across one another's bodies, exploring, enjoying the sensations. Then Sue lowered a hand and took his manhood in her grip, and using the soap that had pooled there, she slowly began rubbing back and forth, while her tongue licked his lips seductively.

Henry wasn't idle while she caressed him, his right hand having slid between the juncture of her thighs, feeling the moistness waiting within. Slowly, with one finger and then two, he penetrated her, while also rubbing the place he knew would give her the most pleasure. Spreading her legs wider, she thrust forward, inviting him to go deeper.

But then, having enough foreplay, he spun her around, and with her hands on the tile wall, he entered her, and for the next few minutes, both were lost in the joys of being one with another person.

The slapping of two wet bodies and their moans of pleasure were muffled by both the shower spray striking the floor and the steam hanging in the air—or so they hoped. Now that would be an awkward meal with the others if the sounds of their lovemaking were being overheard.

Finally, Henry couldn't hold back any longer, and with a muffled curse, he exploded with her, just as her legs began to shudder so bad she almost fell over, if not for Henry holding her up.

Both spent, they separated and leaned against the wall, breathing heavily from their exertions and their simultaneous climaxes.

"Wow," she gasped. "That was incredible."

He grinned. "Right back at ya."

"So much for getting clean first, then play."

He shrugged. "Hey, the heart wants what the heart wants."

She pointed to his still semi-erect member. "I don't think it was your heart that was doing the wanting just now."

He pushed off from the wall and pulled her close, once more kissing her passionately. But this time it was more than simple lust. He knew he loved her with all his heart, a love he hadn't felt since his late wife Emily. And in many ways, he thought he loved Sue even more than he had Emily, as the circumstances were so vastly different. Though he might not want to admit it, at least not to himself and disrespect his late wife's memory, it was possible that Sue, was in fact, his true soul mate in life, and it was Emily who had simply been filling the seat until Sue came along.

Sex had never been as intense with Emily as it was with Sue, and though he had always loved Emily, now looking back, he realized there had always been a piece of himself that he'd held back. Not so with Sue. He'd given himself over to her body and soul. She completed him.

Finally, she pushed them apart and grabbed the soap again. "Okay, now that that's out of the way, let's get back to washing you up."

He nodded and let her wash him, feeling like a child coming in from a day of playing in the mud, his mother having to wash him because he was so filthy.

She was careful around his wounds, but he told her not to shy away. He wanted her to get in there good, even open the wounds a little if need be, anything to make sure they were clean. Infection in a world without hospitals could be a death sentence.

When she was finished, he thanked her, the two finally leaving the shower to towel off.

"I'm like a prune now," she said while examining her fingers. "We were in there way too long."

"Not long enough for me," he said with a grin.

She smiled back. "Twice in a week. It's a new record for us."

"Yeah, I think I could stay here forever, or close to it. We got food, shelter, and nothing trying to kill us except some homicidal spider droids, and maybe a crazy janitor."

She finished wrapping his upper arm with a fresh bandage. The wound on his back got an antibiotic spray to protect it from infection, then had to be left alone, as there was no way to cover it due to its length and location. But the wound had barely broken the skin, and other than bleeding when first given, had already been healing nicely even after a day.

They each wrapped themselves in towels to then go and grab some fresh clothing, and as they prepared to leave, Henry stopped and seemed to be staring at something on the far wall.

"What are you looking at?" she asked.

"I'm not sure. Something doesn't look right." He padded with bare feet over to the wall to get a better look, then bent over and picked something up. Against the white floor tile, the object had caught his attention, seeming out of place.

As he examined it, he felt a slight breeze, as if a door had been opened and closed. Moving to a set of lockers, he peered around the corner to see there was a service corridor, a fire door just clicking closed as he watched.

Sue joined him, looking down on the object in Henry's hand. "What is it? What's wrong?"

"It's a service medal, like the ones pinned to Adam's chest." He looked at the now closed fire door, then back to Sue. "The dirty old pervert was watching us."

Sue took that in for a moment and then grinned as she looked up at Henry. "Well, if he was, I bet we put on one hell of a show."

Chapter 5

Upon Henry and Sue leaving the shower room and entering the dormitory proper once more, both were concerned about their lovemaking having disturbed the others.

They needn't have worried, for the others were all sleeping soundly at the far end of the dorm, like Henry had suggested.

Together, Henry and Sue silently padded across the floor and donned new clothes, which was how they planned to sleep, only leaving their boots off for comfort.

As he buttoned his shirt, he glanced over to the egress of the dorm, where they had entered earlier in the day. Henry saw that while he and Sue had been showering, chairs had been piled up before the opening, as well as two beds pushed across the area. If Adam tried to come in while they were sleeping, he would make a hell of a lot of noise, thus warning the group of his arrival.

"We need to block that rear exit as well," Henry said, realizing if he hadn't seen the service medal on the floor and discovered that there was a doorway there, blocking the main entrance to the dorm would have been redundant, as Adam or anyone else in the complex could have just snuck in through the side door and caught them all unawares. Henry still didn't know if the old man was alone or not, though it seemed that way. But assuming would get a person killed if they weren't careful.

It didn't take long for Henry and Sue to stack some more furniture precariously before the hidden door, the items taken from the kitchen. They made the pile so that the chairs on the very top were carefully balanced, so even the slightest jar to them would set it all tumbling down the pile, and sound the alarm.

Finished with the barricade, it was time to go to bed, and with that conscious thought, suddenly, like he'd been slapped in the face, Henry felt a wave of exhaustion hit him. He blinked when it rolled over him and he was barely able to keep his eyes open. Since arriving at the complex, they had always been moving, and even after they ate, there had been the arrival of Adam, which kept everyone on their toes, despite full stomachs and lack of sleep.

But now, with his stomach full, bathed, and the exertion of having sex, why, it was all he could do to walk down the center of the dorm and find a bed near Jimmy. His younger friend was snoring softly, but Henry could have cared less. Looking at Sue, who was nearby, and had followed him to the others, the second he saw her weary features, he knew she felt the same way.

The beds were too small for two people together, unless they really wanted to work at it, and there was no reason for them to bother. Picking a bed side by side, they touched hands briefly, fingers caressing one another, then both dropped down on their perspective beds, and with long sighs of utter relaxation, were sleeping soundly before their sighs were fully complete.

"What the hell is this shit? What have you people done?"

The harsh voice, filled with annoyance, floated throughout the dormitory, rousing Henry from his slumber. Blinking sleep from his eyes, he realized they had all slept with the fluorescent lights on, all of them so exhausted no one had bothered to turn them off for the red lights that were for sleeping.

Despite forcing sleep from his brain, he felt remarkably rejuvenated after days of constant running and fighting. And to sleep in an actual bed was a bonus.

But Henry was also irritated at his lack of alertness. Normally, even when sleeping, he always had one ear listening for signs of danger. Apparently, even one day in the installation, with its running water and soft beds, was enough to make him lose his edge—and mistakes like that were what would get him killed.

They had all been lulled into a sense of security, though it might have been false.

Adam was still swearing up a storm as he tried to gain entrance to the dormitory. Henry saw the other companions were awake as well, though all had the same groggy expression he wore.

"Get hard, people, He's either coming to kill us or tell us we're accepted." Henry quickly slid on his boots, not bothering to tie the laces, the others doing the same, knowing time was of the essence. "Fan out so he doesn't have a single target with that room sweeper of his."

They did as instructed, Jimmy going to the far right, Cindy the left. Mary went to the left but higher up, Sue going across from Mary. Henry couldn't hide. He needed to go help Adam gain entry. If the man was coming to free them, then stopping him from gaining entry wouldn't be a good way to begin their new friendship

No one had a weapon to use, the dormitory devoid of anything useful. The frames of the beds were made of solid welds, so nothing could be taken from those to make a shiv or something that would cut or slice.

The kitchen had only soft plastic utensils that snapped from the slightest pressure. Any drawers had turned up nothing, not even a pen or pencil. The shower stalls were also one solid piece, with large bolts holding them in place to the wall or floor. In time, it might have been possible to extract some form of weapon from the surroundings, but in the end, it was simpler to just rely on what nature had already given them, such as teeth and sharp fingernails.

The search for possible weapons had been conducted when they'd first arrived and found themselves trapped in the dorm, and once they had done their best, they'd accepted their situation, to then bathe and have some fun sexually. All but Mary, who was the odd man out. But she'd found an old, dog-eared romance novel in a drawer when searching for a weapon, and had ended up reading it until falling asleep. She'd barely read a chapter before her eyes had drooped and she'd nodded off.

Adam could see Henry approaching, his vision clear through the tangle of furniture. "Well, sonny," he yelled in annoyance, "are you gonna help me clean this stuff out of the way or not?"

"That depends," Henry replied as he stood off to the side. "Are you here to free us or kill us? What's the verdict?"

"Verdict? If you mean did you pass the test the answer is yes. You people have no records I can find in the database, so you have never been arrested for being a terrorist. That's good enough for me, and as the Leader of this installation, I grant you freedom."

Though not fully trusting Adam, as the old man's answer could be a lie, Henry helped him remove the furniture, while he directed the others to stay back.

"You do realize that if I wanted to kill you," Adam explained, "I could release the gas inside here, too." He cackled his dry laugh. "I don't need to come inside myself to kill you if that was the case."

"Yeah, I figured as much but still, if you wanted to come here in person, we weren't gonna make it easier for you."

"Fair enough, sonny, fair enough."

The furniture was set aside and Adam entered. Henry knew then the old man spoke the truth for the M-5 he carried was hanging by its lanyard, not held level in his hands to shoot Henry.

As Adam entered, Henry waved the others to join them. "It's okay, guys. We passed the test. We're okay."

Adam nodded. "That is correct. You're all cleared. You may now enjoy the complex in its entirety. Feel free to explore all you want."

"What about our weapons?" Jimmy asked.

"They are where you left them. Feel free to retrieve them whenever you like." He grinned his toothless grin. "Like I said, you have been cleared. You now have full access to the base." He raised a finger to get all their attention. "But stay away from the north side of the complex on level two, near the bio-research labs. I live there and I like my privacy."

"Fair enough," Henry said, the others nodding.

"Clean up this mess, too." He gestured to the discarded furniture. "I keep this place ship-shape and I will not have newcomers coming in here and messing it up. You understand me?" He didn't wait for a reply, and Adam turned to leave but then paused, turning back. "The spider robots have been recalled, too."

Mary spoke up. "But I thought you said they couldn't be turned off?"

"No, dearie, that's not what I said at all. After so much time elapses and they don't find their prey, they return to their birth, recharge, and wait for the next alarm to be sounded."

"But I heard you say…"

"Leave it, Mary, it doesn't matter," Henry told her.

Adam left, as there wasn't anything more he had to say.

The companions stood looking at one another, for a moment, not knowing what to do.

Cindy broke the silence. "How about we go to the caf for breakfast and then do some exploring?"

"Sounds like a plan," Henry agreed. They all went to get ready to have breakfast, and others went to use the bathroom.

Henry paused to talk to Mary. "I heard Adam say the droids couldn't be recalled, too."

"Then why did you stop me?" she asked.

"Because the old fart is nuts, that's why. He probably doesn't remember what he did five minutes ago, let alone yesterday.

Arguing with him wouldn't have accomplished a thing, and getting on his bad side is still something we should try not to do—at least until we get our weapons back."

Mary considered his words, and finally nodded. "Yes, I see your point. I guess it would have been silly trying to get him to see reason."

"Right, so come on, let's go eat so we can check this place out. I bet there's a lot to see down here."

They found out after checking the time that they'd been awoken at four in the morning. But they had gotten a full night sleep, and everyone felt ready to go exploring, despite the early hour. Not that they could tell the time of day while being within the bunker.

In the cafeteria, they quickly finished a meal of reconstituted powdered eggs with thawed and cooked bacon. Sue had done most of the cooking again, but Henry helped. Though his late wife Emily had done most of the meal preparing in his home, Henry hadn't been that bad of a cook himself.

As he cooked the bacon, he thought back to the last time he'd eaten some. It was the last time he'd seen his late wife alive. He remembered it had been turkey bacon, Emily feeding him that due to his high cholesterol. He'd been pretty angry about it at the time, if he recalled correctly. Thinking back to that moment in time made him morose, but when Sue had asked if he was okay, he'd pulled himself out of his funk and had nodded he was fine, then he'd kissed her, and squeezed her ass playfully, which made her squeal and laugh. After that he'd focused on the present, and made sure not to let his mind wander into the melancholy past.

"Do you really think we can trust the old coot?" Jimmy asked as he finished off the last of the bacon. "I mean, the guy's totally off his rocker. Can we believe anything he says?"

"I know, right?" Cindy added. "He talks about us having been checked out for being terrorists. That's the most ridiculous thing I've ever heard. There are no more terrorists, not since the deaders took over."

"Maybe so," Henry agreed, "but he knows this place a hell of a lot better than we do, and by that I mean we know nothing, so for now we might as well play along." He stood up. "Let's get this stuff cleaned up and go retrieve our weapons, then it's time to do some exploring."

Jimmy clasped his hands and rubbed them together. "Aliens. I wanna see the aliens they got down here."

No one replied to Jimmy's foolishness.

"Whoa now, hold on there a second," Jimmy said. "Just hold up, everyone." The others stopped moving and looked at him. "Let me get this straight. The idea of aliens being down here is crazy to all of you, but the idea of dead people walking around, eating living people and all that shit, well, that's just as normal as the sky being blue. Is that right?"

Everyone looked at one another.

"You know, he makes a good point," Mary said. "A few years ago walking dead people was the stuff of movies, and then look what happened."

"He makes a decent case, I suppose," Cindy said, defending her boyfriend.

Henry sighed. "Fine, all right, we'll go look for aliens. But if we don't find any you need to let this go, Jimmy. All right?"

"Sure, Henry, sure, but you'll see, we're gonna go into some lab with test tubes and shit and, bam, there'll be these large glass cylinders with little green men floating in them."

"I thought they were gray with big heads and eyes?" Sue asked, getting into the fun as they began to clean up their meal trays.

Adam had been adamant about them cleaning up and no one wanted to anger the old man over something so foolish. Besides, after so long of struggling day to day just to survive, doing something as mundane as cleaning up after a meal seemed almost relaxing.

Jimmy clapped his hands together as if Sue had hit the nail on the head. "That's right! Gray guys, like in Close Encounters. Those are the ones that probe your ass."

"No they're not," Mary rebutted. "Stop talking like an idiot."

Cindy laughed. "Sorry, Mary, but that's the only language he knows."

"Yeah, he is fluent in Idiot." Mary laughed.

Henry had to get in on this. "Oh, I don't know, girls. I think he's pretty fluent in Moron, too."

Everyone laughed louder.

Jimmy laughed at first, too, not fully hearing their words, just caught up in the fun, but then it dawned on him what they were truly saying. "Hey, cut it out, guys. When did it become the 'rip on Jimmy' hour?"

Henry returned from the kitchen where he'd carried the pans they'd had the food in, patting Jimmy on the shoulder. "Jimmy, old boy, every day is 'rip on Jimmy,' it's just that most of the time you don't know we're doing it."

"Ha-ha, you're so fucking funny. Keep it up, old man, you know, a few more years and you and Adam are gonna look like twins." He touched Henry's graying hair, Henry snapping his head back, irritated. "Sure, a little more gray hair here, grow a beard, and presto, just like Adam."

"I'm starting to regret saving your ass by removing that bullet," Henry snapped.

Jimmy smiled and crossed his arms. "Oh please, that's such a load of horseshit. You'd hate it if I died. Life would be so boring."

Mary joined them. "He's got a point, Henry. Since we first got together years back, you can't say things haven't been interesting."

"Yeah. I keep life fun." Jimmy began limping out of the cafeteria. "Come on, already, let's go get our guns. I miss my shotgun, and I know she misses me, too."

Sue came fast-walking from the kitchen, having placed a handful of trays and dishes into a sink for washing later, and as she joined Henry, Mary and Cindy began to follow Jimmy.

"What'd I miss?" Sue asked and wrapped an arm around Henry's waist.

Henry shrugged. "Not much. Just Jimmy being Jimmy."

"Oh, then it was business as usual?"

Henry nodded. "Yeah, pretty much."

Chapter 6

"There they are," Cindy said, moving ahead of the group.

Before the five companions, still exactly where they'd been dropped, piled neatly on the floor, were their weapons.

Jimmy limped over and picked up his shotgun, cradling it like a baby. "Come here, you sweet thing. Did you miss Daddy?"

Mary rolled her eyes as she recovered her.38 and her knife. "Oh, please."

Jimmy stuck out his tongue at her. "You're just jealous. Me and my baby here have a connection you'll never understand." He took his hunting knife and .38 when Cindy handed them to him, tucking each away.

Cindy moved closer to Jimmy, getting in his face. "You better be talking about me, lover, or tonight's gonna be a lonely one in bed for you."

He leaned in and kissed her. "Oh, Cindy, you know you're the only one for me." He winked at her. "But perhaps, maybe a three-some could be discussed later?"

"Cut it out, you two," Henry snapped, uneasy at standing in the empty passageway, exposed. The blast panel that had been dropped to stop the spider droids from killing them was gone, retracted back into the ceiling, but there were still residual signs that the sec droids had been there. Scratches on the floor, which were cut off abruptly where the panel had seated onto the floor, showed just how hard the droids had tried to get past the barrier. Deep gouges in the concrete were visible, and even the walls showed defacing, where the droids had attempted to get around the panel from the sides.

Henry couldn't help but keep his attention focused down the corridor, as if he expected to see a horde of the gleaming, silver spider robots come charging at him at any moment. His Glock was gripped tightly in his hands, the knuckles white as he squeezed the weapon. It didn't take long for the others to sense the tension and also become on guard.

Jimmy moved next to Henry so that the two were shoulder to shoulder, both men looking down the hallway. "I'd love to be able to sic those droids on Vincent and his gang. Now that would be something to see."

"Uh-huh," Henry said, barely listening, as he stared warily ahead.

"Relax, old man, the whacko said the droids are gone. We're fine."

"Yeah, I know, but still…"

Sue handed Henry his panga, which he put on his hip, then she gathered up a duffel bag, Cindy and Mary doing the same.

"We're really low on ammo," Mary said as she peered into the bag she held.

"That's our next stop," Henry said. "But first we need to deal with Jimmy's wound once and for all. Then I need to check something out."

"I'm fine, really," Jimmy protested but Henry wouldn't hear it. Soon, they were back in the Medical Bay, which was still a mess thanks to the attack of the spider droids.

"Okay, Jimmy, on the table again," Henry instructed, Jimmy doing as he was told.

"What's this all about? Another shot?"

Henry shook his head. "Nope, we need to get that wound stitched up or it'll never heal right." He went to a cabinet leaning against the wall from where it had been knocked over. After rifling through it, he came back to Jimmy with sutures on a tray. "Lay back and shut up. This'll be over in a few minutes."

Jimmy opened his mouth to speak but Cindy placed a finger on his lips. "You heard the doctor, lover. Shut up and let him work."

Henry unwrapped the leg and cleaned it again, and after making sure it was in good shape, he stitched it as best he could. He wasn't a doctor, so he sewed like he had learned to do when hemming pants. It seemed to do the job, and when he was finished, he cut the thread and wrapped the wound with new bandages.

"There, you should be good to go."

Jimmy sat up and slid off the table, then tested his weight on the leg. He limped in a circle, comfortable with his mobility. "Not bad, old man, not bad at all."

Henry tossed Jimmy a bottle of pills. "Here, take these orally every six or so hours. It's another antibiotic I found when getting the sutures. Should keep you from having your leg rot off from infection."

Jimmy caught the bottle and shook it once, the pills rattling inside. With an annoyed grimace on his face, he shoved it into a pocket. "Will do. I like having two legs just fine, thanks."

"Okay, now that we're done here, I'm gonna go check on that other thing." Henry glanced at Mary and Sue, who were sitting to the side, talking quietly. "You two coming along? We should stay together for the moment."

"Right behind you," Mary said, Sue only nodding.

Henry left the Medical Bay and began walking down the corridor, in the same direction the spider droids had retreated to when recalled. The others fell in behind him, and soon they were standing before the elevator that had brought them from above ground.

Without saying a word, Henry pressed the call button to the elevator, the door opening immediately. The car was still in the same position it had been when the group had been let out.

"We leaving?" Jimmy asked suddenly. "What about the armory?"

"We're not leaving, not yet, but I want to see if this works." Henry stepped into the elevator, the others right behind him. The door closed and it began to rise, their stomachs dropping right out from under them due to the speed. Eventually, the door opened and once more was the long corridor before them. Their footsteps echoing off the walls, they made their way all the way back to the outer door that led into the warehouse.

"What now? We're leaving, even after all the shit we just went through?" Jimmy persisted. "What about Vincent and his cronies?"

"No, Jimmy we're not leaving yet," Henry repeated. "I wanted to see if Adam was on the level when he said we now have complete access to the base." He gestured to the hallway they were in. "And it looks like we can leave whenever we want, just like he said." Henry studied the door leading outside, the keypad on the side of it. He spotted another panel and opened it. Within, was a monitor screen, and everyone muttered to themselves and to one another at the image on the screen.

The picture was a live feed of right outside the door, where instead of an empty building, the Skullfuckers had set up a temporary camp.

From the way they acted, the biker gang had been there since the companions first entered the underground complex. The camp had been created so that the shed was in the center, the bikers' motorcycles lined up on both sides, surrounding it. Torches were set up in ten feet intervals to push back the darkness that suffused the interior of the warehouse. On the far wall of the outer building, holes had been punched out of the walls to let in light, but it was still early and the sun hadn't risen yet.

Adam had spoken the truth when he'd told Henry about the bikers. Even as they watched the bikers in the camp, one of them got up, walked over and threw something at the door. A second later, the camera feed went white for a moment, then re-focused, though now flames blocked the image. Henry noticed there were three different buttons below the monitor, each with a number below it. He pressed the second one. Now the screen showed the shed, taken from an angle that suggested the camera was mounted to the high ceiling. The shed door was on fire, a Molotov cocktail having been thrown at the door, the bikers cheering at the action. Henry couldn't hear anyone cheering as there was no sound, but the way they were yelling and pumping their arms, it sure looked that way. The fire burned out quickly with nothing but the fuel from the Molotov to sustain it. From the amount of scorch marks on the door and stone frame, it hadn't been the first time it had happened. Another biker came over to the door, and with a sledgehammer in his meaty fists, began to pound on it.

From inside the shed, the companions barely heard the thud-thud of the blows, so thick was the door.

Pieces of cement around the door had been chiseled away, only to reveal the steel plating beneath. Even the actual shed, which looked like it was built from concrete blocks, was nothing more than a façade for the metal structure beneath.

"Unless that asshole has a German Panzer tank up his ass," Jimmy snickered. "He's not getting in here anytime soon, if ever."

"Yeah," Henry agreed. "But we're not getting out either. Adam told us this was the only way in or out; the other exits were de-stroyed. I doubt he lied. We can check it out for ourselves any time we want." He shook his head. "So we're not going anywhere soon unless we want to take our chances with them." He pointed to the camera, and Vincent, who sat on his Harley in the center of the circle by a fire. Meat roasted over the flames, an animal a biker had hunted, perhaps deer. Bed rolls could be seen scattered around the warehouse floor as well, accentuating the idea of them having taken up permanent residence.

Henry pressed the third button, the screen flicking to the rear of the shed. Even here, a few bikers were hanging out—one bearded fellow with his old lady were screwing, using the wall of the shed for support. She had her hands pressed to the wall, and he was standing behind her, thrusting hard and fast while grabbing her hair with a meaty hand and pulling back. Her eyes were closed, mouth hanging open slightly, a look of lust covering her features. Her shirt was pulled up so that her breasts were exposed, both full and firm. They swayed back and forth each time she was penetrated from behind.

"Oooh, the porno channel," Jimmy said, his eyes going wide. "Does this thing have a zoom button?"

Cindy slapped him on the shoulder and made a disgusted face. "What, I'm not enough for you?"

"Ah, come on, babe, of course you are. But I'd be lying if I said I didn't miss porn. All men watch it."

"Is this true, Henry?" Sue asked. "Do all men watch porn?" Her question was implied, without her outright asking him, if he too watched pornography.

Thinking fast, Henry went for a time-honored tradition when it came to men, their wives or girlfriends, and porn. He changed the subject. "If we tried to open this door and run for it, we wouldn't get far, especially without a vehicle. It looks like we're trapped here, people, for as long as Vincent decides to stay."

"Yeah," Jimmy said, "But we can wait him out. We got food, water, comfy digs. We can treat it like a vacation."

"Yeah, a forced vacation." Henry got Mary's attention. "You have that map on you still?"

"Sure. Why?"

"What's the code to open this door again, I want to make sure I have it right."

She pulled out the map and unfolded it. Henry had a look in the light of the single fluorescent bulb overhead. Reading the code, he used the tip of his panga to scratch it onto the frame of the door. "This way if any of us got here before the others the code is here for all. Adam's the only one left and he won't come up here, so who cares if it's here or not."

"Good thinking," Cindy said, smiling. Now, anyone could leave at any time, if they had to, despite walking into certain death from the waiting Skullfuckers.

Having seen enough, Henry nodded, and closed the panel, and with the others following, they returned to the elevator. Entering it, they rode back down, once more safe within the bowels of the earth.

When they were again gathered in the corridor, Mary asked, "So what now?"

"Now we go to the armory and see what we can get to replenish our supplies," Henry stated.

Jimmy slapped his hands. "Oh boy, I hope they have lots of goodies here." He started walking, Cindy by his side. He was still limping but it was fading every hour as he healed. "I want a bazooka and a grenade launcher. Maybe a few mortars, an Uzi and an M-60..." He trailed off as he walked, Mary shaking her head as she followed him. That left Henry and Sue alone for a few moments. Henry began to walk, Sue beside him.

After a full minute of them walking, and neither said a word, Jimmy's voice echoing from up ahead, Sue said, "You know, Henry, you never answered my question from before."

"Question?" he deferred. "What question?"

She stopped walking and stared at him, her arms crossed over her chest, her head cocked at a slight angle, as if saying, "Oh, come on, we both know what question."

He was on the spot, no way to change the subject, a deer caught in the headlights. So he did what he had to do given the situation.

"Honestly, Sue, I never did. It just didn't interest me. Nothing beats the real thing in my opinion. That stuff is just so fake."

"Oh, Henry, you're sweet." She moved up close and kissed him, then turned and began walking away, Henry right behind her.

He smiled wanly, before forcing it down.

The truth was; Jimmy was right. All men had watched porn when it was available before the crash of the internet and the world around it, even the men who said they didn't. But knowing the truth would do nothing but anger Sue, so he did what any man would have when cornered by his woman on that particular subject.

He lied.

The instant the group entered the armory, they knew they were in the right place due to the odors in the air. The scent of gun oil and grease, mixed with the aroma of steel was easily detected.

"Holy shit," Jimmy gasped upon taking in the massive room. Floor to ceiling were shelves filled with nothing but firearms, explosives, knives, and any other weapons of war imaginable. "It's like I've died and gone to Heaven."

"I've never seen so much stuff in one place," Cindy commented as she moved into the room, everyone gawking the same as she was.

Glass-doored cabinets lined each aisle, in which there were over fifty, twenty-five to a side. There were also tables where weapons could be machined and repaired.

The room was so large Henry had to squint to see the far wall. As he walked down one of the aisles, he read some of the labels on the doors. "Remington, Luger, Kalashnikov, Uzi, Webley, Smith and Wesson, Colt, Schmeisser, Browning..." He trailed off, getting tired of reading, shaking his head at the unbelievable array of ordinance. He stopped at a large table, where there were rows of explosives. He read off some of the labels once more, a few of the names he'd never heard of before. "Emulex 90, Hydronite, Austinite," were some of the ones he listed. Near them, but not too near, were also blasting agents and detonation cords, as well as safety fuses. C-4 was there as well.

He was drawn to the Hydronite, which were white sticks of dynamite but with a bigger punch. Something about the sticks being white instead of the red he was familiar with intrigued him. He'd remembered back in Pittsfield, when Jimmy had been sent to find an old van to retrieve the cases of leaking dynamite inside it, the van having been discovered by the companions on their travels. Jimmy had done the job, and had even managed to get back to the town intact, though it had been pure luck that one bump too many hadn't blown him and the vehicle he'd been driving into a thousand bloody pieces.

Cindy stopped by an assortment of rifles, one in particular catching her eye.

Jimmy joined her. "Watch ya lookin' at, babe?" He was chewing something; he blew a bubble.

"Where'd you get bubble gum?" she asked.

Jimmy grinned, showing her the bubble gum in his mouth. "I found a whole pack in one of the drawers in the kitchen where we're sleeping."

She frowned slightly in distaste. "It must be stale."

Jimmy shrugged. "It's not that bad." He gestured to the gun she was admiring. "What's up with that?" he asked again.

"This," she said, taking down one of the rifles from the metal rack. There was a label card below where the rifles were, and she began reading the small print. "This is an AR15 rifle." Her eyes scanned the card and she gave Jimmy the highlights. "This is the model before the M16. But it's mostly the same other than some adjustments."

"Like what?" he asked.

"Well, for one, the charging handle was relocated to the rear of the receiver. But it takes the standard 5.56 mm rounds the M-16 does. The mags are the same, too. Has adjustable front and rear sights, as well."

"You gonna take one?" Jimmy inquired, curious.

"Nah, I like my M16, but I'm gonna load up on ammo, that's for damn sure." She grabbed a duffel bag from another shelf and began piling empty magazines and bullets on a table to load the mags later.

Henry came up behind the couple, Mary and Sue close by. "Cindy has the right idea, guys," he said. "I know you see all these guns and you want them all, but we don't know how they'll work out in an actual firefight. But we do know about the ones we already have. No one should be getting used to a new weapon if bullets are flying around. So just load up on ammo for what we already own, and make sure to get plenty of oil and cleaning supplies. I'm gonna see about getting some spare parts for us in case we need them later, and the last thing is to take some explosives. Actually, I'll do that." He pointed to Mary. "Get as much .38 ammo as you can carry, though, as both you and Jimmy use it. Sue, find rounds for your .22, and if you like something bigger, grab it. That .22 isn't forever you know, you need to upgrade sooner or later."

"What about me?" Jimmy asked. "I wouldn't mind adding an Uzi to make up when my shotgun isn't optional."

"Good point, Jimmy, okay, you alone can take an Uzi. But the rest of you don't get greedy. What we have works well and has worked for a good long time. All our guns are in good working order, too; we know they're reliable. Don't take chances. It's not worth it."

Everyone split up, loading up on ammunition, the corresponding caliber stocked below each firearm. A few decent knives were added to their pile of acquirements, as well as a new sharpening stone for Henry's panga. He found a new leather sheathe as well, as the one he was using wasn't in the best condition. One time too many he'd re-sheathed the blade without a proper cleaning of the blade, and he didn't want to think about the gunk that must be inside it. There was a rack of machetes, and for a brief moment he pondered taking one, but in the end declined. He needed to take his own advice. He knew if any of the others snuck an extra gun into a bag, he wouldn't be upset. Temptation was a bitch, and when the items being dangled before you were guns that might save your life, it was hard to simply walk away empty-handed.

They spent hours inside the armory, gathering what they wanted, exploring, and checking out the massive collection of weapons. Finally, they decided it was time to take their finds and leave.

Jimmy helped matters by declaring he was hungry. "Hey, it's been hours since we ate. I'm a growing boy, I need to eat."

"Actually," Mary said, "I could eat, too."

"Me too," Cindy agreed.

Henry raised a hand to stop the others from trying to convince him. "Hey, you're preaching to the choir. I'm pretty hungry myself, but I wanted to finish up here before we left."

Jimmy picked up a small duffel bag and slung it over a shoulder, wincing when he put too much weight on his bad leg. "Then let's go already."

Everyone gathered the overflowing bags they had packed their new gear in, and one at a time, walking in a line, set off. Henry was last in line. He stopped before he closed the armory door, looking back at all the weapons and ammunition. He'd probably never see this much in one place again, he thought, wishing he could take it all. But a long time ago he'd learned that carrying too much was just as bad as carrying too little. When the concern was speed, being weighed down with too much gear could get a man killed. There needed to be a balance on the exact amount. Still, seeing all the oiled weapons gleaming under the overhead lights, he wanted them all.

Pulling his eyes away, he turned and followed the others, the door clicking closed behind him.

Chapter 7

After the companions' new gear and ammunition were dropped off in the dormitory, Henry set up a booby trap to make sure it wasn't messed with, then they went to the cafeteria to eat.

The trap was a simple smoke grenade with the pin pulled, wedged under a duffel bag so that if the bag was moved in any way, the grenade handle would open, and three seconds later someone would get one hell of a surprise, if not be killed. Even a smoke grenade could kill if a person was standing right over it when it went off. Highly unlikely but still a possibility.

For the meal this time they enjoyed frozen hamburgers cooked well done, lathered with mustard and ketchup, depending on the diner.

Jimmy had commented that he wished they had been able to use hamburger buns, but only meat had been stockpiled in the freezers. Large metal tins of flour had been found, and Sue promised when she had more time to focus on cooking, she would see if she could find all the ingredients to bake bread.

Once the meal was finished, and the table had been cleared, everyone gathered around a map of the base, which had been removed from a wall in a corridor where it had been mounted. The maps were everywhere, showing with a red dot where the person reading it was at any given moment.

Adam hadn't been seen since that morning, and it seemed the man had been true to his word about leaving the companions alone.

Now that there was time, the group was able to study the map in more detail. The complexity of the installation was amazing, with miles upon miles of hallways and corridors, elevators and stairwells, hundreds upon hundreds of research labs, experiential laboratories, and anything else government minds could conceive of to create when no one was watching. Exits and entrances were clearly marked, and using a marker, Henry circled each one of them.

The motor pool was at the farthest part of the complex and would take an hour to get to if walking. There had to be an egress for the vehicles to come and go, so he had high hopes of finding another way out of the complex once he got there.

"I want to see for myself that there aren't any other ways out of here," he told the others as he circled one exit at a time. "I'm not just taking the word of a crazy old coot 'cause he says so."

"But I want to see the aliens," Jimmy said, sounding a lot like a five-year-old whining he wanted an ice cream.

"Then go do what you want, Jimmy," Henry said, annoyed. "We might as well all split up into two groups anyway." He gestured to one of the circled exits. "Sue and I can go check on the exits with Mary, and you and Cindy can go hunting for aliens, Jimmy."

"Ah, I think I'd rather go with them," Mary said. "If it's okay. I know what a motor pool, looks like."

Henry shrugged. "Sure, it's fine with me." He glanced at Sue who nodded, not minding either.

"Okay, then let's head out. We'll meet back in the dormitory in three hours." He looked at Cindy, Mary and Jimmy. "Make sure you're back in time. If you're not there in three hours, Sue and I are gonna assume the worst and come looking for you, and this place is huge so I don't even what to think about something like that."

"Don't worry, Henry," Mary said. "Cindy and I will make sure Jimmy's back in time." She glanced at Cindy who nodded slightly in agreement.

Jimmy looked at the women, then at Henry, realizing something was going on. "Hey, wait a second. I don't need a babysitter. I can tell time. I'm not a kid anymore, you know. I'm an adult."

Mary patted his arm as they wrapped up their meeting to head out. "Oh, Jimmy, it's so cute you think that."

Splitting up at a junction in the corridor, the two teams went their separate ways.

Henry and Sue walked silently together, each taking in their surroundings.

Any doors that weren't locked were checked, while any that were locked he ignored. He was curious what might have been beyond those particular doors, but at the same time didn't think it would be worth the trouble, as the only way to see what lay within them would be to blow the locks with some of the explosives they'd acquired. And then Adam would know about it as well and it wasn't worth risking the old coot's anger, especially when he had control of the complex.

What could possibly be in those rooms that mattered? They had found the Armory unlocked and fully-stocked, they had food, hot running water, and beds; all basically the essentials of life nowadays.

When Henry and Sue reached the motor pool, and began walking through it, Henry found the egress he expected to find, only it wasn't in the state he was hoping for.

Whistling as he inspected the cave-in, he kicked a rock back onto the collapse as he glanced at Sue. "Well, so much for this way out."

"What do you think happened here?" she asked as, she too, studied the debris.

He shrugged and pointed to the ceiling, which the collapse was even with. "Hard to tell. Those might be scorch marks over there.

If so, then someone planted charges and took it all down. Adam said all the exits were blocked off with the exception of the elevator we used; guess he wasn't lying."

"But why would all the other exits be blocked off like this one?" Sue asked. "It all doesn't make any sense."

"A lot of what Adam says and does doesn't make sense." Henry walked away from the collapse, barely glancing at the vehicles inside the motor pool. There were a few military jeeps, an APC, and an assortment of cars and motorcycles, all civilian models, the latter probably having belonged to personnel on the base. None of it mattered. Without a way to get them out, the vehicles were worthless. "Come on, I've seen enough. Without a backhoe and a team of engineers, no one's gonna be getting out this way anytime soon."

"Okay, where to next?" she asked.

"There's one more place I want to check out."

Jimmy was on the hunt for aliens, and he was acting like a boy in a candy store as he went from door to door, hoping the next one would open onto a room with gray forms floating in giant beakers. Cindy and Mary followed close behind, as if they were the parents of a rambunctious child.

Over the next two hours, the trio did come across laboratories, some that would have required them to don biohazard suits to enter through airlocks after entering large foyers, but none of them went to the trouble.

"Reminds me of Pineridge a little," Mary said to Jimmy, who nodded in agreement.

"Where the fuck are the aliens and their ships at?"

Cindy grinned. "Oh, so now we're looking for flying saucers, too?"

Jimmy stopped limping down the corridor they were in, the hallway resembling all the others they'd traversed since leaving Henry and Sue. "Of course we're looking for saucers, too. How the hell do you think the aliens got here?" He pointed to a door. "Maybe behind that door is the saucer that crashed at Roswell. We won't know if we don't check." He opened the door, and they all crowded at the doorway, peering inside.

"It's a broom closet," Mary said flatly.

Inside the small room were janitorial supplies; a mop and bucket, a shelf with cleaning chemicals, and a small stainless steel sink.

"Well, it could have been something else." He began to pout.

Mary rolled her eyes and stepped away from the door. "Look, Jimmy, I've had enough for today. What say we go back to the dorm and wait for Henry and Sue to return? You can go alien hunting tomorrow—but without me."

"But I want to find the aliens." He actually managed to sound like he was whining like a little boy who was told to go to bed, but wanted to stay up a little longer.

Cindy sighed and began rubbing his arm to console him. "Sorry, babe, but I don't think there are any down here. It's probably just a myth people made up about this place." She gently nudged him the way they'd come. "Mary's right. Let's go back. Maybe we can watch a movie. We've never done that before. It'll be nice to do something normal for a change." She leaned in closer to whisper in his ear. "And like at the movies, we can mess around some."

That perked him up and got him out of his funk. "Well, all right, if we get to mess around."

Mary scrunched up her face. "Ah, I don't want to hear about that, thank you."

Jimmy flashed her a sly grin as he gave Cindy a hug. "Oh, Mar', you're just jealous."

"No, I'm really not." She turned and began walking away, Jimmy and Cindy following.

"I wonder if the aliens are on the north side of the base on level two, where Adam said not to go. That would make sense; he's keeping them hidden for himself." The women ignored him. Cindy moved up to Mary, the two walking side by side.

"Hey, Cindy," Mary began, "Did I ever tell you, back when Jimmy and I first met, that he tried to get with me?"

Cindy's eyes opened wide and she smiled, enjoying the tidbit of Jimmy's past she'd never known. "No, I didn't know that. Tell me everything."

"Ah, no, Mary," Jimmy said quickly. "We don't need to go into that. I was a different guy back then. Besides, the past is the past, water under the bridge and all that shit."

Cindy turned and glared at him. "Quiet, you. I want to hear this."

"But…"

"I said hush." Cindy nodded to Mary. "Okay, girl, please continue."

Mary sent a sneaky peek over her shoulder to see Jimmy slightly uncomfortable. Like they were siblings, this made her feel really good for some reason. "Okay, so we were still working at Pineridge Laboratories, but had just left it, and we were in this Delta 88 he was driving. We came across this car with a deader mom and her two eaten kids. So Jimmy goes and…" She continued the story, Jimmy having to hear it from her point of view.

Once in a while Cindy would look at him, her face asking the question, "Really? You did that?"

For Jimmy, it was a long walk back to the dormitory.

* * *

It took almost an hour to find what Henry was searching for. He didn't know where he was going at first, assuming he needed to go in the same area that the other research laboratories were located in, but had struck out. Then he tried a place on the map simply marked MT.

It was on the same level as the dormitory, only was at the far west side, near the edge of the base. It had taken almost twenty minutes to walk to it, and Sue was getting impatient when Henry finally came up to the doorway he wanted.

A sign mounted on the door had the words: Matter Transfer Station. Security Clearance D-3 Required For Entrance.

The door was locked, and there was a keycard reader mounted to the wall next to the door, which was made of a metal alloy Henry didn't recognize. "Damn it, I really wanted to see what's in there."

"Why? What did you think was inside?" Sue asked.

He shrugged. "Don't know, but the name makes me think of something out of Star Trek. You know, 'Beam me up, Scotty' and all that. Maybe they figured out how to do it for real." He shook the reinforced door handle again, as if the action would somehow open the door. Of course, nothing happened. There was a low humming coming from inside, and when he put his ear to the door, the sound grew louder. But as to what the humming belonged to was a mystery.

"Oh, Henry, that's just science fiction."

"You think so? Zombies were once fiction and now they're part of everyday life, or were until recently." He sighed. "I bet there's some cool stuff inside there." He turned to face Sue. "We might have to come back and blow the lock off this door."

"But you said Adam would know and that wouldn't be a good thing."

"Yes, I know what I said. But in this case…" He trailed off, thinking. "In this case, there might be a way off this base using what's inside there."

She crossed her arms and shook her head in rejection of the idea. "There's probably nothing more important in there than some kind of plant or tree research."

"Yeah, maybe. It just might be wishful thinking on my part." He let out a long, frustrated sigh. "Okay, you win. Let's go back and join the others. We'll be getting back right in time if we leave now anyway." He began walking the way they'd come, but marked the location of the MT lab in his memory. The complex was a warren of corridors, but it was actually easy to reach the MT lab from their living quarters. Two lefts and a right, then there was a main access corridor that went on for more than half a mile, where he then took one right and was at the door to the MT lab.

The next two days passed slowly, with equal parts exploring the complex mixed in with down time, where they did everything from taking long naps in the dorm, to watching movies in the rec room, cleaning and stripping their weapons, and sneaking off for a little hanky-panky.

Mary was left out of the last one of course, but she didn't mind the others going off for a little fun. She didn't mind being alone, either. True, it would have been nice to have a lover like the others, but at the same time, she had the freedom not to have to worry about another person in that way.

Of course, she felt a deep love for the others, and though there was no sex in the equation, in all other matters it was basically the same.

Jimmy had joked once when he and Cindy were heading off to find a secluded place to mess around, that she could come along as well. Cindy had slapped him hard and apologized to Mary profusely. Jimmy had just grinned that knowing grin he always used, and Mary was barely fazed by it. Jimmy saying something like that was as normal to her as the sky being blue.

But though she was alone when the others went off together, it wasn't like she didn't know how to take care of herself sexually. When she used the shower and knew she was alone, she'd make sure to spend a few extra minutes washing between her legs, and in no time would find herself orgasming so hard her legs could barely support her. Yes, a man would have been nice, but she got by just fine on her own. Of course, she hadn't told the others any of that. Sometimes, no matter how close they all were, some things still needed to remain a secret between each other.

Besides, it wasn't like she was a nun. A year or so ago she'd become close to a man named Lyle, who had joined the companions, and had then taken them to a place called Cement City. Once there, the group had gotten into a spot of trouble, and were set to be hanged by the neck until dead. But at the last second, before the noose was around their necks, they were offered an alternative, and had quickly agreed to save some of the townspeople, who were kidnapped by raiders and were holed up in an old Ford car factory. If the people were rescued, then the companions would receive their freedom in exchange. With some of the companions left behind as collateral to make sure the others didn't run away once freed, the rescue-raid had been executed. But like most things where even the best-laid plans couldn't cover every contingency, there were hitches; some turning deadly.

Lyle was killed in the retreat, though he'd helped save his sister, who was one of the people taken by the raiders. He'd also been Mary's salvation. When a raider had shot at her, having her dead to rights in his gun sight, Lyle had thrown his body in front of her, making himself a human shield. He saved Mary from certain death, but in doing so made the ultimate sacrifice. His body became riddled with bullets meant for Mary. He'd finally died on the factory floor, in her arms.

Just before he succumbed to his wounds, he asked her a question. "Could you have loved me?" Mary had nodded slowly, and with tears in her eyes of a future lost before it could begin, she told him she could have loved him easily, and sometimes, when she was alone, she had to fight the grief that to this day still overwhelmed her. She had found love, only to lose it just as quickly, which in many ways was worse than if she'd never found it to begin with.

Mary stood up from her bed, placed the book she was reading down, stretched, and began to slowly have a walk around the dorm. Two more days had passed uneventfully, and she was feeling the first onslaught of cabin fever. Though the complex was huge, in the end she still felt the weight of the tons of rock and dirt over her head. She wanted to be out in the sunshine again, feel the warm air on her skin.

As she moved around the large room, she decided to make the rounds to see what the others were up to. She found that Jimmy and Cindy were in the rec room watching an action movie. They were sitting so close they were one lump under the blanket draped over them, and every now and then Cindy would giggle like a school girl. Mary smiled at this. It wasn't a big secret what they were up to under that blanket.

Henry and Sue were sitting in the kitchenette, talking while holding hands from across the table. As Mary entered, they both looked up and gave her a welcoming grin.

"Hey there," Henry said.

"Hey there, yourself," she replied. "I'm not interrupting anything am I?"

"No, we were just talking," Sue said and gestured for Mary to sit with them.

She did so. "I don't know about you two, but I'm feeling restless."

Henry nodded, and after glancing at Sue, replied, "Yeah, I know what you mean. It's hard dealing with what's basically nothing to do all day. Hell, I've cleaned my Glock so many times I know I can do it in the dark if it came to it."

"I know, right?" Mary agreed. "Me too." She sighed and glanced at Sue, who leaned over and rubbed her shoulder against Mary's. "I thought when we first got here that I'd like it here," Mary began. "I mean, for a change, it's nice not to have to look over your shoulder when you just need to use the bathroom—and not have to go in the woods and use leaves for toilet paper." She looked up at the ceiling, then waved a hand to signify the installation. "I mean, all the food we can eat, running water, and nice beds. Compared with how most people are living topside, we're living like kings."

"Perhaps, Mary," Sue said. "But we're still trapped down here. In a way we're no different from prisoners, only our cage is much, much bigger and nicer than normal."

Mary looked at Henry. "Any change with the bikers?"

Henry shook his head. "Nope. They're still up there."

"Maybe we can use some of the explosives in the armory to deal with them," she suggested.

"I thought of that, but no matter what I come up with it won't mean we get away clean." He sat up taller, getting into it. "I thought maybe I could use some of the dynamite and then just open the door up there and toss it at them. But there's no guarantee it'll work. Not even a little. Sure, the explosion would kill some of them, but you saw how they're scattered around the exit. And there's no way to get them all with just explosives, not without us taking serious fire. And the trick would only work once. After that, they'd back away from the door to ensure it doesn't happen again. Or worse, would figure out a way to jam the door from opening again. All they'd have to do is pile a few bikes before the door and it would never open, and we wouldn't have the weight to force it open."

"I see you've really been thinking about this," Mary stated.

"Well, of course I have. I want to get out of here as much as you do. It's nice and all, but it's been days and enough's enough. It's time to move on." He leaned in conspiratorially. "Not to mention Adam is a wild card. I don't want to kill the old fart after he helped us, but I also don't like the idea he's always skulking around somewhere down here with us." He frowned. "'Sides, he might crack at any time and kill us with that damn gas he's always talking about."

"Then maybe we should just kill him and be done with it?" Mary suggested, being pragmatic rather than thinking like a coldhearted killer.

"Believe me, I've considered it, but in the end I won't murder someone in cold blood." He locked gazes with her. "You know as well as I do what we've had to do to survive, and the wake of bodies we've left behind, but I never killed anyone who didn't deserve it, and I don't want to start now. No matter how hard life gets. We all gotta live with our choices. So far, I'm okay with all of them, no matter how tough some of them were at the time."

Mary reached out a hand across the table for Henry to take and he returned the gesture. Sue looked on silently. She knew of the bond the two shared and had accepted it a long time ago.

Clasping hands, Mary smiled, her eyes picking up the warm feelings as well. "Henry, I agree with everything you said. I don't want to go down that path either. If we do, then we're no better than the people we fight."

There was a shifting of clothing and footsteps from close by, and everyone turned to see Jimmy and Cindy standing at the opening to the kitchenette, listening to the tail end of the conversation.

Jimmy coughed slightly to call attention to himself. "Hey, guys, if you're all done with your little love fest, I could go for something to eat in the caf. You in?"

Mary, Sue, and Henry each looked at one another, sharing another private moment, then they all smiled at Jimmy.

Henry stood up, went over, and clapped Jimmy on the shoulder. "Sure, Jimmy, food sounds fine. And it's nice to see you're as sensitive as ever, and as always your timing is impeccable. What would we ever do without your two cents?" He walked into the dormitory, not waiting for a reply.

Mary and Sue stood up and walked by Jimmy as well, both merely shaking their heads at him as they passed, a look of slight disappointment on their faces.

Jimmy watched them walk away before he turned and stared at Cindy, who had quickly picked up that she and Jimmy had interrupted what looked like a rather personal moment between Henry and the women.

"What did I say wrong?" he asked, his face a mask of bewilderment.

"Oh, lover, the fact you gotta ask is the problem right there." She kissed him on the cheek lovingly, her softened features letting him know she accepted him for who he was, faults and all, before following the others, leaving Jimmy standing alone in confusion.

Chapter 8

It was mid-afternoon on the fifth day inside the underground complex, and everyone was restless. But with nothing to do about it, they tried to make the best of it.

The gym had been found on the third day, and everyone except Jimmy had taken up exercise for the past two days. Jimmy's bullet wound was practically healed, and if the younger man had to run, he knew he would be in good enough condition to do so, despite any pain it may have caused.

More and more, Jimmy had been pushing for an attack on the Skullfuckers, and to then run for it in the ensuing chaos. Every time he suggested it, Henry shot him down, explaining how the plan was foolhardy. Jimmy would rebut, sometimes with his voice raised a little too high. Arguments ensued, and it was plain to see that everyone was getting on each other's nerves.

Even the most loved family, trapped together for a long enough time, would begin to show cracks in the perfect foundation of their relationship.

After lunch, when everyone had gone back to their living quarters to relax, Jimmy had decided he wanted to explore the last part of the complex not seen yet. The north side, which Adam said belonged to him, and that the companions were not allowed there, could contain the mysteries Jimmy longed to find. They hadn't seen Adam since that first day, the old man leaving the companions to themselves.

Jimmy's reply when Cindy brought that up was, "Fuck that old bastard. I'm going and if you won't come, I'll go alone."

"No, lover, I'll go with you, even if it's just to keep you out of trouble and watch your back."

He'd kissed her in gratitude, and the two had set off. When asked by Mary where they were off to, Jimmy just winked and mimed having sexual intercourse with his fingers, one index finger jutting sideways, with the other hand shaped into a circle.

Mary had made a disgusted grimace. "Uggg, too much information," before returning to what she was doing. Henry and Sue were off someplace on their own, and Mary assumed they were doing the same thing.

So the couple had left the dormitory, walking side by side through the long corridors. It took over twenty minutes to reach the juncture that would take them to the north side of the complex. When Jimmy reached the juncture, there was no hesitation when he turned and set off down the new corridor.

"There's gotta be aliens down here somewhere," he said while rubbing his hands anxiously. "If they weren't in the rest of the place, they must be in this part somewhere." He imagined stepping into a section of the base that was huge. In the center of the room would be a silver spaceship, saucer-like in shape. Cables and wires of all sorts would be connected to it, and lights would flicker here and there across the smooth surface. But that wasn't the half of it. Jimmy's mind was filled with everything he'd ever seen in movies and on television. He imagined there would be rows and rows of six-foot tall glass tubes. In each one would be a various alien; some gray, some with tentacles, and others looking human, only with two heads. His mind was going crazy, thinking of all the cool things he was going to find, and all he had to do was open the next door in front of him.

But he quickly found that almost all the doors were locked, with keycard readers the only way to access what lay beyond each portal.

They had spent over an hour searching for rooms that were open, but so far they were out of luck. Jimmy was so frustrated at finding nothing that he was seriously considering using his shot-gun to see if he could blow the lock off one of the reinforced doors. But just before he raised the subject with Cindy, footsteps and someone talking could be heard coming from around the corner of the hallway that he and Cindy were presently in. The sound of cackling and coughing came a moment later.

"Shit, that's gotta be Adam," Jimmy hissed.

"What do we do?" Cindy whispered, unsure of their next move.

Jimmy looked back and forth, before pointing to the end of the corridor, where it dog-eared to the left. "There. We can hide around the corner till he goes by." They ran off down the corridor, Jimmy limping heavily, while behind them, Adam's voice was getting louder.

When they reached the corner, they barely managed to swing their bodies around it when Adam appeared. He was carrying something, and both Cindy and Jimmy's eyes went wide when they saw what it was.

A corpse.

Female at one time, the body was now desiccated to mummy-like status. The body was dressed in a pink dress, a floral hat propped on the head, which wore a blonde wig. The dried skin on the face was pulled tight to the skull, a rictus grin showing when the gaping visage was facing Jimmy and Cindy. Gold earrings were in each of the shriveled ears, and bright red lipstick was on what was left of the tattered lips.

Adam turned away from Jimmy and Cindy, walking further down the corridor.

"What the fuck is he doing what that body?" Jimmy whis-pered.

"I don't know," Cindy replied, her mouth an inch from Jimmy's right ear. "But we need to follow him and see."

"Yeah, I agree. Okay, come on, but don't let him see you."

She glanced at him annoyed. "No shit."

They began tailing Adam, waiting each time he was on a long stretch of corridor, and when he turned a corner and disappeared from view, they would dash to that corner, peer around, and continue to follow.

They did this for a full ten minutes, realizing they were actually working their way back to the main complex, when Adam stopped in front of a set of double doors with a key card reader. But most doors in the complex had key card readers to gain entry, other than janitorial rooms, bathrooms and the like.

Swiping a card, the reader went from red to green. Adam pushed through the right-side door and was gone.

"Okay, move, before the door closes," Jimmy hissed. They rushed across the distance to the door, just catching it from closing by a fraction of a second. Jimmy was almost back to full health and he'd made the run easily other than with a limp.

Jimmy had a finger between the door and where it would connect with the second, closed door, keeping it from shutting completely, but other than that he didn't know what to do. Adam could be heard right on the opposite side of the door, so if he opened it even an inch there was a possibility they would be discovered. Jimmy told Cindy as much when she asked what they were going to do next.

"So then this was all for nothing, unless we want to barge in there and confront him," she said, whispering softly. "Maybe we should go find Henry and tell them what we saw."

Jimmy stood at the door, his finger stuck, thinking of what to do next. "No, I don't want to tell Henry shit until we know more." An idea came to him as he considered his options, and with his free hand, he reached into a pocket and pulled out the pack of bubble gum. "Here, give me a piece," he whispered. "I can't open it with one hand stuck here."

Cindy took the gum, confused. "You get the urge to chew gum now? What the hell's wrong with you?"

His eyes went wide and he glared at her, frustrated she wasn't cooperating. "Just do it, okay? I've got an idea."

Muttering what an idiot her boyfriend was, Cindy did as he asked, and when Jimmy opened his mouth, she popped the gum between his lips. He nodded in thanks, grinned, and began chewing profusely.

Thirty seconds later he took out the partially chewed gum and stuck it into the doorjamb of the door, right where the retracting bolt was, so that he forced the gum inside the lock. Coughing could be heard, and more mutterings—and they were coming closer.

"Shit, he's coming back," Jimmy hissed. "Go, go, he's coming." They turned and ran back to the corner, letting the door close the inch on its own. Once more, as if it was perfectly timed, just as they rounded the corner, Adam appeared through the doorway. He was clucking softly to himself, scratching at his beard, the M-5 slung across his shoulder. The corpse was nowhere to be seen. He began walking directly to where Jimmy and Cindy were waiting, and Jimmy leveled his shotgun, thinking the jig was up. If Adam discovered them, the only option would be to kill the old man before he could do something. Henry might not like it but it was Jimmy's call at the moment. His knuckles went white as he gripped the shotgun, his finger caressing the trigger, his legs braced to absorb the recoil.

But when Adam was no more than five feet away, he suddenly stopped and turned around, realizing he was going the wrong way. Shaking his head from the mistake, he turned and went off in the opposite direction from where Jimmy and Cindy were, and as he tottered off, they stuck their heads around the corner, watching his retreat.

"Wow, that was close. Okay, he's gone," Jimmy said, and stepped out into the hallway. Cindy followed, and walking on tiptoe, though there was no reason to do so, they crossed the space silently to the double doors.

Jimmy glanced at Cindy over his shoulder as he grasped the door handle. "Okay, let see if my trick worked." With a gentle shove, the door popped open easily, the gum having done its work, preventing the double doors from locking. With one more look at Cindy, who nodded that she was ready to see what was inside, Jimmy stepped through the doorway, Cindy close on his heels.

The first thing they both noticed was how cold it was inside the room, their breath steaming from their mouths each time they exhaled.

The second thing, despite the air conditioning being on full blast, was the odor; a smell they knew all too well.

The third was to find was what lay within the large, banquet-style room, and as they took it all in, Jimmy would have dropped his shotgun if it hadn't been hanging by its lanyard, he was so shocked.

Cindy let out a gasp of awe, her eyes jumping back and forth as she stared in horror. "Oh my God, what is this place?" she breathed.

Jimmy walked around a little, looking every which way. "That guy is sicker than any of us ever could have imagined." He bent over, peering at one particularly grotesque item, then pulled back, not wanting to vomit on his new boots.

But as he was leaving, he came across something that rocked him to his very soul, simply by imagining if it had come to pass. Picking up a piece of cardboard about four inches long and two high, he held it up so Cindy could see it, and read what was on it. Her eyes went wide when she did.

Dropping the cardboard back on the table, he quickly retreated to the exit, where Cindy was still standing. She hadn't moved at all while Jimmy had ventured deeper into the room. Nor did she want to. She wanted to stay in the relative safety of the doorway that would lead to freedom, so she could escape the house of horrors spread out before her.

When he reached Cindy, Jimmy had to grab her by the arm and tug her with him, as she was too focused on the interior of other room, as if she was hypnotized. "Come on, babe, we need to get the hell out of here, now."

"But… but," she began but couldn't get the words out.

"Yeah, I know." He pulled her harder and she was torn from her fugue state. "We need to tell Henry and the others about this shit, and fast."

"Uh, okay, yes, that's a good idea. They need to know about this. Oh my God, Jimmy, if we hadn't found out, if he hadn't known. We all could've…"

"Yeah, I know, but we know now and soon Henry will, too." He pulled the door open and stepped out into the hallway, and as the plain white walls, floor and ceiling surrounded him, he let out a sigh of relief, now that he was free of the vault of horrors. He realized the smell was still with him, as if it was stuck inside his nose.

With Cindy stumbling behind him as she regained her wits, they rushed off to the dormitory to inform the rest of the group on their discovery.

Chapter 9

When Jimmy and Cindy returned to the dormitory and filled in the others, Henry wasn't happy in the least upon learning that Jimmy had gone into the north side of the complex, despite Adam's firm warning not to. But his reaction quickly changed when he learned what Jimmy and Cindy discovered, and in no time he had everyone gather their weapons, so that they were fully armed. Then they set off to see the room firsthand for themselves.

It was a quick run to reach the double doors in the north complex, no more than ten minutes, and as the companions stood before the doors, Jimmy grabbed the handle and said, "Now you'll see I wasn't bullshitting you." But when he pushed the door, it didn't open. Confused, he tried again, and even gave it a shove with his hip, then winced slightly from the pain in his leg. His leg was healing nicely, but if he put too much pressure on it, the wound would let him know about it.

"I thought you said the door was jury-rigged to open?" Henry asked, the others gathering around him.

"It was," Jimmy replied. "I put gum in the locking mechanism."

"It's true, Henry," Cindy added. "I saw him do it myself and it worked when we came in the first time."

"Maybe Adam found the gum?" Mary suggested.

Henry shook his head, denying her theory. "Doubtful. If he had, I think we would have heard about it already—and not in a good way." He glanced at the security camera mounted a few feet away on the wall. It was silent and still, but for all he knew, Adam was watching them even now. So if that was the case, stealth was a waste of time, and he needed to see what was inside that room.

"Jimmy, use your shotgun and shoot out the lock, we don't have to screw around here. I need to see what's in there."

"But if I do, Adam could hear the blast. You want that?" Jimmy asked.

Henry nodded. "Yeah, I do, 'cause if what you say is inside there, then Adam and us have a reckoning to come to."

"Okay, old man. You got it." Jimmy waved the others back. "Don't want any shrapnel hitting anyone." He stepped to the side so he could avoid anything blowing back into his face, and shot the lock, a large hole appearing in the doors in the exact center, breaking the seam.

Inside the corridor the boom of the shotgun was loud, but it couldn't be helped. The second the lock was gone, Henry stepped forward and kicked in the doors, sending both open to slam back against the wall holding the doorframe.

The others were right behind him, and as Jimmy crossed the threshold, he glanced down at what remained of the lock, which lay on the floor, smoking. Within the scattered parts, the wad of bubble gum was visible. "See, there's the gum, just like I said. It must've given way enough for the lock to pop back in." He looked up, wanting to vindicate himself with Henry, but the older man was already standing in the center of the room, his mouth hanging open in awe and disgust. The lock was forgotten, as there were more important things to deal with.

Sue moved up beside Henry, as she too gazed around at the circle of horrors.

"See?" Jimmy said as he joined them. "I told you I wasn't shitting ya." He spat on the floor in disgust. "Whoever did this is one sick fucking bastard."

"Or flat-out mad," Sue commented. "He must be insane to have done this."

Mary turned around in a circle, taking it all in. "It must have taken him years to accomplish this." She sniffed. "Why doesn't it smell too bad in here? I would think it would be terrible to even try to breathe without a mask."

Henry pointed to one of the A/C vents. "The air's on full blast, the cold is keeping it all from just rotting. More like they just dry out slowly."

"You mean like beef jerky?" Jimmy asked. "Shit, this place is one big dehumidifier."

Sue took Henry's hand. A chill was running down her back and she needed to touch him to feel safe. Standing inside the room, surrounded by it all, it was just too much.

Henry went over to one of the tables and peered closer at what was seated there. "I guess we now know the mystery of where the personnel on this base ended up."

"Uh-huh," Mary said, speechless.

They gathered in the center of the room, staring at the chilling tableaux before them. They had seen some sick shit in their travels across the deadlands that were once America, but each of them agreed what was before them now took the cake.

"It's like a wedding straight out of the deepest bowels of Hell," Mary finally said in disgust.

The analogy was pretty spot on, given to what they were witnessing.

The banquet-sized room was filled with circular tables from end to end, a stage set off to the side, where a band sat with instruments. The tables had been done up with formalwear, fine China plates to expensive glasses with tall stems, the Sterling silver utensils complete with multiple forks and spoons for all the imaginary courses that would never be served.

In all the chairs and on the stage, there were people, but the term 'people' was to be used as loosely as possible.

For every single person was nothing more than a mummified corpse, their visages nothing but sagging, dried flesh, empty eye sockets and yawning mouths. Jimmy's descriptive term of beef jerky was correct, for every corpse had been mummified, the internal organs removed. Each corpse was dressed in fine clothing, from suits, to tuxedos, to military dress uniforms. All walks of life could be seen, and many of the chairs were occupied with small forms that were obviously children, or had been at one time. Though the cadavers were mummified, it was still plain to see from a cursory inspection how some of them had been killed. Many had throats with long slashes in them, the wounds now having been sewn back together, while others had bullet holes in their heads, the exit wounds much larger when the holes could be seen peeking out from under hats or wigs. Though it couldn't be seen by the companions, any corpse not directly shot in the head still had a small hole at the temple, where Adam had spiked the body so it couldn't become a zombie, or if it had been a zombie before being killed, it was a way to take it down without destroying the entire body.

The house of horrors didn't stop there. Even animals were done up, set up in poses so that they lay at their masters' feet. In the center of the room, where there was a dance floor, cadavers had been posed using ropes and wires, as well as steel poles, so that they looked as if they were dancing. On the stage, the dead band played on for eternity, trumpets, clarinets and guitars, all glued to their bodies, or secured with wire. Soft music played over hidden speakers, on a continuous loop, but what was even more macabre was that under the music, the sounds of a party could be heard, as if Adam had been attempting to give life to his creation.

One corpse, wearing full military dress, still had its key card pinned to its lapel. Henry saw that the security clearance on the card was D-3. Remembering that was the clearance level needed to enter the MT lab, he took it from the cadaver and pocketed it for later.

Jimmy wandered around some more from when he and Cindy were there alone earlier, and he ended up in the rear of the room, where he found yet another room. He returned a second later, looking as white as a ghost. "Oh shit, I think I'm gonna be sick," he said and then had to lean on the back of a chair to prevent from falling over.

"What is it?" Mary asked, joining him, the others right behind her.

Jimmy just pointed. "All the way in the back. You can't miss it." Turning, he headed for the open doors leading to the corridor they'd entered from. "I need to get outta here for a second, I need some air."

While Jimmy went to the hallway to get a respite from the horrors around him, the others moved to the back room, and when they found what Jimmy had discovered, they all blanched in shock.

"Like what out front isn't bad enough," Henry said, his voice low.

"Oh my God, this can't be what it looks like," Sue gasped.

Mary went to one of the beds, of which there were ten, and she inspected the corpses before her. "I'm afraid so, Sue."

"Jesus Christ," Henry gasped. "The sick bastard's got his own harem here. One for each day, with three more for some extra variety."

"Shit, Henry," Cindy said. "Despite how gross this is, I can't believe the old codger can still get it up?" The others all looked at her in astonishment and she paused and realized what she'd just said. "Oh shit, sorry, guys. I think I've been around Jimmy too much. That's something he would say."

"Yes, unfortunately, it is," Mary added and then returned to examining the corpse before her.

All ten beds had cadavers in them, each one wearing some sort of sexy lingerie. Many had their legs spread wide, while others had their mouths locked open. On some of the tables near the beds, an assortment of lubes, Vaseline, and jellies had been lined up, some of the containers barely half full.

"He's been…" Sue said, but then had to stop and start again. "He's been…"

Henry finished for her. "He's been fucking these corpses." He couldn't believe it. "And from the looks of it, daily or more. Christ Almighty. I knew the guy was off, but this?"

Cindy got everyone's attention. "Henry, everyone, follow me. I almost forgot the other thing we found you gotta see."

"Is it worse than this?" he asked.

"Maybe," she replied. "I'll let you be the judge."

Everyone filed out of the back room, Cindy leading the way. She brought them to an empty table in a far corner, where five empty chairs were placed around a table before a place-setting for each one.

Cindy picked one up and handed it to Henry, who read the name on the card. "Mary." He dropped it and picked up another one. "Sue."

Now the others went to the table and picked up the remaining cards.

"Mine says Jimmy," Sue said.

Mary held her card aloft. "I got Henry's name."

Cindy held a card aloft. "This one's got my name on it."

They looked at one another, the meaning clear to all.

Henry tossed the card back on the table. "The bastard was gonna add us to his collection."

Before another word could be said, there was the report of a powerful gun in the corridor. Everyone turned to face the exit, weapons coming to their hands instantly.

"Jimmy's out there," Mary said quickly.

"And that wasn't his shotgun we just heard," Henry added.

Four muzzles were trained on the open double doors, waiting for what came next. Seconds ticked by, the tension hanging heavy in the air, fingers caressing triggers, ready to shoot instantly.

They didn't wait long.

Jimmy appeared in the doorway, his hands held above his head, plaster covering his face and shoulders.

Cindy let out a sigh of relief to see her lover unharmed. The gunshot must have been a warning shot to alert the others, and the blast had gone into the ceiling, the falling plaster and debris then covering Jimmy.

Right behind Jimmy, the M-5 digging into the younger man's back, was Adam.

The old man's eyes blazed with anger at the group invading his sanctum, his face flushed red with fury.

"What the fuck are you people doing in here?" he shouted, spittle flying from his lips, some getting trapped in his white beard. "Drop your guns or this asshole gets it." His eyes were wide, filled with rage from the intrusion.

Henry took a step forward, his Glock never wavering. "You kill him and you're dead before Jimmy's body hits the floor."

"Thanks a lot, Henry," Jimmy said, hating feeling helpless.

"Shut up, Jimmy," Mary snapped. "Grownups are talking." Her .38 was lined up with Jimmy's right shoulder, hoping Adam's face would appear, but the old man was smart and he stayed well behind Jimmy, using him as a human shield.

Henry was already considering if he could shoot Adam through Jimmy, say in the arm or a place that wouldn't do too much damage to his friend. Jimmy would hate him for it, but if it would save his life, Henry would do it. But Adam was thin in stature and he hid behind Jimmy's torso easily, nothing protruding from the sides to get a shot at.

"You can't be in here!" Adam screamed. "I wasn't ready for you yet! I still needed to get more beds for the women!"

"Okay," Mary said, "if he means what I think he means, I'm going to have nightmares about it for a long time." She didn't want to even think about Adam using her body, and Cindy and Sue's also, for sex after they were dead. She gripped her .38 even tighter, wanting desperately to shoot the sick old bastard.

Jimmy locked eyes with Henry, and he mouthed, "Get ready," then he sneered and turned his head slightly so Adam could see his face and the contempt there. "Let me tell ya, Adam, we've come across a lot of sick fucks as we've gone from place to place, but you take the cake. Seriously, you fuck dead chicks? What's wrong, can't get a living one to put up with your small dick?"

"Shut up or so help me I'll kill you where you stand," Adam hissed between clenched teeth.

Jimmy ignored him, on a roll now. "You sure you wanna do that?" Jimmy rebutted, acting calm despite his stomach doing flip-flops. He was playing a dangerous game and he knew it. "If you shoot me with that gun, you're gonna blow half my insides out. That's gonna make a mess of my corpse, isn't it? For when you prop me up like a department store mannequin."

"So now we know where the people of this base went to," Henry said, glaring at Adam as the old man poked his head around Jimmy's briefly, then retreated. "You killed them all, didn't you?"

"Yes, I killed them. Why wouldn't I? They walked around here all superior; no one even looked at me! They acted like I was invisible. When the rotters took over everything, families of base personnel came here to stay until it was over, but year after year it only became worse. The world ends and I still have to empty the trash barrels and mop the floors. But I showed them. I learned how this place works, how to release the gas, how to control the lights and air. It didn't take me long to kill them all, and when a few got away and hid, I found them, too." He began to rant, as he relived the indignities of living on the base. "Those damn Generals and their families, strutting around here like they were so much better than me. Like their shit didn't stink. I had to clean up after them, and let me tell you, sonny, their shit stunk just as much as mine—if not worse!"

"So you killed them all to get even because they didn't acknowledge you," Henry said. "Even the children."

"Damn right I did," Adam spit. "Now I'm the Leader of this place, me, and no one else!"

Jimmy spoke up. "Aw, poor little Adam. No one liked him and they teased him all the time. What's the matter, Adam, you sad 'cause you're a loser? And a crazy one at that?"

Adam's eyes went even wider in anger; he was so furious that words wouldn't come out. Sputtering, he raised the muzzle of the M-5 to whack Jimmy on the side of the head, to show Jimmy he wasn't a loser, that he was powerful. That was the gamble Jimmy had hoped for, that Adam wouldn't just pull the trigger and kill Jimmy, that the old man wanted to inflict punishment first, to prove he was the man in charge and not a simple janitor.

Jimmy felt the barrel of the M-5 whack him on the side of the head, making him see stars, but he went with the blow, rolling to the floor and away from Adam, who was caught standing out in the open, his human shield suddenly gone.

"You all die now!" Roaring in anger, Adam leveled the M-5 and squeezed the trigger of the room sweeper, sending hot lead spraying across the room, directly at Henry and the others.

Chapter 10

As Adam began firing the M-5, so too did the companions, though they had to dive for cover first. Kicking cadavers out of the way, Henry flipped one of the tables over, sending fine China and silverware flying, the latter landing on the floor and making music as it clinged and clanged. Sue was right behind him, and as the table landed heavily, bullets thudded into it. The table was heavy and made of thick wood, and it absorbed the rounds without them punching through to the other side, which would have been fatal to Sue and Henry.

Mary and Cindy dived to the side as well, and together they upended a table to hide behind.

Adam was screaming like a madman, standing out in the center of the room, as he fired every which way. The M-5 was devastating within the confines of the banquet hall. Desiccated corpses, all set up in poses, were blown apart into a thousand pieces. Heads disintegrated as bullets punched through brittle skulls, sending bone fragments flying off in all directions. Glassware was shattered, glass shards ricocheting throughout the entire room.

With his ass high in the air, Jimmy crawled across the room until he joined Cindy and Mary.

Cindy pulled Jimmy close just as a spray of bullets struck the floor where Jimmy was an instant ago. She glared at him. "Way to piss him off, Jimmy!"

"What? You think this is my fault? In case you weren't listening, he was going to add us to his little menagerie anyway. Killing us is killing us, no matter how mad the fucker is."

"He has a point, Cindy!" Mary yelled as she hunched down behind the table. The reports of the firearms were deafening, and already it was difficult to hear anyone speak.

Jimmy blinked, surprised. Mary never took his side—on anything. He could say the sky was blue and she would adamantly deny it and say it was gray. She just liked to disagree with him it seemed.

"Well, whatever the reason, he's out for blood now," Cindy shouted, and when there was a lull in Adam's firing, she popped up and sent a tri-burst of rounds at him with her M16. "I'm just glad Henry told us to arm up, or we'd be in a heap of trouble right now."

"Cindy!" Henry called, and when she turned around, she could see Henry peering out from behind his table.

"What?"

"I'm gonna draw his fire. When I do, you and Mary take the bastard out." More gunfire struck his table and he had to duck back.

"Okay, ready when you are," she replied.

"On three." He raised his fingers and counted down, and on three, popped up and fired at Adam, who was still standing in the center of the room, the idea of self-preservation not even crossing his mind, he was so angry.

Adam was hit twice in the chest. He spun around, stumbling backwards, but then recovered and shot at Henry, who ducked back down, the top edge of the table become nothing but splinters. Cindy and Mary had used that time wisely, and they began firing at Adam, hitting him more than five times throughout his body.

One round tore apart his right elbow, bone and blood spraying the wall behind him, making him hold the M-5 one-handed. Another round caught the side of his neck, blood seeping from the wound instantly. When he was struck in the chest, he went flying backwards from the impacts, and Henry poked his head around the table, figuring the fight was over. The man was shot multiple times; he was dead.

But the old man still moved, and as Henry stood up, Glock leading the way, Adam, wheezing terribly from broken ribs, fired off a burst of bullets that sent everyone once more diving for cover.

Jimmy was the one to voice what they were all thinking. "What the fuck? He should be dead meat."

Henry peered around the side of the table again, keeping his face close to the floor. Adam was on his feet again, though by the looks of it, it was only by sheer force of will. His janitorial uniform was torn apart over his chest and torso from the bullet hits, exposing the dark-black bulletproof vest he was wearing beneath it.

"The son-of-a-bitch is wearing Kevlar," Henry hissed angrily.

"Damn right I am, sonny!" Adam shouted. "And you're not, which means you're all dead!" He began firing again, the room getting sprayed left to right. But then the firing ceased, and the only sound in the room was Adam squeezing the trigger on an empty weapon. "Shit!" he yelled and threw the gun to the side; he couldn't reload with his right arm a bloody ruin.

Henry knew the time to end the fight was now. He stood up, Glock already moving to track Adam and kill the man. A head shot would finish him off nicely. But Adam wasn't sticking around, and he turned and hobbled out of the room, just as Henry, Sue, Cindy, and Mary began firing. Bullets missed the man by inches, the wall becoming pockmarked with bullet holes. One round hit Adam in the back in the center of the vest; the force of the blow sent him flying forward and out the double doors and into the hallway.

Everyone, moving warily, went after him, but as they reached the doorway, Adam fired at them, using Jimmy's .38, which he'd picked up from where Jimmy had dropped it when Adam had caught him unawares. Adam ignored the shotgun, knowing he wouldn't be able to use it with only one good arm.

With Adam wheezing even harder and coughing, Henry stayed behind the doorframe, knowing if they waited the old man out, he might just die on his own.

But then that option faded away when Adam began talking. "You think you've won, don't you? Well, you have not. If I'm going to die, I will take this entire place with me. You'll all see. I have contingencies for situations like this." He fired the .38 again before hobbling down the corridor, firing every few seconds to keep the companions at bay. When the .38 clicked empty, he dropped it to the floor and kept moving, trailing blood from his shattered arm and neck as he went.

Henry peered around the doorframe and saw Adam was gone. "Okay, let's move. We need to find him and finish this. You heard what he said. If there's even an ounce of truth in it, we need to stop him before he does whatever the hell he said."

Jimmy went into the corridor and picked up his shotgun, then retrieved his .38 as well. The latter was quickly reloaded with bullets he had on him. "How humiliating," he said as he reloaded the .38. "He shot at me with my own damn gun."

"Just be glad he didn't kill you with it," Henry said and moved out, his eyes downcast, scanning the floor, following the blood spatter Adam was leaving. Like breadcrumbs left by Hansel and Gretel, the trail couldn't have been easier to follow.

Running, only stopping at each corner, not wanting to dash out to find Adam standing there, ready to shoot them, the group made good time running after the old man.

After reaching a junction in the corridor, Henry spotted Adam at the far end, just as the man pushed on the handle to a fire door that would lead down to the lower level. Not having time to aim, Henry fired a quick double tap, the rounds ricocheting off the door, missing Adam's head by inches. The old man spun around and flipped Henry off, and coughing and hacking, went through the doorway and was gone.

"Damn it, I almost had him," Henry said, as he began to follow, the others right behind him. When they reached the fire door, Henry slammed his hands on the handle but the door remained closed, Henry slamming into it with all his weight to stop himself. There was a small window at head height above the handle. Henry peered through it, just able to see that Adam had used his Kevlar vest to jam the handle on the opposite side so the door wouldn't open. The fire door was made of metal, and their firearms wouldn't be enough to get it open.

"Everyone get back," Henry ordered, and when they had backed away, he shot at an angle at the small glass window to prevent ricochets hitting him. His three bullets struck it but the glass didn't shatter. It was reinforced with metal inlay and was bullet proof. They would need to find another way to reach Adam; time they didn't have if the old man spoke the truth about having some sort of doomsday scenario planned.

"I wonder where he's going," Jimmy said.

"Nowhere good, that's for sure," Cindy added.

Mary pulled out a map of the complex, which she'd been carrying for a few days as she made her way around it. "If I'm reading this right, this fire door leads to a stairwell that will take him to the nuclear reactor for the base."

"The fucking nuke generator?" Jimmy said. "What the hell could he do down there?"

"A lot." Henry thought back to what he knew about nuclear energy, and his face took on a look of ultimate worry and concern. Immediately, he realized they needed an alternate plan in case Adam wasn't reached in time. His mind raced with what to do, and he could only come up with one idea, as far-fetched as it sounded. Reaching into his pocket, he pulled out the D-3 security key card he'd taken from a corpse and handed it to Cindy. "Here, take this. I want you, Sue, and Jimmy to get as much food, water and the rest of our gear, as much as you can carry, and go to the MT lab to see what's there. If my guess is right, see how it all works."

"What the hell are you talking about?" Jimmy asked, wanting to chase after Adam, not go on some crazy errand for Henry.

"Don't argue with me, all right?" Henry snapped. "Look, if Adam's gonna do what I think he is, even if we kill him it won't matter. It'll be too late."

"Then let's get out of here," Cindy said. "We can get that food and take the elevator up top, throw some grenades at the bikers for a distraction, and run for it."

Henry shook his head. "That won't work. Listen, honey, if Adam isn't stopped in time, there won't be anywhere in this state we can run to. Listen, just trust me here. If that lab has what I think it does, it's our only chance of surviving to see tomorrow."

"What about me?" Mary asked. "What'll I do?"

"You're coming with me. I need someone smart like you to help me figure out the nuke computers." He pointed to the map. "We need another way to get to the nuke reactor. Find one, and hurry." He looked at the others. "What the fuck are you three standing around for? Go!"

Sue blinked, as did Cindy. Henry didn't normally curse like he just did, which gave weight to the seriousness he felt about the situation. Turning, they set off to do as instructed, while Mary pointed to the far end of the hallway.

"This way," she said and ran off, Henry right behind her.

They had to backtrack for almost three minutes before finding another set of stairs that would go down to the level they needed. With Henry leading the way, they raced down the new set of stairs, and came out into a hallway that was much paler than what they were used to, the walls a dull gray. The nuclear reactor was on the lowest level, an area not for normal personnel.

Henry wondered if that was truly so, then why were they able to simply come out on the level without any further security? But his unspoken question was answered a moment later when he rounded a corner and approached a security checkpoint. There was a desk where a soldier would have sat, and another keycard slot was set into the frame of a large, reinforced blast door. Beyond the door would be the beginning of the nuclear reactor area; but how would he and Mary get past that blast door?

The odds were Adam was already in the reactor core, doing God knew what. If there was a chance in hell of stopping him, time was running out fast.

Henry went to the door and banged on it, the dull thud of his fists lost in the thickness of the door. "Damn it, there's no way past this."

"We could get explosives," Mary suggested. "Blow the door right up."

Henry shook his head. "We'd need such a powerful blast that we'd probably just end up caving in the entire hallway." He walked over to the desk, looking down at it. There was a calendar blotter from five years ago on the desk, a lamp, a land-line phone, and a ballpoint pen.

"Maybe you're wrong, Henry," Mary said hopefully. "After all, you're just guessing that Adam is going to do something with the reactor. Am I right? You think he's going to mess with the reactor?"

Henry spun around on her, and stepped towards her, his face so filled with fury that Mary took three steps backwards until her shoulders came up against the wall.

Henry's eyes were wide as he glared at her. "Of course he's gonna mess with the reactor? What the hell have I been saying?

He's wounded bad, probably dying! He took some good punches to the chest. I bet he's got busted ribs or worse. We ruined his plans for adding us to his little display of bodies, he's pissed off and wants revenge. If I was in his shoes and crazy as the Mad Hatter in Alice in Wonderland, I'd do the same thing!"

"Okay, Henry, calm down," Mary said, trying to calm him.

"Calm down?" Henry yelled. "Calm down? Don't you get it, Mary? If he does something to the reactor it'll cause a meltdown. The entire state of Nevada will end up glowing for the next hundred years. Everyone in the state will be dead or dying in a matter of weeks if not days. And we're gonna be at ground zero when this place goes up!" He roared his anger at the ceiling, turned around, and grabbed the desk, flipping it onto its side. The contents went flying, the lamp shattered, and the rotary phone separated, though no dial tone was heard, and never would again.

His shoulders heaving, Henry stood perfectly still. He closed his eyes and concentrated on breathing. Mary stood silently behind him. She'd never seen him like this before and it scared her.

Finally, Henry let out a long breath. "I'm sorry, honey, I didn't mean to take out my frustration on you, but I can't begin to tell you how much trouble we're in right now."

Mary swallowed the knot in her throat, considering her words carefully. She didn't want Henry to lose control again. "I...I understand, Henry. Let's not dwell on it, okay? Let's just focus on how we're going to find Adam."

"Okay, it's just..." He stopped talking, his eyes having spotted something jutting out from under the blotter, which had fallen a few feet away from the desk. Going over to it, he kicked the blotter aside, exposing a key card that had been under it. "Well, I'll be," he said while picking up the card.

"What is it?"

Henry had a wide smile on his face as he swiveled on his heels and ran to the blast door, holding the card even with his chest. "It's a security key card. Adam must have put it there for when he needed to get through here. It makes sense. He was the only one alive down here, so why worry about the security passes, and why carry them around all the time. He just hid one here for when it was needed."

"I guess he didn't come this way, so it was still here when we arrived," Mary said, understanding the reasoning.

Henry nodded and slid the card into the wall scanner. "Right. I bet the way he went, he took the card with him. So if we'd managed to follow him exactly we would have been stuck for good with no way to reach him in time."

The key card slid into the unit, the light changing from red to green. A hiss of hydraulics sounded within the wall, and the blast door began to retract sideways. The instant it was open enough for him to slip through, he was moving, Mary right behind him. Henry pocketed the key card, not wanting to end up trapped on the wrong side of the blast door.

"Which way do we go?" Mary asked as they stared down the long hallway before them.

"For now we go this way, but where he is now is anyone's guess. Wherever the main control room would be is our best shot though." He began running, Mary right at his side.

The hallway ended in a T, and they had to decide which way to go. Once more there was a diagram on the wall and Mary quickly studied it, before pointing to the right. "This way; the main control room is down here."

They set off again, running at full speed.

Coming up at another security break, Henry again used the key card, the door opening at once. Charging through the doorway, he came to an instant halt when he entered a massive room.

One side was nothing but blinking lights and monitors. The opposite side was a large glass wall; inside the clear wall the cement housing of the reactor core could be seen, where the fuel rods were maintained.

Chairs lined the computer consoles and monitors on the former side, and sitting in one of the chairs, leaning to the right as he struggled to remain upright, was Adam. He was punching buttons, moving knobs, a large monitor screen above him showing a mechanical arm as it moved around thin cylinders submerged within water. Henry had a pretty good idea what Adam was doing, and if he was correct, it spelled certain doom for everyone.

Adam didn't turn around when Henry and Mary burst into the room, his attention focused on the dials and readouts.

Raising his Glock, not wanting to shoot for risk of missing Adam and damaging something vital beyond him, Henry yelled out, "Adam, stop what you're doing or you're dead!"

Adam slowed his manipulations of the controls and shifted his head so he could glance over his shoulder. Seeing Henry standing there, across the room, his eyes went wide in anger. "Fuck you!" he shrieked, the sound of his voice telling Henry that the man had completely gone off the deep end. "Now you die! We all die!"

Henry knew he had to stop Adam, and though it was risky from so far away, he began firing at the sitting man. One round went wide, striking a steel plate near Adam's feet, but the next bullet found its target. It struck Adam directly in the center of the left knee, hitting him on the back of the leg, shattering the fragile joint, snapping the bottom of the femur, the patella also, and tearing ligaments to shreds. Adam wailed in pain as he reached down to grab his shattered leg, his hand covering the gaping hole there. Blood squirted out of the hole, and he rubbed his leg with his hands; as if by doing so he could somehow smooth out the pain.

Henry began running at Adam, firing as he moved, Mary right behind him. She held her fire, letting Henry handle the situation. She was still slightly confused as to what exactly Henry was doing, so she let him take the lead. Fanning out, she leveled her .38 at Adam, keeping him covered as Henry ran closer.

Adam let go of his shattered leg and went back to work, his hands now coated in sticky blood, leaving dark red splotches on each knob or dial he touched.

Bloody spittle dripped out of the corner of his mouth and into his beard, and one time he coughed, spraying the controls with flecks of crimson. He had internal bleeding, perhaps a shattered rib had even punctured a lung and even now the old man was drowning in his own blood. Just like when a dying elephant went on its final journey to the graveyard where its kind went to die, Adam too, knew his time was short, that he was dying.

On the monitor in front of Adam, the image of water being drained could be seen, the cylinders becoming exposed to the air. Suddenly, alarms began to sound throughout the room as red lights began flashing. Adam hit a switch, silencing the alarms, and went back to work.

Henry fired again, this time the bullet striking Adam in the back, on the right shoulder. The man screamed in shock, the force of the round sending him spinning to the floor. He tried to sit up, but only slumped back to the cold cement.

Upon reaching Adam, Henry stood over the dying man, looking down at him with the Glock leveled at the crazy man's face. "Fix what you did and do it now or so help me I'll blow your brains out all over the floor."

"Then do it, sonny! What do I care? I'm already dead; we all are!" Adam began to laugh, but it quickly degenerated into a coughing, hacking fit.

Henry stared at the maniacal face, the Glock almost shaking in his grip he was so angry. The madman's face glared up at Henry, the white hair and beard now dappled with red, the floor around Adam slowly becoming slick with blood. Adam was bleeding out from his multiple wounds, and knew it. There was no threat that Henry could make that would make Adam listen, not if the old man was ready to die.

Muttering a silent curse for how everything was going down, Henry realized the futility of arguing with Adam for a moment longer, and without so much as a grunt in reply to Adam, he shot the old man in the forehead, silencing him forever. Brain matter exploded out the back of the skull, painting the floor pink and red, as Adam's corpse jumped slightly. The legs twitched for a few more seconds, as neurons sent one final impulse to the extremities, then the body went still.

Henry was already moving. He grabbed Adam by the ankles and dragged him away from the chair. Plopping down into it, he ignored the blood splatter coating the seat. "I should have done that the second I saw him that first day we got here, goddamn it. Mary, come over here. We need to figure out how to fix what he did or it's all over for us."

Mary came to his side, ignoring the blood she stepped in to do so. "I don't know what to do. All of this is nuts. Do I look like a nuclear technician?" She leaned in close so that Henry had no choice but to look her straight in the face. "I was a secretary for heaven's sake!"

"Yeah, and I wrote software, but it had nothing to do with nuclear energy." He studied the controls, trying to figure out what to do. Each button or dial that had a bloody smudge on it were the ones Adam touched, but in what order he did so was unclear. "Help me, damn it!"

Red lights started flashing and alarms began to sound again, making it hard to speak.

"I don't know how!" Mary yelled. "I don't understand what Adam did."

Henry pointed to the monitor screen, and did his best to explain what was happening, what Adam had put in motion before his death. "We need to get the water that's drained away back into that pool, and cover those rods again."

"Why?" Mary asked. "What happens if we don't?"

Henry stopped trying to figure out the controls. He swiveled in the chair to face Mary. He hoped if he explained exactly what he believed was happening, once she knew, she would be of more help. "Okay, listen close 'cause there's no time to go through it again."

She nodded for him to continue.

Henry pointed to the monitor, where the rods were becoming hard to see, as what looked like steam to him began to fill the screen. "Those are fuel rods for the reactor. Uranium, if I'm right. Radioactive as hell, but that's what makes the fuel to run this place. See, the distilled water covers the rods, and they're so hot they make the water boil. That produces steam that's then captured and pumped into turbines, which makes the power for this base. You follow me so far?"

She nodded. "Sure, go on."

"Okay, but what happens if the water's drained away, exposing the rods and not keeping them cool?"

"They start to get even hotter?" Mary asked.

"Right, they get even hotter; three thousand degrees Celsius hotter to be exact. But as they keep getting hotter they start to melt, and as they do, they give off hydrogen gas. When enough gas builds up, this place is going to be one giant bomb."

"Then why are we standing here? Why didn't we make a run for it past the bikers instead of chasing Adam down here?"

Henry shook his head. "Because when this place blows, the radioactive gas will be released into the air and everyone within miles of this place is going to be irradiated as the rods literally begin to melt into the earth itself."

"So you're saying there's no place to run?"

"Yeah, pretty much. Our only hope is to stop the meltdown before it begins."

Mary moved to the chair beside Henry, her eyes staring at the myriad of controls. The monitor on the screen showed nothing but steam, the rods completely hidden from view.

"So we need to figure out how to get water back onto the rods or else," she repeated, Henry nodding. Mary looked at all the dials. "But there's no way of knowing what to push here. We could be here for weeks and never figure it out."

Before Henry could reply, every monitor began flashing the words, **RADIATION LEAK. ALL PERSONNEL EVACUATE!**

"What does that mean?" Mary yelled over the claxons filling the room.

"It means our time's up. The exposed rods are too hot to stop now and the radiation can't be contained now that all the water's burned off!" He jumped up, grabbing his Glock from the panel where he'd placed it. "We need to go before we get hit with a lethal dose of radiation."

"But what about the rods?" she yelled. "You said we need to cover them again!"

"It's too late for that. What's done is done. All we can do now is run for it and hope for the best. Come on!"

They ran out of the room, the key card once more opening the door to exit. Behind them, when Henry glanced over his shoulder, he saw a display appear on every monitor. **THIRTY MINUTES**

TO MELTDOWN began to flash as a timer appeared, counting down the time remaining before the plant went critical. The warning lights also changed color, warning of the approaching doom.

As Henry and Mary left the reactor room behind and Mary sprinted around the desk Henry had flipped over in his frustration, she called out, "How the hell did Adam even know how to do that? He was a janitor for this base for Pete's sake!"

Henry was right by her side, the two of them moving fast, their legs eating up the distance as they dashed through the hallways.

"He's had years alone down here to figure it all out," he guessed. "Nothing but time to read and study. There's bound to be manuals somewhere for how to operate the reactor, and he would've had to learn to make sure it was all running smoothly. Computers do most of the work but sometimes a human might've been needed when there was a glitch. Nothing goes on forever if it's automated."

Ten minutes later, they reached a junction that split up into three corridors, and Henry grabbed Mary and stopped her. "Hold up, this is where we split up."

"What? Why?" She didn't understand and was getting tired of always being one step behind what Henry was thinking.

"No time to explain, you just get to the MT lab where the others already are. If I was right about what's there, it means we're not dying here today. Go, I'll be right behind you by no more than ten minutes. I promise."

"But there's less than twenty minutes left!" she yelled.

He turned and ran off, towards the armory, as a hidden speaker in the ceiling began counting down the remaining time before the reactor went critical. The lights dimmed and only the red ones began to flash, which was the sign to evacuate the base.

"Where the hell are you going? What's so important you need to do it now?"

"I have some unfinished business. Just go already!" he called over his shoulder, before rounding a corner and disappearing from sight.

Mary stared at the empty space where Henry had been for another five seconds, and with an annoyed look on her face, she turned and ran off to join the others.

Chapter 11

The Skullfuckers had settled down for the long wait, knowing they couldn't get inside the bunker, nor could the companions get out—at least that was what Vincent believed.

He'd almost lost Henry's trail, only to find it again thanks to one of his brothers, an Indian they called Cochise. The man was an expert tracker, and was proud of his native heritage. He'd once bragged to Vincent that he could track a man over solid rock or through a running stream. Vincent hadn't believed it, but he hadn't really cared either. At the time, he'd been so high on cocaine that nothing had mattered anyway, well, other than the pleasure he'd been feeling.

But when the trail for the companions had grown cold after the fiasco at the corpse-sea, Vincent had called Cochise over to him and asked for help. The man was happy to oblige. After all, it was his brothers and sisters who had been killed as well.

It hadn't taken the man long to pick up Henry's trail, though doing something that appeared mystical in nature, like tracking a jeep across hard pavement, wasn't necessary.

Cochise had spotted transmission fluid, and once he found the first drop, the trail was as easy to follow as if Henry had drawn a painted line.

Back when LAW rockets had been shot at Henry, one of the resulting explosions had managed to send shrapnel up into the transmission pan of his jeep, and a small leak had begun. So as long as Henry used the jeep, he left a trail.

Once the bikers found the jeep abandoned, Vincent had grown concerned that his prey was lost for good, but once more Cochise proved himself and soon the biker gang was hot on the companions' trail again.

But they had escaped once more, and though Vincent didn't know what lay beyond the metal door, he knew sooner or later either he would find a way inside, or Watson and his people would have to come out. When that time came, he would be waiting to pay back Henry in blood.

More than six days had passed without an occurrence, and though at first the men wanted vengeance for their slaughtered brothers, now a few of the men wanted to leave, and only Vincent's iron will kept them under his thumb. He wasn't leaving until Watson and his people came back out. Watson had to leave eventually, and when he did, the biker President would be waiting to kill him and his people.

So after so long with nothing happening, no one noticed when the steel door opened a few inches, then a few more.

A lone arm came snaking around the door, and just as it was spotted by one of the Skullfuckers, the arm tossed something, to then quickly withdraw.

Instantly, the bikers were up and moving, firing at the door en masse. Like rain hitting a metal roof, bullet after bullet spanged off the already pockmarked metal, the bikers yelling and screaming. Buckshot from shotguns struck the surrounding cement that made up the shed, leaving hundreds of small holes in the outer wall.

The bikers yelled their fury, Vincent the loudest of them all.

In all the chaos of the door opening, no one had noticed the object that was tossed, as it wasn't large, perhaps no bigger than a coffee can that had once held coffee grounds.

The metal can rolled across the ground towards the bikers, who didn't see the object as dangerous. Why would they? It wasn't a grenade, or anything else that seemed a threat.

The can made it all the way to the feet of one of the bikers, who looked down as the can bounced off his boots. Curious as to what it might be, he stopped firing and bent down and picked it up.

The plastic lid was secured to the can, so he removed it to see what was inside, never once thinking it might be a mistake.

Vincent noticed the man, who instead of shooting was playing with something, so he also stopped firing and went over to him.

"Brother, you better have a fucking good reason for not using your piece," Vincent warned as he stepped up to the biker, and just as he finished speaking, Vincent saw the man's eyes go wide with what sure seemed like fear—and it wasn't from Vincent's words.

Like the man was a child who wanted to show a friend the pet he had in the can, the biker tilted the coffee can so that Vincent could see inside it.

The second Vincent saw the contents, his eyes went wide as hell, and he opened his mouth to scream, managing to get out, "Watson, you fucking piece of shi...!"

Then there was nothing, as a brilliant white flash consumed him, as well as all of the Skullfuckers in the vicinity. The ceiling became coated in a generous amount of blood and gore, and what wouldn't stick began to rain down onto the devastated area in loud, wet plops.

If Henry had bothered to glance over his shoulder at the monitor to the side of the door, he would have seen the screen splattered in blood, the donors of the droplets numbering in the dozens. For a few brief moments, a single eyeball was stuck to the screen, or rather the camera lens mounted to the ceiling. It hung there perilously, then slowly slid down the lens until it fell back to the ground, directly into the massive, smoking crater that was left behind, the edges strewn with dismembered corpses and motorcycle parts.

Henry didn't need to see the results of his actions, knowing all too well what they would be. He barely heard the explosion as he raced back to the elevator that would take him below ground once more, a thin smile on his lips. Three white sticks of Hyrdromite had been crammed into the coffee can, a grenade with the pin pulled used to detonate the explosives. He probably hadn't needed to use that much of the dynamite-like substance, but he wanted to make damn sure no Skullfucker remained alive.

He'd learned a long time ago to never leave an enemy behind. That was how a man got shot in the back down the road, and though the meltdown would probably kill every biker there, he didn't want to chance it. Besides, after everything Vincent had put him through, Henry wanted the satisfaction of knowing he had been the one to take the man out. And in that brief instant before the biker President's world went white, Henry knew that Vincent knew who had been the architect of his demise.

The elevator door opened deep underground and Henry was off and running again, while the hidden speakers all around him continued to count off the remaining time. As he ran past the hidden laser beam, he inadvertently woke up the spider droids once more, and as one group, the sec droids filed out of their charging units and headed off in search of prey.

Once more, their clickety-clacks filled the corridors of the base as they went on the hunt anew.

Henry turned a corner as he made his way to the others, and ran smack dab into the approaching spider droids. His mouth dropped open when he saw them, and though he pulled his Glock from its holster and began firing, he couldn't help but be amazed at his bad luck.

It sure seemed like the universe wanted him dead.

He shot two droids right between their glowing eyes just as they scooted in and nipped at his legs, the impact of the bullets sending them flipping over onto their backs. Then he was off and running again, knowing there was no time to mess around.

The droids were fast, and they nipped at his heels as he powered through the passageways, knowing that if he wanted to survive to see the next hour, he had no choice but to lead the sec droids right to where his friends were waiting.

Rounding a corner, he almost fell when his boots slid out from under him, and his hands slapped the wall to hold himself up. Then he was moving again. The spider droids took the corner with ease, their legs gripping the floor easily.

Other than the sound of his own breathing in his head, the constant clickety-clack filled his ears. A sound he would hear in his nightmares if he lived to see another day.

Entering the matter transfer room, the door propped open, he removed the chair in the doorway and saw the others were waiting impatiently, Mary was there, too, and each of them was standing on a raised, glowing platform in the corner of the room, their gear also on the raised dais. On three sides of the platform, the walls were made of some translucent material made for conductivity.

On the wall, a small display was counting down to zero, only five minutes remaining. A muffled voice from hidden speakers in the hallway proclaimed five minutes to meltdown

"You're sure cutting it close, Henry," Cindy said as Henry jumped onto the glowing dais.

"Spider droids right behind me!" he yelled. "Get hard people!"

"What?" Jimmy screeched. "You've gotta be kidding me!"

Henry turned and fought to control his breathing, as he pointed to the door. Already there were dents in the door as the indefatigable sec droids began chewing through it.

Despite the high tension, there was nothing to do but wait, so it was a chance for Mary to get more information on where exactly Henry had gone off to.

"I made sure that no matter what, Vincent and his cronies are never gonna be a problem again," Henry explained and quickly filled them in on what he'd done.

"Seems like overkill if this place is gonna go supernova," Jimmy said when Henry had finished.

"Maybe, but I like knowing they're all probably dead," Henry said. "No one could have survived that blast." He nodded to Sue. "So I was right about this room, and you figured out how it all works here?"

Sue nodded. "Cindy and I had a hell of a time, but we found something like a manual and read through it. If we did it right it'll work. That is, if it works at all."

"What do you mean by that?" he asked, breathing heavily from his mad dash to the MT lab.

"She means," Mary added, "that the unit has only been used once before on living matter, and that was on a test animal. It's never actually been used on human beings yet."

He blinked in surprise at hearing that, as it certainly wasn't the news he wanted to hear. "So what happened to the test animal? Did it make it?" The timer was counting down from two minutes.

Jimmy had to add his two cents. "No, it didn't, old man; the damn bunny rabbit arrived on the other end dead as the proverbial fucking doornail."

"Oh, that's just wonderful." Once more, Henry wondered if the universe truly wanted him dead.

"So what do we do now?" Mary asked. "We don't even know if this thing works."

"We're out of options, Mary, so if it doesn't, then we're all dead, either from those sec droids, or a meltdown, or both." Henry's voice was low, ominous, and though he hated to sound so negative, it was the truth.

One minute remained on the countdown.

The sound of tearing metal filled the room and all eyes went to the door, where the first spider droid was forcing its silver body through the hole it had made. More tears appeared in the metal, and in seconds the heavy door was nothing but Swiss cheese, the droids spilling into the room, their red eyes once more seeking the flesh of the companions.

"Take them out!" Henry screamed. "We only need to hold them back for a minute!"

Scampering over the tables and desks, the spider droids charged the group of humans, who were trapped in the corner of the room on the glowing platform. They had backed themselves into a corner, and if in the next minute nothing happened and they remained where they were, the group would be at the mercy of the spider droids.

"Well, old man!" Jimmy yelled over the booming of his shotgun, his voice barely heard from all the firepower erupting within the room. "At least if the droids kill us, we won't have to worry about this place going boom."

"Shut up, Jimmy!" Henry yelled.

"Yeah," Mary added. "Shut up, Jimmy!"

"Hey, just trying to help," he quipped as he shot a droid directly in the face, the blast of pellets sending it flying backwards, its silver chassis peppered with tiny dents. One eye had been shattered, but the remaining one glowed even brighter as it righted itself and renewed the attack.

It was a losing battle, the droids coming at the group from all sides, and only the fact they had their backs protected thus far had prevented them from being overrun.

Focused on keeping the killer droids at bay, the companions didn't even see when the display on the wall finished its countdown, the numbers becoming all zeros and flashing repeatedly.

Something behind the wall began to hum, the sound growing louder with each passing second. Soon, the noise was so overwhelming that everyone had to hold their hands over their ears, faces scrunched up in pain. Thin bolts of electrical lightning erupted from the platform under them, shooting up into the ceiling, where another panel the same as the one on the floor was. This static charge seemed to halt the droids, perhaps messing with their circuitry.

Which was a good thing, for the companions were helpless to defend themselves any longer, as their bodies were subjected to energy forces that were unimaginable to them.

His eyes squeezed tightly shut, Henry managed to peer through his cracked eyelids to see the digital display had counted to zero, which also meant that the reactor had just gone into full meltdown.

There was a massive rumbling deep within the bunker, a sound so loud it overrode the oppressive humming.

The walls began to shake, the ceiling cracked, pieces of plaster falling inwards.

All the companions had fallen to their knees, the pain of the humming too much to bear. The spider droids surrounded the glowing dais, a few trying to cross the energy barrier but failing miserably. More than one had its circuits fried as it attempted to lunge at the helpless humans.

The entire room seemed to tilt on its axis as the explosive pressure of the detonations deep underground roiled throughout the bunker, consuming everything in its path.

Henry forced his eyes open one last time, and as he did so, he looked around, seeing all his friends lying unconscious. He could feel himself slipping into darkness as well, but he managed to fight off the coming blackness for a few more heartbeats.

The sound of the humming had grown to such a high pitch that it couldn't be heard by human ears any longer, but it could be *felt*, deep down to his very being.

A soft mist began to rise up around the companions, but Henry didn't know if it was from the cycling of the matter transfer system or if it was simply smoke due the fires raging throughout the bunker.

There was a massive crashing sound from outside the torn door of the room, and he shifted his head to the side, the very effort almost too much to manage.

He could only watch, helpless as the door to the room was blown clear off its hinges to rebound off the far wall, and a massive fireball of orange, yellow and red flowed into the room. The deafening sound it made was like a living thing, as if it was some inhuman demon or animal filled with an unrelenting hate for anything that lived. It was devastation given form, one that's only reason for existence was destruction, to consume anything in its fiery wake.

The heat caressed his cheeks, seeming to wrap around him in its hot embrace.

A flash of silver floated before him but it was gone as soon as it appeared.

There was only a bright light before him, one so powerful it blocked out everything else.

Try as he might, he couldn't remain conscious, and though he fought with every ounce of his iron will to stay awake, he slipped into a dark oblivion, one he wondered if he would ever awaken from.

Chapter 12

Henry Watson slowly opened his eyes, his vision blurry. He couldn't make out a thing as he lay immobile. Dizzy, he closed them again, instantly feeling better.

His breathing was labored, and he slowly rolled onto his back, making it easier; he let out a long exhale.

Mentally, he did a diagnosis of himself, wondering what had happened and where he was. Disoriented, he had trouble remembering anything before waking up.

His stomach felt queasy, nauseous, and he idly wondered if he was going to vomit.

His right hand slid down his body and touched the gun holster on his hip. The holster was empty, his Glock missing. He slowly moved his left hand down his side and at least felt comforted to find the handle of his panga where it should be.

Groaning, he tried to sit up, and as he did, his elbow hit something that scraped across the floor. Reaching out, he discovered it was his Glock. Had he dropped it before lying down? That seemed an odd thing to do.

Moving his head from side to side as he fought to push back the fuzziness, he felt something on his stomach, then little pressures that moved up to his chest. Eight separate pressure points pushed down on his body, each one not enough to cause much discomfort. But even though confused, he knew deep down it wasn't right.

Knowing that whatever had happened he needed to get up, and worried he could be in danger, Henry forced himself to sit up on his elbows, his head pressed against a wall that was warm to the touch. With the strength of an iron will, he forced his eyes to open.

Only to find himself staring into the glowing red orbs of a spider sec droid.

He didn't move, not so much as blink; even his breath hitched in his throat.

The droid sat on his chest, staring at Henry, unsure of what to do. So far, the human prey had made no signs that its processors deemed dangerous.

Instantly, Henry's memory came flooding back. Area 51 in Nevada, the madman called Adam, Vincent and his biker gang, and the nuclear meltdown of the reactor deep underground.

The desperate gamble to use an experimental matter transfer system, something pulled right out of Star Trek if Henry was to believe it. And finally, as the seconds counted down, the entire base exploding, just as the spider droids arrived to renew their attack on the beleaguered companions. The matter transfer had actually worked! It must have, for if not, he wouldn't be alive, and there was no question that Area 51 had gone into meltdown. All those ramifications would normally have been something to ponder; such as considering how in the hell his atoms had been broken down and sent across time and space like a proverbial email, only to be reassembled whole on the other end.

But at the moment, there was most definitely more pressing matters to attend to, such as the deadly sec droid perched on his body like a curious puppy.

Henry stared at the glowing red orbs that seemed to be studying him, and to his disappointment, he realized that another one had managed to join the first one on the ride out of the complex.

A clicking sound to his left made him carefully shift his head an inch. Out of the corner of his eye, he spotted yet another sec droid. It was moving over Jimmy, who lay unconscious, as were the others. Sue was lying on her back, her mouth open, a sliver of drool rolling out the corner of her mouth. Mary and Cindy lay together, arms entwined, only a foot from where Sue was. As he watched each of his friends, he saw their chests rising and falling evenly, letting him know they were alive, though still unconscious.

Ever so slowly, Henry moved his right arm out and snaked his hand across the floor, until he managed to grip the stock of Jimmy's shotgun. With his eyes never moving from the sec droid's glowing orbs for eyes, he carefully pulled the shotgun towards him. It took everything he had not to jump up and buck the droid off his chest, but he knew that would be a very bad move. The killing machine might fall off, but would be on him again before he managed to stand up.

The droid shifted its stance on his chest slightly, Henry feeling the pressure of its legs, but still, it didn't move; only studied.

Henry was counting the seconds, knowing if he could get only a few more, he would be able to kill the damn thing that had followed the companions through time and space.

The muzzle of the shotgun was maneuvered into position so that it was only inches from the droid's face—if that was what it could be called. The pincers opened and closed ever so subtly, as if the droid was dreaming of what it was going to do to Henry.

When the shotgun was in position, Henry turned his face away from the droid, not wanting to be hit with blowback, and squeezed the trigger of the shotgun, wincing as he did so, as he expected to hear the deafening report and feel the blast of the weapon as it bucked in his hand.

But instead of instant sound and violence, all he heard was a soft 'click.'

The shotgun was empty.

"Well, that sucks," he muttered low in his throat. Snapping his eyes open, he moved his head to stare into those red orbs once more, but instantly he saw something had changed. It wasn't something he could put his finger on, but more of a feeling; the droid had just changed from whatever mode it had been running into something far more deadly.

He knew he had to move, now. Before it was too late, and he had to get the sec droids away from his friends.

He reached around and grabbed the shotgun with his other hand as well, so that he was gripping it like a baseball bat, then he pushed off the floor, the sec droid skittering off him as its legs tried to grasp his clothing.

The time for caution was over; only action would save the day now.

The spider droid had barely landed on the floor before Henry was swinging the shotgun, the stock connecting with the silver carapace and sending it across the room like he was playing golf.

There was a whining of servo motors from his side, and Henry turned to see the other spider droid now focused on him. Henry moved faster than the droid could react. "I haven't forgotten you either." He moved in and used the shotgun as a club again, sending the droid flying across the room to hit the wall and fall behind a row of computer consoles.

From past experience, he knew firearms wouldn't do the job on the hard shells of the droids, so using the shotgun as a club was only out of desperation. But as adrenaline flushed his system, he became focused, the nausea evaporating, his mind becoming sharp.

He lunged for one of the duffel bags filled to the top with explosives and ammunition, then pulled out a hand grenade. But he needed one more item, and as he dug through the bag, he found it a second later.

Duct tape.

Something the group never went anywhere without due to its versatility. There had been rolls of it in the Area 51 armory, and

Henry had made sure they'd taken one for each bag the friends carried.

The two spider droids were already up-righting themselves, and the first one to be struck by Henry was skittering back at him. He put down the grenade and duct tape and picked up the shotgun again. As the droid came at him, he swung for the fences, once more sending it falling backwards, where it hit the second one, knocking it to the side.

As the two droids gathered themselves for a concerted attack, Henry went back to what he was doing, knowing he had seconds if that. Using the duct tape, he pulled off a large strip and rolled it into a ball, doing his best to keep the sticky side facing outwards. Then he took the grenade and attached it to the sticky tape-ball.

Pulling the pin on the grenade, the only thing preventing it from going off was his grip on the handle, which once released would detonate in seconds.

He jumped off the raised platform he was on and charged at the spider droids, just as they were about to do the same to him. Reaching the first one, he raised his foot and stomped down hard on it, forcing it to the floor, its legs spreading out beneath it like a crab. It was strong, and Henry knew he couldn't keep it there for long. The soft sound of hydraulics moving and shifting within the silver shell filled the room as the droid fought its aggressor. The second droid was about to attack when Henry leaned over grabbed it, picking it up. He stuck the grenade to the second one's back, while struggling to keep the pincers away from him as the metallic legs went wild, flailing every which way. It was hard to hold it, the damn machine bucking in his hands, and he knew he could only maintain his grip for another second, which was a good thing because the grenade would blow at the same time if he didn't get rid of the damn thing.

He removed his booth from the spider droid he was stepping on and ran to the door, using his elbow to hit a switch on the doorframe. The door slid to the side silently and Henry heaved the spider droid out into what was a long corridor. Clicking sounded behind him, and he turned just in time to see the second droid, which seemed angry at being stepped on if that was possible, charging at Henry. Sidestepping the droid, it came right up to him, and with a sweeping kick, he sent it flying out into the corridor to join its brother.

Slapping the door control, he jumped backwards as the door slid closed. His last glimpse of the two droids, standing side by side, was of their duo pair of glowing red eyes staring back at him.

Then the door closed with a hiss and there was dull thud from the hallway. The door buckled in its frame and Henry felt a tremor through the souls of his boots, followed by the spanging of bits of metal and other debris striking the door. As he stood there, everything went deathly quiet, only the sound of his heavy breathing to mar the silence.

He quickly loaded Jimmy's shotgun with shells taken from a gear bag, and picked up his Glock before returning to the door. Pressing his ear against the metal, he listened closely for sounds of the sec droids on the other side.

He heard nothing that sounded like the spider droids were active and coming through the door. He waited for a full two minutes, his ear pressed to the cool metal, and finally decided it was time to see what was going on in the hallway.

When he pressed the button to open the door, it wouldn't move, but the sound of a hidden mechanism trying to work came from within the wall. He tried again, this time using his hands to help shove the door open. At first it wouldn't budge, but with enough force it soon opened an inch, followed by another, and finally he had it open a full twelve inches.

Peering cautiously through the gap, he looked out onto the devastation of the corridor. The overhead lights were hanging down, separated from the ceiling from the blast; they swayed on hanging wires, the housings sparking electricity where they still worked. The far wall was completely demolished, the plaster and paint entirely gone, exposing the now scorched cement that was the true wall, though some of the cement had been damaged, like a giant set of teeth had taken a bite out of it. The floor as well had a large chunk missing, over five feet gone, leaving a deep, crater-like impression. A haze of smoke hung in the air, stinging the eyes.

Spider droid parts were scattered everywhere. Legs still twitched, resembling insect appendages. But both of the droids had been destroyed in the blast. Off to the side, was the upper half of one of the droids, looking like a crab's shell left on the beach after it had molted. Pushing through the gap in the door, Henry stepped out into the hallway to investigate some more, when suddenly, the door behind him slammed closed, leaving him standing out in the corridor alone, with nothing but his panga, Glock and Jimmy's shotgun.

Going to the door, he studied it up and down, and cursed when he realized it had a keycard access to the right of the door, similar to the entries at Area 51. He considered shooting the door but reneged when he remembered how thick it was. Another option was to shoot the keypad or use the panga to see if he could pry it from the wall. Then perhaps he could cross a few wires and jury-rig the door to open. He was about to try when he changed his mind again. Surely, there would be some sort of failsafe to prevent someone from doing such an act, and if so, would it prevent the door from ever opening again?

He began banging on the door with his fist. "Jimmy! Cindy! Mary! Someone! Hey, wake up already! I'm trapped out here!" He pounded harder. "Sue, I'm out here!" He did this for over a minute but there was no response from inside the room.

His eyes darted side to side, watching for security droids, or other personnel that might be around, but so far the place was empty. After all, if anyone had been inside wherever he was, the explosion would have drawn them to his location. But other than the sparking of exposed wires, all was silent.

Why weren't the others waking up yet? Hell, he'd just fought a small war right beside them, complete with explosions, and none of his friends had stirred so much as a finger. Thinking about it, he found it damn fortunate that at least he had woken early. What would have happened if he'd been unconscious as well, while the two spider droids had free reign to do as they pleased to the helpless humans?

He turned and leaned his back against the door, sucking in the acrid air in the corridor. Small fires burned here and there, some already fizzling out, the others soon to follow. He could feel the need to want to cough, but thus far had been fighting it, and he realized breathing in the residue of whatever was burning probably wasn't in his best interest.

If he couldn't get back into the room, then he might as well set off and explore, and perhaps see if he could find a keycard to open the door. His friends were safe enough at the moment. Let them sleep. Hopefully, when he returned, they would have revived. And if they woke before he returned, well, one look around the room, and if they opened the door and saw the devastation in the hallway, and the remnants of the droids, would tell them what happened.

He considered leaving a note on the wall, written on the smoke-smudged wall with his finger, but decided not to. If there were other people around besides himself and his friends, he didn't want to let those people know about the slumbering travelers within the matter transfer room. There was no reason to detail his plans to a potential enemy.

So with no other choices before him, Henry turned and walked down the corridor to see where he had ended up.

He strolled through the lonely passageways for over an hour, finding no other living beings, though he did find countless corpses, all old and dried from age. Many had been shot in the head, telling Henry the bodies were probably once the walking dead.

Sometimes he would come across a section of corridor where there was nothing but dried blood and bits of clothing on the floor or walls. Something bad had happened in these spots, but any remains had been either removed or cleaned up long ago. The blood was dry and flaking, nothing even remotely fresh.

There were no diagrams on the walls, no maps detailing where he was and where other areas were located.

So he scraped an arrow into the corners on the walls each time he reached one, so he could find his way back to the matter transfer room when it was time to return. It was cold in the corridors as well, so cold that each time he exhaled, steam billowed forth. With only a shirt on he was feeling the chill and knew he needed to find warmer clothing, so as he searched the place, that was a main concern, as well as looking for a keycard. It didn't feel like the air conditioning was running full blast however; the cold felt more natural, like something he would have expected in the winter back home in the Midwest. But that little bit of knowledge still gave him no clue as to where he was. One thing was that thanks to the cold, the bodies he found were odorless, and with the temperature so low, nothing had rotted like if it had been warm; no maggots had festered within the decayed meat.

Other than the matter transfer room, all other rooms he'd come across were simple offices. They had all been abandoned at some time in the past, with paper scattered across the floors and what little remained for furniture in disarray.

Then he got lucky. In one of the offices, he found a blue anorak. Quickly slipping into the warm jacket, he zipped it up and immediately felt better. His hands were still cold, but at least he had something warm to wear. He left the hood off, not needing it inside the building or wherever he was.

Overhead fluorescent lights in the ceiling still glowed brightly, though many had burned out over time. He wondered where the power was coming from. Was it nuclear like back at Area 51? Then he thought back to Adam and the meltdown and decided he didn't really care where the power was coming from. One thing he found out soon enough was that wherever he was, it wasn't as big on technology as where he'd come from. There were some security cameras in the hallways, mounted high on the walls, but they were definitely dormant.

As he continued moving through what he believed was another military base of some kind, he came across the motor pool. It was empty, or so he thought at first, but way in the back, behind a large pile of empty crates, and covered with tarps, as if someone had stashed them there, were two snow buggies. Each one had ice spikes jutting out of the hard rubber, and there was a machine gun mounted to the top of each frame, which resembled a dune buggy configuration more than anything else. But these vehicles were entirely enclosed in thick plexiglass, and had single doors on each side. It was lightweight to move across the snow easily; they would be excellent transportation when Henry and his friends left wherever the hell they were. Keys were in the ignitions, and when he started each one, he was pleased to hear the engines cough a few times and begin idling smoothly. The batteries had been on some sort of chargers, the wires running from the engines to a wall socket. There was a large, hangar-like door at the top of a low ramp that led to what he assumed was outside, but there was also a small door to the right as well, so personnel didn't have to open the large door designated only for vehicles.

Figuring this was as good a time as any to see where he was, he moved up the ramp until reaching the door. Some fresh air would be good. After more than a week of breathing recycled air, he was eager to feel the sun on his face again.

There was a glowing keypad on the doorframe, just like he'd seen in Area 51, and at first he prepared to start cursing up a storm, until he saw that right above the keypad, scratched into the cement by a knife or something sharp, were the numbers: seven, four, three, two. He blinked in surprise when he saw the numbers, then actually turned around to see if there was someone standing there, and if there were, that they were going to nod and tell him that, yes, it was just that easy this time.

With a shrug he punched in the numbers, followed by the 'enter' button, and as he did, there was a soft click as the door unlocked. But he wasn't going to be so stupid as to leave the base and end up locked out like he did an hour ago. Turning, he ran down the ramp and over to a work bench, where he found a long tool for getting at hard-to-reach bolts on an engine, and jogged back to the door.

Now, when he opened the outer door, he would place the tool on the ground and prevent the door from locking behind him, much like what people once did when they needed a smoke at work and used a door not made for reentry.

He held the shotgun in his hands, ready to use it if there was a need, and with one last glance over his shoulder to make sure he was still alone, he pushed open the door and stepped out to get some much-needed fresh air.

Chapter 13

The muzzle of the shotgun poked out from between the door and its frame, followed a moment later by its owner.

The thick metal door opened soundlessly, pushing the snow blown up against it, and after kicking some snow away from the door so that it would be able to close when needed, Henry dropped the tool by his feet to prevent the door from closing and locking him outside. Not that he needed to, he now realized, for he saw there was a keypad on the outside of the door to the right of him as well. Of course, he didn't know if the same code would work, but he would have been surprised if it didn't. Still, better to leave the door open slightly to prevent any mistakes or malfunctions on the part of the mechanisms tied to either the door or the keypad.

If he ended up trapped on the wrong side of the closed door, he would surely die before finding safety if the weather was any indication of the environment. Going out alone, he knew he was taking a hell of a risk. If something happened to him, there would be no one to help him. He would die alone, his body soon covered in snow, forever frozen outside the complex. Not a pleasant image to have.

It was still light out but only just, the overcast sky allowing only the barest of sunlight to filter down to the frozen terrain.

He immediately noticed upon stepping outside that it was bitterly cold; an arctic blast of cold that froze the moisture in his nostrils and stung his cheeks, making him want to cough. Few times had he felt cold such as this.

He recalled one time years ago, before the world had fallen into turmoil, when the temperature had dropped to below zero. He remembered having to leave his house to run an errand, and it was so cold that the saliva on his lips had become frozen in only seconds, long before he'd reached his car after stepping outside.

This cold reminded him of that experience.

He stood by the door, not moving just yet. Outside, snow flurries swirled across a flat plain about seventy feet square, the wind howling. Looking left and right, and seeing nothing that could cause him harm, he stepped out into the snowy wasteland. He pulled the sleeves of the anorak down over his hands. It helped, but he knew he couldn't stay out for too long without risking frostbite. His breath plumed before him each time he exhaled.

He took in the bleak landscape before him as he walked farther away from the door. Turning around, he looked back the way he'd come, to see that the complex—for he could now tell that was what it most definitely was—was set deep into the side of a mountain, with a winding trail leading away from it to lower land. Trees dotted the landscape, their canopies covered with a fresh dusting of snow. He had no idea where he might be as far as location. Was this Antarctica or perhaps Greenland? Where could he be that there was so much snow and ice, the temperature so cold, the land so barren?

The snow buggies would be able to handle the terrain easily, he was pleased to see. The trail also would be simple to navigate. So at least there was a route out of the complex when the companions were ready. Of course, they would need to stock up on winter gear, but there was still more of the complex to search, and hopefully once it had been checked from top to bottom, more supplies would be found.

The shotgun was already getting cold under his palms. His Glock and panga were on his hips, safe from exposure under his anorak. Turning forward once more, he gazed out at the jagged peaks surrounding him on all sides, their snow-covered tops layered with fresh snow and ice. Hopefully, if there was a need to travel that way, there would be a trail through those mountains. He didn't relish trying to go at them on foot.

There was a large mound of snow a little to the side. He walked over to it, for some reason thinking it didn't look right. When he reached it, he kicked at the base with his boot, and sure enough, a frozen arm appeared when the snow was knocked off it. Using the butt of the shotgun, he scraped away more of the snow to find an entire pile of frozen corpses. Most seemed to have head wounds, resembling zombies, but a few looked as if they had died in other ways, mostly bites and tearing, like wild animals had been at the corpses. When the bites had occurred, whether pre or post mortem, was also unknown. From a cursory glance, Henry figured he'd found a body dump after the zombies had been destroyed, but he might have been incorrect. Still, bodies lying out in the open air was nothing new to him, and as long as the people who did it were long gone, it wasn't of much interest to him.

Far to the north, a thick black cloud of ash hung in the sky, the origin unknown. It wasn't smoke; that was for sure. Not by the way it hovered in the sky, barely moving.

Spotting movement far off in the valley below, he watched for a moment, seeing two white shapes almost blending in seamlessly with their surroundings. If they hadn't been moving he would never have seen them. The bears' white coats weren't as white as he first thought; the fur was more of a dirty-white, with splotches of mud here and there. Judging their size compared to their surroundings, the bears were quite large.

He felt his heart skip a beat when the monstrous bears turned towards him, and began to come his way. Though the animals posed no such threat being so far away, Henry couldn't help but get the shotgun into a better firing position. Both bears looked huge, even from a distance, and even one would have been difficult to kill, let alone both of them. Gauging the distance, they had to be at least a quarter mile away, only the wide-open plain allowing him to see them at all. And to take the winding trail down to the plateau would have taken even longer in distance.

No, the bears were no threat to him; best to see what else he could see and get back inside where it was warm, and where it was undoubtedly safer.

As he turned around to return to the warmth of the complex, it was ironic that it was the two bears being spotted that probably saved his life in the next second, for by seeing them, he'd made sure the shotgun was in his hands and ready to fire, despite the cold. Otherwise, the weapon might have been held in a more relaxed pose, one where he never would have been able to use it instantly.

A third bear, appearing as if from nowhere, its white coat blending in seamlessly with the terrain, attacked him from behind, jumping onto his back and forcing him to the ground so hard that the wind was knocked out of his lungs. But through it all, Henry held onto the shotgun, gripping it tightly in his fists.

A hundred things raced through his mind as he was thrown forward, as he went through the list of potential enemies that could be attacking him. One that didn't come to mind was that of a bear.

With the wind knocked out of him, not understanding what had happened, he scrabbled to his feet as quick as he could, his boots slipping on the snow and ice. At first glance, the bear being so white, he didn't fully understand what was attacking him. Before he could move away, and just as he stood up, he was pummeled to the side by a huge paw, where he went flying to land heavily in the snow once more. But reflexes from years of fighting everything from the walking dead, to wild dogs, to feral human beings, had made Henry act without thinking. To react to danger the way a normal man would simply blink if dust blew in his eyes. Because of his instant reaction, just before he was hit, Henry squeezed the trigger of the shotgun, the blast of pellets hitting the bear—which was tall as he was when it stood on four legs—in the right shoulder, missing its face by inches.

Dark red dappled the white fur on the shoulder, but other than that, the animal only seemed more enraged at being shot. The bear nipped at its shoulder as if it could somehow bite what was stinging it away. For a few moments, the bear moved around in a circle, much the way a dog would chase its tail as it tried to get at the wound, but finally it gave up and focused on the prey before it. It growled low in its throat, shaking its head angrily, sensing that the cause of its pain was the prey before it.

Henry barely hesitated as he forced himself to his feet, wincing at the pain in his right arm at the elbow. The fingers didn't want to work on that hand either. When he'd landed, he'd struck rock or ice hidden beneath the snow, and his arm tingled with pain. Glancing past the bear, he could see the partially-opened door to the complex through the swirling flurries. The door was too far away to try for, that was for damn sure. The bear would be on him the second he tried to make a run for it. Glancing left and right, there was nothing but snow and rock; nowhere to run in those directions either.

He had no choice but to stand and fight and the let the cards land where they did. If this was the day he took the last train west, so be it.

But he still had options, few though they were. This wasn't a fight to the death for him. He didn't have to kill the bear, only wound it enough to slow it down so he could try to escape into the complex. This wasn't some macho battle for survival between man and beast where only one would walk away alive. He didn't care what he had to do to escape the bear's clutches, and no matter how demeaning it might be, if it let him get away in one piece, it was all good in his eyes.

That included using firearms against the bear's naked claws.

So leveling the shotgun at the bear, he squeezed the trigger, hoping to end the fight before it began. As if sensing the coming barrage, the bear darted to the side, only a few pellets creasing its tough hide. Its long claws protruded from its paws, allowing it to move easily across the ice and snow, while Henry slipped and slid, while fighting not to fall over, his boots terrible in the snowy conditions. He didn't want to think what would happen if those dagger-like claws sank into him. He'd been lucky thus far. When the bear had attacked him from behind, its claws had been re-tracted.

"Shit," Henry muttered as the shotgun blast went wide, before trying to line up another shot. Only the bear was faster, and it came at him, a massive paw coming up and swiping the shotgun from Henry's hands. The weapon spun off into the storm to land on its barrel, before falling over and stopping. Henry threw him-self to the side, half-running, half-falling, as he chased after the shotgun. He managed to reach the weapon just as the bear came at him, its narrow head on its long-curved neck reaching down for him, its long claws ready to tear and rend his body. By sheer luck alone the large paw missed him by less than an inch, though one razor-sharp claw caught and tore the side of his anorak. Its hot breath exploded from its gaping jaw, warm and wet, saliva dap-pling Henry's face before it instantly froze.

Henry rolled across the ground, always moving, always one step ahead of the bear, the animal following so that it was right on top of him, looming over him like a living blanket. A paw came down inches from his head as he rolled to the side, a voice telling him his luck was running out.

Spittle flew from the bear's mouth as it chased after its prey. Huffing and puffing, the animal was unstoppable it seemed. Powerful, majestic, it was a creature of the wild, built to kill.

When the bear caught up to Henry, who lying on his back, the bear let out a howl in victory. Desperate, he jammed the shotgun up under the bear's chin as it towered over him.

"Gotcha, you bastard," Henry hissed, unable to stop the grin from appearing on his face as he prepared to end the battle

His finger tightened on the trigger until it was all the way back, and he braced for the kicking weapon to shove itself deep into his shoulder. He also expected to be pelted with blood and gore as the blowback of the blast took off half the bear's head. But there was no violent report, only a metallic grating sound from deep inside the shotgun. Not understanding what was happening, he squeezed the trigger again, then again, only to get the same result.

That was when reality sank in and he knew what the problem was.

The rough treatment of the shotgun had somehow jammed it!

"Shit," Henry hissed between clenched teeth.

The bear reared up over him, seeming gigantic from Henry's prone position on the ground, its white coat glistening in the pallid light, its teeth bared for the kill.

Chapter 14

Henry knew he was about to die; there was no other way around it.

The next few fractions of a second seemed to happen in slow motion. He watched the bear's mouth open wide in expectation of tearing into his throat, saw the claws extending even more from the giant paws.

Deep down inside himself, he couldn't believe that this was how it would end. After years of battling the walking dead, cannibals, all measure of evil human beings, to finally be killed by a bear of all things, out on a bleak plateau in the middle of…

He still didn't know where the hell he was.

That made it worse for some reason.

To die and not even know what part of the planet he was on seemed somehow wrong.

He was about to close his eyes, because he sure as shit didn't want to see the deathblow coming, when out of his peripheral vision he spotted something gray moving fast directly towards him and the bear.

He barely registered the moving shape before something connected with the bear right at the shoulder, while sharp teeth sank into the bear's neck, just behind its short right ear.

The shape was almost as large as the bear, and the force of the impact sent the animal sprawling off of Henry, who suddenly found that he was suddenly lying on the snowy ground free from harm. Snow flurries drifted down and landed on his face, melting immediately. One landed on his left eyelash. He blinked it away, the briefest glimpses of the complicated pattern of the flake visible before it was destroyed forever.

Turning his head to follow the bear, he quickly discovered he'd been saved by a giant wolf, its gray and black fur a patchwork of missing places from past battles, the fur not having grown back over the deep scars left in its thick hide. The gray head was almost the size of the bear's. With a black streak going down the center of its skull, giving the head a streamlined look.

Fur and blood were flying off in all directions, both white and gray, as the two animals battled for dominance. Getting to his feet, Henry took in the scene in awe, then his gaze shifted to the beckoning door of the complex only twenty feet away. The shotgun was left on the ground, as it was useless.

But the doorway might as well have been a hundred miles away, for the fight was a constantly moving tableau, and there was no way for Henry to get by them without risking getting caught up in the turmoil.

A low growl from behind caused Henry to spin around, his eyes going wide when he saw three more wolves standing there, their heads held low, their flanks razed.

"Seriously?" Henry said under his breath. He flicked his eyes up to the sky briefly, as if asking what the hell God had against him. The three wolves didn't move, luckily, for he would never fend off all three at once. They merely watched him, their gazes locked on his body.

His right hand snuck under his anorak to pull his Glock free, but as he tried to grip the gun, his fingers wouldn't wrap around it. His fingers were still messed up from his fall. They tingled, and he was confident he would recover full dexterity in time, but at the moment that was the one thing he didn't have.

With no other option, he reached down with his left hand and gripped the hilt of the sixteen-inch panga, pulling the blade from its sheathe in one fluid motion. As if on cue, the exposed metal caused one of the wolves to dart forward, its mouth open wide to sink its teeth into Henry.

He waited for the last possible moment to react, hoping the wolf would think its prey was too terrified to move, and at the last possible moment, just as the wolf launched itself at Henry, he jotted to the side while spinning his upper body by the waist only, the panga swinging around in a full arc.

The wolf rushed by Henry as if it was a bull and Henry the bullfighter, the snow and ice on the ground causing it to slip and slide. Its claws extended to halt its momentum, but not before it slid past Henry, who was even now bringing down the panga with the entire force of his upper body behind it.

The sixteen inches of razor-honed steel bit deep into the back of the wolf, about halfway down its spine. The blow was so powerful the entire blade disappeared into the wolf's body, where it was then stopped by skeletal bone and muscle.

With its spine severed, the wolf was done for, even if the animal didn't know it yet. Spine severed, the legs refused to work, and the animal dropped heavily to the ground, taking Henry with it, as he wasn't about to let go of his panga, the only weapon he had to defend himself with competently. The wolf didn't get up, its paws twitching as it lay on its side in the snow. A pool of dark red blood seeped out of its wound to soak into the frozen ground.

Jerking the blood-slick blade free of the carcass, droplets of blood flying off into the air, he spun around to face his next foe, but the remaining two wolves weren't moving. These two were smaller than the others and weren't as brash to attack. They'd seen one of their number go down, killed by the human, and they weren't as eager as their fallen brother to fight.

But they smelled the fresh-spilled blood, and Henry could see if given enough time, the two might get up enough courage to try anyway, especially if they did it together.

Hunger was a great motivator, after all.

Glancing over his shoulder at the wolf and bear still fighting, Henry didn't see the battle letting up anytime soon. Both were evenly matched. Though the gray wolf was smaller and seemed to have a few more wounds on its hide from the fight, it was holding its own well against the slightly larger bear.

Seeing he had a few precious seconds to alter his tactics, Henry switched hands with the panga, the fingers on his bad hand barely able to grip the hilt. But he didn't need to fight with the hand, only hold the blade for a moment.

He then pulled the Glock with his left hand, crossing the arm over his body. It wasn't a smooth motion, awkward at best, but he managed it, all the while never taking his eyes off the two wolves before him, while letting his peripheral deal with the battle to the side. For a fleeting moment, he wondered what would be the result if for some reason the Glock malfunctioned as well. It would bode ill for him for sure. With two inoperative guns and only the panga for defense, the animals would make short work of him.

Leveling the Glock at the two wolves, he fired twice, both rounds striking the ground at their feet, causing ice chips to fly upwards like shrapnel. The ice slivers stung their legs and caused them to back away, which gave Henry the seconds he needed to make his move. He didn't shoot them directly for fear that if the rounds weren't killing shots, it would make the wolves engage him, but a warning shot might make them simply back away. Exhausted with hands that weren't cooperating, he wasn't confident of a kill shot if he tried, no matter how close the targets were. And once more, killing wasn't mandatory, just slowing the enemy down so he could escape back into the complex.

Swiveling on his heels, he lined up his next target, namely the two battling animals before him. He only wanted a path to the complex door, and safety, and could have cared less which animal he hit. He knew if he shot one, the opponent would gain the upper hand. The Wild Kingdom battle for survival that was now going on meant nothing to him. The wolf might have saved him from being mauled by the bear, but he knew without question that if the wolf was the victor over the bear, it would then turn on Henry without a moment's thought.

He didn't aim for any specific creature, only lined up the two of them as they rolled across the ground, and fired three rounds in quick succession. By luck or chance, or because the bear was a slightly larger target, all three struck the bear in the side, causing it to howl in pain and rage. Immediately, blood appeared on its fur. But the bear kept fighting, as if the bullets were only an annoyance. But then, as seconds passed, the animal's movements began to slow, the wolf getting in more bites, its claws doing more damage as it sank deep into the once-white fur.

Almost in the blink of an eye, the battle had turned in favor of the wolf. The powerful beast didn't hesitate, and its strong jaws opened wide before snapping shut on the bear's neck like a vise, directly below its chin, locking on and not letting go.

The battle began to ease as the bear struggled to free itself, but lacked the strength to do so.

Henry spotted his chance to make a run for it, but just as he began to run, taking a second to grab the fallen shotgun and slinging it over his shoulder by its lanyard, the other two wolves overcame their fear and charged him.

One bit him on the lower leg, above the ankle, its teeth sinking into the top part of his combat boot but not finding the flesh beneath. Still, Henry could feel the pressure of the teeth as they pushed on his skin. The second wolf came at him high, lunging for his throat. Henry instinctively raised his right arm to protect himself, and the wolf bit into the steel of the panga, the blade cutting its mouth terribly, blood shooting from around its teeth.

As the wolf fell back, wounded, it tore the panga from Henry's grip, the fingers still weak and not strong enough to hold onto the hilt. There was no time to even try to retrieve the fallen blade. He fired down with his left hand at the wolf biting into his boot with the Glock, the round punching into the beast's skull from the top. Dead before the animal even knew it, the wolf's head slammed down to the ground with the force of the impact, its teeth ripped from their purchase. Henry kicked out and freed himself, before turning and running for the door. He made a wide arc around the wolf and bear that still fought on, though the bear was moments from death.

"You're welcome," Henry tossed out as he passed the gray wolf, hoping for a little appreciation for shooting its adversary, but knowing he would receive none.

With his boots crunching on the snow and ice, and blinking the snow flurries from his eyes, he made a mad dash to the doorway, expecting to feel the weight of the last wolf punching into his back and forcing him to the ground. His heart trip-hammered in his chest as he crossed the few remaining feet.

He made it without incident, however, and he yanked the door open as he simultaneously kicked the tool in the door frame back into the complex. Never slowing, he darted inside, while glancing over his shoulder briefly to see if he was being followed.

His fear was unfounded, for nothing was even close to him that could be deemed a threat.

Safe inside the doorway, and knowing he could slam it closed if need be, he paused to finish watching the scenario of life and death playing out before him.

The bear was on its last legs, the gray wolf still having a firm grip on its enemy's throat. The wolf that had bitten Henry's panga was up once more but it wasn't moving around, and only stared and watched the alpha wolf fight. Blood seeped from its muzzle where the panga had sliced deep into its gums.

The bullets Henry had fired into the bear must have struck something vital, and the rounds were definitely taking their toll. There were a few huffs and puffs by the bear as it gave one last try at freeing itself, then it went limp, sagging to the snow. The wolf held on for another full minute, never ceasing its grip, just in case the bear was faking, but finally it released its vise-like lock on the bear's throat and stepped away to admire its kill.

The bear's fur was sodden with crimson where Henry had shot it, the circle of blood twice as large as before. If he had to guess, Henry would have figured loss of blood was one of the bear's downfalls in losing the battle.

The gray wolf turned and looked across the area, and when it spotted its two dead brothers, it howled and began searching for the human. Henry's eyes locked with the gray wolf's gaze, and for a moment it was as if the wolf was speaking to him with its penetrating eyes.

Having seen enough, Henry pulled the door closed, blocking out the light and cold. The silence inside the motor pool was deafening after being outside, with the wind blowing, the battle for survival raging, and all the other sounds the average human never noticed, but took for granted as background noise, something that would always be there.

He was breathing fast, adrenaline pumping through his system, the fight or flight instinct still prevalent in his mind.

Walking down the ramp, he paused halfway and had to lean against the wall, as a wave of dizziness overcame him. Closing his eyes, he pressed his back against the wall before sliding down it, realizing he needed some time to regain his composure.

Again he was drawn to his heart beating in his chest, and as he struggled to control his breathing, slowly, his heartbeat slowed to a more normal rhythm.

He stayed there, not moving, for a good deal of time, thinking of everything that had occurred, and how close to death he'd just come. But once more, he'd slipped through the Grim Reaper's clutches, and if he had his way, he would continue to do so for many years to come.

Though he may already own a ticket to the last train west, he was going to make damn sure he didn't redeem it for a long time to come.

When he felt more like himself, he stood up, and with one last look at the closed door, remembering what lay beyond it, he turned and walked back into the complex, and his slumbering friends.

Chapter 15

When Henry reached the door to the matter transfer room once more, he realized he was right back where he'd started. As far as gaining entry, he still didn't have a key pass to get him inside.

But time had passed so he tried banging on the door again, calling out to the others. Surely, they were awake by now. If they weren't, then he needed to consider that something was seriously wrong with them.

He didn't have to bang long before a muffled voice could be heard from the other side of the door.

"Charlie? Is that you?" It sounded like Mary's voice.

Henry didn't understand what she meant and said, "Who the hell is Charlie? It's Henry, I got locked out. Open the damn door."

"I don't know any Henry," Mary said. "But Charlie 'is' someone I know given where we are."

Then it came to him, what she was doing, and he muttered a curse that he hadn't remembered. But then they had never been in a position to use the all clear passwords they'd set up years ago for just a situation as this.

The idea was that if one of the group was captured, and forced at gunpoint to try to gain entry to where the others were holed up, different names would be used, certain ones declaring whether that lone person was under duress or was fine and safe.

The name Charlie was the call sign to ask the question, and if Henry was fine, he was to ask for Jane, and whether she was all right. But if he asked for Claire, then it meant he wasn't alone and that under no circumstances should the door be opened.

"I hope Jane is okay in there," he called and then there was silence. He counted in his head for a full twenty seconds, and was about to repeat his sentence when the door popped open and a two- inch crack appeared. Moving his head to the opening, Henry found he was now staring down the barrel of a .38.

"You're saying Charlie's okay, too?"

He crossed his arms over his chest and stared at her, ignoring the gun aimed at his head. "Mary, I just said I was fine. Now open the door, please. And you shouldn't have opened the door at all if you had any doubts."

He could see Mary's face beyond the gun, and he saw the way she scrunched up her face as she made a decision. The door popped open.

He entered the room, and looking past Mary standing before him, saw that the others were finally awake, and in different positions on the floor, as they struggled to pull themselves out of the fugue state they'd woken to find themselves in. The scent of vomit hung in the air, and Henry figured someone's constitution hadn't managed to hold back after waking.

Mary was able to see past Henry into the corridor. Her eyes went wide at the destruction. She opened her mouth to ask what it was all about when Henry raised a hand to halt her. "Later, honey, it's not important."

Sue came up to him, hugging him so tightly he thought he would pass out. "I woke up and you were nowhere in sight," she said. "I was so worried." Then she looked at the jacket he wore and the rips in it, where the stuffing was poking out. Her eyebrows went up in a question and once more Henry waved it off as unimportant.

"I'm glad you're all on your feet again, so we can search this new place together to see if we can find anything of use. I walked around a bit and found nothing worthwhile… well, except transportation out of here. But we need to find warm clothing. Thermals, gloves, the works, before leaving."

"So it really worked, huh?" Jimmy said, amazed. "We actually were transmitted somewhere else like in a sci-fi movie. Fuck, that's something else." He waved his hands in the air, showing that they were whole, then pulled his waistband apart, as if he was inspecting his penis. "And it all got put back the right way."

Mary walked over and acted as if she was peering down his pants. "Hmmm, maybe some of those things shrank when they were reassembled."

"Ha-ha, very funny." Jimmy joined Henry, who was placing the shotgun on a bank of computer consoles. "I was wondering where that went."

"Yeah, about that," Henry said. "It jammed on me when I went outside. Almost got me killed."

Jimmy picked up the shotgun and inspected it, seeing the new scratches and scrapes, as well as the moisture coating it from being tossed in the snow. "Well, no wonder, old man, you've been treating her like shit."

Cindy went beside Jimmy, wrapping an arm around him affectionately, her eyes locked on Henry. "So, Henry, do you know where we are? Does this place have people in it?"

He shook his head. "I found nothing that told me where we are and all I saw were long-dead corpses." He quickly filled everyone in on what had occurred since he'd woken first, detailing the two spider droids, destroying them, and then going outside and being attacked by the bear and wolves. He left out most of the details that Sue would have worried about, her thinking of Henry fighting for his life, with no help coming, causing her distress. Besides, glossing over most of it suited him just fine. When he thought back to the fiasco outside with the bear and wolves, he was pretty damned embarrassed about all of it. He'd made some bad choices it seemed, and had almost gotten killed for it, so better to keep most of what happened private.

They talked for another fifteen minutes, while the group regained their composure, and when it was time, they left the room behind and went out into the complex. Jimmy made a few jokes about the demolished corridor upon seeing the small crater and spider droid parts scattered about, as they moved off deeper into the complex.

With more eyes to search, even the offices off the hallways were checked, and it was Mary who discovered where the complex was located in an itinerary she found in a desk drawer. Gathered in a junction of two corridors, their gear bags on the floor around them, the companions discussed their options on moving forward.

"Makes sense she's correct," Henry said, explaining about seeing nothing but snow for as far as he could see when he was outside.

"Shit," Jimmy spit, "Alaska? I hate the fucking snow."

"It won't be so bad, Jimmy," Henry explained, "I found a few snow buggies we can use. I checked; they started right up. We can load them up with maps, and anything else we can carry, and head out in style."

"Where will we go?" Sue asked.

Henry considered her question before answering. "I say we go to Anchorage. It's the largest city in Alaska. With the deaders gone there should be people there."

"What if there's not?" Mary asked. "For all we know, this entire state could be a ghost town."

Henry nodded, thinking the same thing but not wanting to voice it. "If we don't find anything, I figure we come back here and try that matter thingy again. See if it sends us somewhere else."

"What?" Jimmy said loudly. "That's crazy. For all we know it might send us back to Area 51, which is probably glowing in the dark right now."

Mary shook her head. "No way, Jimmy, that would never happen. When I was reading up on how it works, I clearly remember reading about some kind of redundancy. It knows if a particular station is bad and won't accept a transmission."

"So there's more of them?" Henry asked, not having given it much thought till now.

Mary nodded again, her hair bobbing around her face; she brushed it away absently with a flick of her hand. She was becoming excited. "Oh my, yes. As we've found out, there are bunkers all over America, right?"

Henry didn't say anything, but when she didn't continue, he said, "Yes, I suppose so."

"Right," she nodded. "Well, for what I read it seems there was a matter transfer room in almost every bunker we've been to and sometimes they're in places that are more private. Remember when we were at Fort Knox? It's possible there was one there somewhere."

"Jesus Christ," Jimmy said. "Imagine that shit. While us simple folks were driving around in cars and flying on airplanes, government assholes were hopping from place to place in the blink of an eye."

"I don't know about that, Jimmy," Henry said. "I woke up feeling pretty terrible. Not the way I want to travel, thank you."

Mary butted in. "I read some notes that I found in a desk. It's a side effect. They were trying to figure out how to stop the nausea but never got the chance."

"So every time we use that thing we're going to feel like we're massively seasick?" Sue asked.

"Yes, that's a good way of looking at it," Mary told her.

"One thing at a time, people," Henry said, taking charge of the conversation. "I don't know about you guys but I've had enough of bunkers and government bases for a while. I say we move out tomorrow at first light, after a good night's sleep." He pointed to the gear bags. "These go to the motor pool and get loaded into two snow buggies, then we make sure they're fueled and ready to go." He began ticking items off his fingers. "Mary and I will go see if we can find food, ammo and pyrotabs to name a few things. We're pretty stocked from what we took from Area 51, but if there's more here we should take what we can." He paused and remembered one more thing, gesturing to the anorak he still wore. "And you all are gonna need jackets like this, and if we can find them, gloves and hats for us all too, plus thermals for under our clothes. If not we can wear multiple layers. No one travels around alone. The place looks deserted but I'm not taking any chances. We travel in pairs at all times. This place is smaller than the last one so it's easier to move around, too."

Everyone stood looking at him, as if waiting for him to continue. Finally, he clapped his hands and said, "What are you waiting for? Go!" He pointed down the left-hand corridor. "The motor pool's that way. Go all the way to the end and you come right to it."

Talking quietly amongst themselves, everyone began moving away, and were soon walking down the corridor, leaving Mary and Henry behind to go off in a different direction. Sue had paused for an extra moment near Henry, and after she glared at Mary to turn around to give them privacy, Mary walked over to a diagram on the wall and began studying it, which gave the couple a minute of relative privacy. Sue hugged Henry and kissed him passionately.

"I thought we were dead back there," she whispered into his ear. "I really did. When I woke up and you were missing, I thought you hadn't come with us." A tear welled up in the corner of her eye and rolled down her cheek. "I thought I'd lost you."

Acting stoic, Henry wiped the tear away. "It'll take more than a nuclear meltdown to kill me, Sue. You should know that by now."

She sniffed and laughed slightly. "Yes, I suppose I should." She kissed him again, before moving her lips so close to his ear that her breath felt hot on his skin. "I'm glad we get one more night inside someplace like this. I want to show you how happy I am we're still alive." Her tongue flicked out and licked his ear, and then she pulled back, picked up her two gear bags, and jogged off after Jimmy and Cindy awkwardly, as the bags were weighing her down. The young couple was walking slowly while they waited for her to catch up. Cindy had seen Sue delay to talk to Henry, so had made Jimmy slow down to wait.

Mary had been glancing quickly over her shoulder, waiting for the conversation to end, and when she saw Sue leave, she walked over and joined Henry.

"What was that about?" she asked, having an idea, a slight smile creasing her lips.

Henry shrugged. "Sue just wanted to tell me she was glad we're all okay."

"Oh really? It seemed more personal than just that."

Henry began to walk, Mary askance of him. "Mary, do you really want me to go into details?"

She shook her head adamantly. "No, no I don't. I know body language so I think I know what she was telling you, and the old saying about 'too much information' comes to mind."

Henry didn't reply, though he did his best to hold back the smile coming to his lips. The two walked off in search of supplies in silence for a while.

* * *

That night, dinner was a simple meal taken from the supplies acquired from Area 51.

Both the cafeteria and armory were found empty of supplies, the former nothing but trash scattered everywhere, and the latter so empty not even a single bullet casing was found.

With the remnants of the meal pushed aside, everyone sat around talking. On the side of the table they were gathered around in a section of the dormitories in the complex, a map of Alaska was spread out, the route to Anchorage mapped out as best they could, given where they believed they were now and where their eventual goal resided. Going to the coast seemed a viable option, and even if the city was devoid of life, they hoped to find a boat or ship and sail back to the American mainland.

No one wanted to try and use the matter transfer again, not unless it was a life or death prospect. The technology was still too new for them to want to risk it, and the feeling upon waking was an equal deterrent.

The snow buggies had been fueled and loaded with all the gear, and one stroke of luck was that warm winter clothing was found in a storeroom, enough for a hundred men. Everything from parkas to gloves to thermal underwear; all still wrapped and sealed in plastic. Not only had everyone taken a pair of thermals to wear at the moment, but extras were loaded into the buggies. Tents, sleeping bags, and heating supplies were also found in a separate storage room, and these too were added to the buggies.

There was no running water anywhere in the facility, so there were no chances of showering or even a light wash. But with snow outside for as far as the eye could see, lack of water wouldn't be an issue, and later, if needed, snow could be melted down for washing and other uses. It felt weird using a real toilet and having to leave their waste in the bowl, but it couldn't be helped. By the end of the day, the odor had become rather ripe. A few blankets were hung across the entrance to the bathroom and bathing area, which blocked off most of the odor from permeating the air in the main dormitory. There were no doors leading to the bathrooms and showers, only a wide opening where there were first sinks, and around a floor-to-ceiling tiled wall, were the toilets and non-working showers.

Once the buggies were packed, the meal eaten, everyone simply wanted to go to bed early, knowing the coming dawn would have them leaving the complex and once more traveling the long road to new destinations.

Henry folded the map of Alaska and stuffed it into a pocket, then set his wristwatch alarm to five in the morning, knowing without natural light it would be easy for them all to sleep well into the day. Before retiring, furniture was built up around the entrances to the dormitory, so that if they had been wrong, and there were people somewhere inside the complex, the occupants would find it hard to reach the sleeping companions without making noise. Henry added one more touch to prevent a surprise in the night. Finding some empty wine bottles in an office, he smashed them and spread the pieces across the floor, knowing the crunching glass would alert them to intruders. He left one small path open to the bathrooms, and from a casual glance, the path looked invisible unless a person knew what to look for in the maze of glass shards.

With pleasantries concluded, everyone went to bed, and soon, Jimmy was snoring loudly, causing Mary to put her pillow over her head to muffle the noise. Cindy tried to push Jimmy to a better position but failed miserably. Used to it, and exhausted, she rolled over so her back was to him and drifted off to sleep.

Henry didn't care that night about Jimmy's snoring. Far too weary from the stress of the day, he quickly dropped off to sleep as soon as his head touched the pillow. Sue was curled up beside him, her head on his chest.

Henry woke sometime in the middle of the night, unsure where he was or what was happening. But it only took him a moment to realize what was occurring.

Sue, crouched down on the bed, under the military green blanket, had taken his manhood into her mouth while he slept.

His body responding even as he slept, he quickly rose to her ministrations, and soon found himself gasping as she took him deeper into her mouth. Lowering his hands to her face, he caressed her cheeks, and she slid her mouth off him for a second and kissed his palms, before quickly resuming her ministrations, the blanket rising and falling in time with her head the gloom, the red lamps mounted to the walls the only illumination.

She began to move faster and faster, also wrapping one hand around his shaft to increase the friction. Lost in a world of pleasure, Henry found himself reaching climax, and he muttered something about being close, warning her of his impending orgasm. But all she did was go even faster, her hand twisting a little as her lips caressed his entire length.

When he exploded, she never stopped, remaining in the same position, only separating from him when he had stopped bucking his hips and his body settled back to lay prone on the bed. Crawling out from beneath the blanket, she curled up close to him, nuzzling his neck with her nose.

"Can I have a kiss?" she joked.

"I'll pass right now," he said back lighthearted, his breathing slowing, his heartbeat resuming to a more regular rhythm. "What was that for? Not that I'm complaining, of course."

"Of course." She moved closer to him, draping a leg over his thighs. "I told you earlier that I was going to make you happy later. I just wanted to be a woman of my word."

"Well, you sure as hell did," he breathed. "Do you want me to do you now?" He whispered softly, not wanting to disturb the others who were around them in their own beds.

She shook her head, only the outline of her face seen in the gloom. "No, it's fine. I just wanted to make you happy."

"You always make me happy," he said, hugging her close and kissing her on the forehead. "I don't even want to think what life would be like without you."

She laughed, and quickly pushed her face into Henry's chest to muffle her voice so she didn't wake the others. "You'd be a wreck without me."

"Damn straight I would." He yawned.

Sue could see he was slurring his words slightly from exhaustion. She patted his chest with her hand. "Go back to sleep now, we'll talk more in the morning."

"Okay, that sounds like a good idea. I love you," he said and was snoring before he finished the sentence.

She lay quietly, looking at his features in the gloom, studying his face. His firm jaw, the small wrinkles around his eyes, his hair with streaks of gray running through it. As she took all of him in, she realized she loved him more than she had ever loved a man in her life.

"I love you, too," she whispered. "More than you could ever know." Placing her head on the pillow, she moved closer to him, wrapping an arm around his body, feeling his chest moving in rhythm to his breathing, feeling his heartbeat through her hand as it lay on his chest.

She wished morning would never come, that she could simply stay like she was, holding Henry in her arms, forever.

Chapter 16

The peaceful tranquility of the frozen plateau was shattered when the large door, used for the egress of vehicles, slowly began to retract into the ceiling, exposing a ramp and the interior of the complex. Hydraulics chugged within the walls, forcing the ponderous door open.

When the door was completely recessed, one at a time, the two snow buggies rolled out into the ever-brightening light of a new dawn.

In the lead buggy were Henry and Mary; the second one held Cindy, Jimmy and Sue. Though Henry would have liked to be traveling with Sue, he needed to know he had someone with him that could fight. They needed to split up into two teams, and in doing so they had to keep their strengths and weaknesses divided as well. Jimmy and Cindy were always a team, but with Jimmy's leg still not entirely healed, he was still a liability. Sue was that added extra manpower to make their party whole.

Henry and Mary had been together for years. They had an unspoken bond that defied being simple battle mates. There were times Sue felt slightly jealous of the bond between the two, but she knew the relationship was more of a father/daughter situation, and though still envious of the time they spent together, Sue knew it was for the best.

Wearing goggles over his eyes, as did the others, Henry slowed the buggy to a stop just outside the door, only giving Cindy enough room to exit the complex as well.

Getting out of the vehicle, he gazed out across the wind-swept plateau, searching for signs of the epic battle between beasts that had been fought there only a day ago.

There was nothing in sight.

Walking over to the where he believed was the exact spot of the battle, he kicked at the few inches of fresh snow, rubbing it away from the ground. There, under the snow, the ice was colored a rich red. Turning, he once more gazed around the area, seeing nothing at all on the ground. No bones, bits of fur, nothing. The two wolf carcasses were gone, as was the bear's, dragged off no doubt to be fed on in a more secure location.

Jimmy hopped out of his buggy to join Henry, his shotgun ready in his hands, having been repaired the previous night. "So, old man, where are these big bad wolves you told us about?"

Henry had decided the others should at least know about the wolves, so he'd filled them in that morning about his recent adventure, though had kept the details to a minimum. Later, he'd given everyone instructions to shoot the wolves as they left the complex if spotted, and now he looked pretty foolish when there was no enemy in sight.

Henry gestured to where he'd shifted the snow with his boot. "See the blood? This is where it happened."

"Then where are the bodies?" Jimmy's eyes were mostly hidden behind his goggles.

"Gone," was all Henry could think to say. Anything else would be supposition and there was no time for that now. As he looked around the area, he spotted a glint of something reflective as the dawn sun caught it. Ignoring Jimmy, he crossed the few feet and once more used his boot to kick at the snow. His face lit up with relief when he found it was his panga, still in the same place he'd dropped it. Blood was frozen to the blade, and with a few taps on his boot heel, it fell right off. Then he wiped it clean with a rag procured from a pocket and sheathed it again, feeling whole once more. That morning, when he'd thought about it, he'd accepted that the weapon was gone, and though it had felt like he'd lost a limb, he knew sooner or later he could replace the sixteen-inch steel blade with a similar weapon, despite the one he'd thought to lose being almost a part of him. He'd had it since the beginning, and other than his Glock, there wasn't much in personal possessions he'd managed to hang on to.

He waved Jimmy to join him and together they made their way back to the idling buggies. Before Jimmy returned to his vehicle, Henry said, "Okay, so we have radios to keep in touch. Mary and I are Team 1, you're Team 2. But we don't know how good the batteries in the radios are, so only use them if you have to. We each have a map, so if we get separated, we meet on the highway that goes into Anchorage." He patted Jimmy on the arm. "We should be there before dark if nothing happens."

"Hey, what could happen?" Jimmy said, having to raise his voice slightly over the wind. "I mean, we always have such great luck wherever we go."

"We're in the middle of nowhere. We shouldn't have any trouble around here. At least, as long as the buggies don't break down."

"Yeah, that's true. Oh, and Henry?"

"Yes?"

"Don't eat the yellow snow."

Henry didn't understand at first, but then he quickly remembered the reference, though didn't find it the least bit amusing. "Sure, Jimmy, you bet. Go close that outer door and then get into your buggy; it's time to leave."

Jimmy went to the large door and punched in the code to close it. Once more, the faint chugging sound of hydraulics could be heard as the door slowly returned to its original position, sealing the complex again. Just as Henry hoped, the code worked on both sides. So if they did need to return, they had a way back inside for the vehicles. When the door rumbled closed, powdery snow cascaded from above, shaken from its perch. Jimmy had to hustle or he would have been covered. Limping heavily, he half-jogged back to his snow buggy.

The wind picked up in intensity, and Henry had to lean forward or risk being blown over. The hood of his anorak fluttered around his face, and he was glad for the goggles on his eyes. Anywhere he wasn't fully covered he could feel the bite of the cold. The gloves he wore kept his fingers warm, but the temperature was still cold enough to make the tips tingle. Though bare-bones, the buggies did have heat, which was a welcome addition, and he was already looking forward to getting back inside, where the heat would warm his already chilled body.

Trudging through the snow, he climbed back into the buggy, immediately relishing the relative warmness of the interior compared to what was outside.

"All set?" Mary asked in the passenger seat.

"Seems like it. You do another radio check?"

She nodded. "Cindy and I have been talking while we waited for you and Jimmy to come back. Sue, too. We're good to go."

Pushing in the clutch and shifting into first gear, Henry eased the snow buggy forward. "Then let's go see Anchorage."

It took over an hour of easy driving to reach the city limits, but there was barely enough left of Anchorage to call it a city.

Stopping the buggies on a bluff overlooking the city, nothing but desolation could be seen. Snowfall covered most of what could be discerned as buildings, but what jutted forth was blackened and scorched. A massive conflagration had raged years ago, one that had consumed the once-sizable city in its entirety, leaving behind nothing but destruction.

Henry's face showed no emotion as he gazed down at the devastation. From where he stood, a few corpses could be seen laying here and there in what were once streets and thoroughfares, fallen zombies that had collapsed when whatever had destroyed them occurred. "Must have been some fire," Henry commented to the others, who were gathered around him, each lost in private thoughts as they took in the scorched city.

"Probably no one was able to fight the fires," Jimmy suggested. "Too busy either dying or trying not to."

Mary shifted her stance at Henry's side. "Anyone who survived would have left there."

"Where would they go?" Jimmy asked.

Mary shrugged. "Anywhere would be better than staying down there."

"What's the next city around here?" Henry asked.

"Fairbanks," Sue replied.

Turning, Henry began walking back to his buggy. "Then we go there next, see if anyone's still alive."

In less than a minute the buggies were driving off, Henry's vehicle taking the lead once more. After five miles of traveling, he spotted something that piqued his interest. Not bothering with the radio, he opened his door and slowed, letting the second buggy drive up beside him.

Jimmy was in the passenger seat and he cracked his door to hear Henry, who stuck his head out of the door to be heard better.

"What's up?" Jimmy asked.

Henry pointed far ahead of them, where the beginning of a shallow valley could be seen, on the edge of a tall mountain. Right at the foot of the mountain, a small grouping of buildings was visible. "Some kind of settlement there. I want to check it out."

"Okay, we're right behind you."

Henry nodded and closed the door, glad to be out of the wind.

"Do you think anyone's alive down there?" Mary asked askance of him.

"Don't know, but there's only one way to find out." He shifted the clutch and drove onward.

When Henry was halfway to what he hoped was a settlement, he could already see the fire damage to most of the structures. Where once short, flat buildings had stood, now there were mostly only skeletal frames of burnt timbers which stood out as a stark contrast to the snow all around.

"Be ready for anything," Henry said into the radio.

Jimmy clicked the speaker and replied, "No one's home here, old man. This place has been toasted good."

"I don't care how it looks. Stay sharp and keep your eyes out. There's an open spot up ahead, I'm gonna park there. Follow me in. But turn your buggy around so we're ready to go if there's trouble."

"Okay, will do."

Henry heard Jimmy telling Cindy to do exactly that, just before the younger man released the button on the radio mic. Henry drove the buggy in a circle, and when the nose was facing back the way he'd entered, he turned off the engine and looked at Mary. "You coming?"

"Sure, though I don't think we're going to find anything good here." Unknown to any of the companions at the time, Mary's words would soon be the understatement of the day.

Jimmy chose to come as well, but Cindy and Sue wanted to stay inside their warm buggy. Henry didn't see a reason not to let them stay; it was a good idea to have someone hang back and watch the vehicles anyway.

Walking down the empty street, nothing but blackened husks of the squat homes lay on both sides. At the end of the small street, and that description was used loosely, the 'street' was barely wide enough to let one of the buggies pass without scraping the destroyed buildings on either side. To the left was a home still relatively intact, despite the scorch marks on more than half of it; most of the burnt roof looked ready to cave in the second someone sneezed too loudly.

"Maybe this place was set on fire after the people left," Jimmy suggested. "They might have gotten out alive."

"Maybe," Henry said, not believing it for a minute. He was proved correct a few seconds later when he stepped over the threshold of the home, treading lightly, to enter its gloom-filled interior. The odor that came to him, tickling his nostrils, was one he'd recognized far too often in his travels for his liking.

It was the smell of death, of rotting human meat. Though the temperature was below freezing outside, within the hut, out of the brunt of the wind, the odor of death permeated everything, the stink of dried blood wafting in the air.

There were the remnants of five people inside the sparsely filled hut. Two adults and three children, one of the kids only a baby.

The parents were in the corner of the single room, their limbs entwined in death, the slash marks to their faces showing an edged weapon had been used. But it was the large gashes to their throats that showed how they had died, bled out like slaughtered pigs, the cuts so brutal that the bone of the spine showed through the split flesh. Their eyes were still open, seeing nothing, glazed over in death.

Blood pooled around the bodies, frozen in time. A human adult body held around nine to ten pints of blood. The red ice pool contained that if not more in quantity.

There were two beds in the room, one on each side. One bed was empty, but the other held two of the children, each not older than eleven or twelve. One had been a boy, the other a girl, but to whoever had come to kill them hadn't cared. Both children had been sodomized and used horribly before finally having their necks broken, the small bodies lying crumpled on the bed like discarded rag dolls.

But it was the youngest child that caused Henry and the others to hold their breath in horror, to almost have to leave the hut, not wanting to look at the unbearable cruelty that had been brought down on the unsuspecting family.

Perhaps angry that there had been nothing worth taking from the poor household, or angry when the baby began to cry at the sound of hearing its parents' slaughtered, the child had been picked up by its heels and slammed against a wall, its fragile head caving in like an eggshell before it was tossed aside like an apple rind.

Even the family dog had been slaughtered, its carcass left to rot with its owners.

"I've seen enough," Henry said and exited the hut, Mary and Jimmy right behind him, all of them with blanched features.

"Who could do something so horrible?" Mary whispered as she leaned against the hut, gathering herself.

"Whoever it was, they're one evil son-of-a-bitch," Jimmy added.

Henry set off to investigate further, but each time he found a partially-burned structure, the same type of carnage was discovered inside. Whoever had been to this settlement had attacked and killed everyone found with a bestial ferocity he'd not seen before. Sure, he'd come across raiders and cannies, but for some reason, the wholesale slaughter of an entire village seemed like a new form of evil, one where only killing for the sake of killing was the rule. Cannies at least ate their victims for sustenance, and slavers would want the villagers alive to sell at the market; both were equally devilish, but at least they held some form of meaning for the killers, twisted as it might be. But whoever had come to this small enclave had arrived with only death in their hearts and a need to do evil.

As they continued through the village, the streets of flattened snow churned with blood long frozen, the trio found a naked pregnant woman lying on her back in the middle of the street. Her face was a network of deep cuts; the lower part of her body, and around her groin area mostly, were mute evidence of the usage she had suffered from her killers' hands.

But that still wasn't the worst of it, not even close.

Mary couldn't take in the rest and had to turn away, a soft sob and a choking cry filling her throat.

"Jesus fucking Christ," Jimmy whispered as he gazed down at the dead woman, his eyes taking the worst of it all in, and though wanting to look away, he couldn't, as if he needed to stand witness to the atrocity before him, that someone needed to remember what had happened here.

The woman's stomach had been slit open vertically, the fetus then yanked from its mother's womb to be tossed onto a nearby fire, the dried cord still attached. The small form was nothing but charred flesh and bone, but just imagining what it had once been was too much to accept.

Turning to face Henry, Mary said, "I want to leave here, Henry, right now."

"Yeah, I can't argue with you there." Henry looked down the street, at the burnt structures, and spotted another home that looked virtually untouched by fire at the very end. "I just want to check out that one, then we can go. But if you want, you can go back to the buggies with Jimmy now."

"What?" Jimmy said. "I want to stay out here. I want to see whatever's left of this place. Someone needs to remember these poor fucks."

Mary shook her head. "Relax, Jimmy, I can wait a little longer. Keep your pants on."

Jimmy smiled. "Mar', I'm at my best when my pants are off." He shook his hips and Mary forced a grin in reply. She understood what he was doing. He was trying to make a joke to break the tension of all the gruesome death they'd been exposed to.

"Sure, Jimmy, whatever you say," she said simply, then went to join Henry, who began to walk to the lone home.

With his Glock in hand, prepared for an attack, though he highly doubted one would come, Henry entered the new structure.

Immediately upon entry, his senses were assaulted by another smell he knew all too well, though it was different from the last aroma in the hut of carnage.

Now the odor wafting in the air was one of dying, of blood still fresh, of bodily waste, of misery. The origin of these odors were all too apparent as well.

In the center of the hut, hanging by a rope tied to a support beam for the roof, was a man—or what was left of a man. At first sight, Henry thought the man long dead, for his belly had been slit from side to side; his insides had spilled out, to coil at his feet in a tangled mess of greasy rope. His eyes were gouged out of their sockets, leaving behind seeping openings that oozed blood along with a clear, ocular fluid, and his teeth had been yanked from his mouth, as if by pliers. The man's lips were shattered and split, from when the torturer had removed his teeth, heedless of damaging the man's outer mouth while completing the action.

For the man to still be breathing was a miracle, and the men who had done this to him, no doubt assumed he would have been long dead by now, despite the spark of life still in him. The head raised ever so slightly, a gurgle eliciting from the cracked and bloody lips.

"Oh my God," Mary gasped as she followed Henry into the hut. "Is he…?"

"Alive? Yeah, somehow." Henry walked over to the man, making sure to stand clear of the intestines on the ground, for there was no actual floor, only more packed snow.

"Water…" the man gargled, so low Henry could barely understand it as a word. It was repeated. "Water, I beg you." The man hesitated before adding, "Or just kill me and be done with it." The words were slurred, almost to the point of being unintelligible.

Henry reached for the small canteen he'd taken from Area 51, part of the supplies found there, that was on his hip, then stopped. The man was already dead, even if he didn't know it yet, and with his entire stomach spilled out on the ground, there was nowhere for the water to go. Still, the man was about to die, and if Henry could help in the passing of life to death, he would. There was an ulterior motive as well. Here was a witness to the death that had descended on the village. Henry wanted information.

Turning, Henry waved Jimmy over, who was at the doorway. "Get some clean snow if you can for him. He wants a drink."

"Use your canteen," Jimmy said, being difficult as always.

With the man's mouth a mass of blood and cuts, Henry didn't want him drinking from the canteen, and he didn't feel like explaining the whole 'no stomach' thing to Jimmy, so he just glared at Jimmy and said, "Do it now, okay? No arguments for once."

Jimmy threw his hands in the air. "Fine, I'll do it. Sheesh." He limped out into the snow to grab a handful, returning a moment later with a ball of snow, which Henry took a chunk out of and placed it in the man's mouth, who flinched at the action, thinking his torturers had returned.

"I'm a friend," Henry said softly. "I won't hurt you."

Sucking on the snow, the man seemed to sigh in relief as the dryness of his mouth, despite the blood, was relieved, and the blood from inside his mouth was slightly washed away so that he didn't taste copper as much with every breath.

"Better?" Henry asked with Jimmy and Mary standing behind him.

"Yeah..." he coughed. "Thank you." The blind man moved his head from side to side, almost as if he was swaying to music only he could hear. Another coughing fit wracked his body; it told Henry that the man's lungs were filling with blood.

Henry knew the man's time was short, so though he felt pity for the guy, he knew he needed to be quick. "Who did this to you? All the people in the village are..."

"Dead," the man slurred, before falling into another coughing fit. He spat blood; a large wad that only dribbled out between his destroyed lips. "Yeah, all dead. I reckon I'm the last one left. I know I ain't got much time left either." His words were clipped, to the point.

"That's a fucking understatement," Jimmy mumbled and Henry elbowed him in ribs.

Henry nodded at the man, glad they saw things the same way. "Look, I'm sorry for all you've suffered, but there's nothing I, we, can do for you." He moved closer. "Tell me who did this to you and maybe they might pay for it one day."

The man actually laughed, which caused his body to shake, and another loop of greasy intestine to slip out of his sliced open stomach. The slick coil splat wetly on the ground. Bloody spray flew from his lips, and Henry made sure to step to the side, not wanting to be hit.

"Justice? There ain't no justice here. Just death." He looked down at his destroyed body with his empty eye sockets, as if he could see his insides spilled out at his feet. He moaned loudly and looked like he might faint, but before he did he pulled himself back from the abyss and turned his empty gaze on Henry. The way the man turned his head to face Henry, it was as if he was locking eyes with Henry, as if the two were the only people on earth, as if nothing else mattered but the words he began to speak. Drawing on whatever spark of life remained within his tortured body, he began to tell a story, his voice firm, the coughing held back so he could tell his tale of sorrow. Though slurred, he did his best to enunciate each syllable, knowing these were probably the last words he would ever speak, before taking the last train west to join his people.

"Never saw 'em before. Must've been forty or fifty. On horse-back. Had guns, real nice ones, too: rifles and pistols. They came ridin' in before dawn, set fire to most of the homes. When my people came out, chased into the cold morning by the smoke and flames, they were waiting." He paused as he fought down a coughing fit, then resumed when he was able. "They came like wolves on a baby doe. Never had a chance. Women were raped, children, then killed. Took anythin' of value, and burned what didn't want. What livestock was here; slaughtered and taken with 'em."

"Why did they do this to you and leave you alive?" Mary asked softly.

The man actually smiled at hearing her voice. "You sound beautiful."

Mary blushed and Jimmy yawned, making Mary glare at him for being so insensitive.

"Never thought I'd still be living. Should be dead by now." He coughed again, unable to hold it back. Blood dribbled from his mouth as the fit subsided. He wheezed a few times, and it didn't seem like the man had more than a few minutes left. It was quiet in the hut, until the man's garbled voice broke the silence. "Tell me somethin'…before I…die?"

"Sure, whatever you want," Henry said.

"My wife…pregnant. Lost sight of her when raiders came. Don't know what came of her. She was beautiful, too."

Jimmy opened his mouth to reply, but Mary stepped on his toe, causing him to yelp and stare at her angrily.

"Jimmy, why don't you go wait outside," Henry said, as he looked at Mary, the two of the same mind.

"Yeah, but…"

Mary swiveled on Jimmy, her fists clenched at her side. "Will you shut up and go outside already?"

"Okay, fine, sheesh, what the hell's gotten into you two?"

When he limped away and was gone, Henry and Mary once more locked gazes, and Mary nodded that Henry should be the one to speak, but when he did, she didn't hear what she thought she would, which was the truth.

"We found a pregnant woman when we arrived. She's alive and fine. She was hiding in a hut that was only partially burned. A support beam landed on her and she's unconscious so she can't come see you. I'm sorry. But she'll be all right. One of us is a doctor and said she'd make a full recovery."

The man's face beamed with happiness. "She's okay? My child, my son, I know it to be. They live?"

Henry nodded, despite the man being blind. "Yes, that's right."

"Good. I can die in…in peace now." He was wheezing harder, his breath hitching in his chest. "Tell her… Tell her I love her. Will you?"

"Of course."

The man's breathing was labored to the point he couldn't catch his breath, and all Henry and Mary could do was silently watch the man die.

"One more thing. Important," he said, but then his head sagged down to his chest, the strength to hold it up too much for him.

"What?" Henry asked, grabbing his chin and raising the head, shaking him slightly. "What is it?" Henry was about to slap the man, hoping to jar whatever life was fleeing back into him, when the eyelids snapped open and he said in a garbled voice, "Russ…Russ. The raiders…spoke…Russ…." Before he could finish his body spasmed and went limp.

Henry released the head, which dropped so low that the chin touched the chest. Henry wiped his fingers on his pants. "What was that last thing he said?"

Mary shrugged. "I couldn't make it out. It was probably nothing. He was delirious." She pointed to the dead body. "What should we do with him now?"

In response, Henry pulled his panga from his side and slashed at the ropes holding the body up. The corpse dropped like a sack of potatoes to the ground; it didn't move. Grabbing a worn and tattered blanket from off the floor, he draped it over the corpse. "That's all we can do. No point in doing more when there's an entire settlement of people that need the same."

"Sad, though, that they can't get a proper burial."

"I suppose. But I'm not wasting half a day or longer burying bodies. They're dead, they won't know the difference."

They walked out into the cold, the sun bright on their faces, even if no warmth was felt. Jimmy was there waiting, and as they passed him, he fell into step behind them.

"The guy kick the bucket or what?"

"Yes, Jimmy, he's dead," Henry said flatly.

"Sucks."

"Yeah," Henry agreed. It certainly did.

They walked in silence back to the snow buggies, where Sue and Cindy were waiting, warm inside their vehicle. When Cindy saw everyone return, she opened the door and got out from behind the steering wheel and asked, "What did you find?"

"Pure evil," Henry said coldly. He noticed Sue looking out of the buggy's windshield at him, and he nodded to her, the gesture letting her know he was okay. He went back to his own snow buggy, Mary doing the same.

"What did he mean by that?" Cindy asked Jimmy as they climbed back into their buggy. Sue leaned forward, wanting to hear, not understanding the conversation, as she hadn't heard Henry's reply from within the vehicle.

"I'll tell ya later," Jimmy said, as he shifted his bad leg to make himself more comfortable. The cold was playing havoc with his wound.

Buggy One began to move, Cindy following close behind it, and soon, the small settlement was alone with its dead.

It wasn't long before the first scavenger crept down the lonely streets, searching for the meat laid out like a buffet. The wolves were hungry, but recently, the entire area around Anchorage had been an excellent source of food. Their bellies hadn't been as full as they had been this winter in years, food having become more plentiful, with human corpses seeming to decorate the terrain like manna from heaven. Human corpses weren't the wolves' first choice of food, but when hunting other animals was scarce, they made do with whatever they could. Survival was all that mattered.

One by one, slinking low to the ground, wary of traps, the pack entered the village and began to feed.

Chapter 17

The display on the dashboard, connected to a barometer mounted outside the buggy, told the tale of the changing atmospheric pressure as each hour passed until the sun went down.

And on top of that, the companions had found themselves in one of the worst snowstorms they had ever recalled experiencing firsthand. On a route that would take them into Fairbanks, visibility quickly went down to zero, the snow falling so hard, the wind so strong, that Cindy couldn't see the rear lights on Henry's buggy, despite it being only a few feet in front of her.

"Tell Henry if he stops without warning, we're gonna go right up his ass," Cindy told Jimmy as she struggled to fight the terrible steering.

But then, as if a light switch had been flicked on, there was a surprise break in the storm, and suddenly visibility cleared. Up ahead, was a steep valley, with some sort of installation near the bottom.

Radar dishes and squat one-story buildings could be seen, and off to the right, in the far-off distance, a massive cement and steel dam overlooked the valley.

Then just as fast as it had dissipated, the storm came screaming back to surround the buggies in white swirls of blistering cold and snow, visibility dropping down to zero once more. Cindy peered through the plexiglass windshield, and realized she couldn't see Henry and Mary's buggy before her.

She was going to say something to Jimmy when the radio crackled and Henry's voice came in strong. "Did you guys see those buildings up ahead before the storm came back down? Over."

"Sure did, old man," Jimmy said. "What about 'em?"

"Looks like some kind of radar installation; maybe military. Make your way there as best you can," he said. "I think I lost you at the turn I made, so instead of trying to find you, or you me, just go there. We'll meet up and hunker down till this storm passes."

"Sounds good, Henry," Jimmy added. "See you soon."

"Sure, over and out."

Jimmy glanced at Cindy, who was squinting, as if that would allow her to peer into the storm better. Her knuckles were white as she gripped the steering wheel tightly.

"You heard the man, babe, head to those buildings," he said.

"What buildings? I can't see shit."

Jimmy pointed straight. "Just go that way. We should come to them eventually."

"Nice logic," she scoffed. "Did you just pull that out of your ass or what?"

He shrugged. "What if I did?"

"What if you did? If that's what you did then shove it back up there, 'cause we don't have time for guessing here."

Sue chuckled from the back seat but said nothing more.

Jimmy frowned. "Look, I have an excellent sense of direction. Just go straight and we'll be there soon enough."

"You better not be wrong," she scoffed, giving in. "Cause if you are and we end up driving off alone into nowhere, and this car breaks down, Sue and I might not live to regret listening to you—you either for that matter."

"Just relax, and let me navigate. It's all under control."

Frowning deeply, she turned her head briefly and stared at her boyfriend, who in sensing he was being watched, turned to look back at her. He smiled widely, an ear to ear kind of grin, and she simply shook her head and refocused her attention on the white-out before her.

Sue was smiling as well. Watching Jimmy and Cindy bicker was better than the soap operas she used to watch on television. Jimmy was the comic relief in a story if there ever was any, and the funniest part of all, was that the young man didn't seem to know it.

She had to admit she was worried as the storm grew more intense. She wished she'd gone with Henry in his vehicle, unhappy at being separated from him.

Thinking of him, she sent a prayer out into the storm that he was safe in his buggy, and of course, he sent another one for Mary's security as well.

Henry handed the radio to Mary after signing off with Jimmy; she took it and placed it between her legs. The storm was unbelievably fierce and for the past five minutes, Henry was doing his best to stay in a straight line, hoping he wasn't deviating from what he felt was the path to the buildings. For all he knew, he was miles off course and driving in the opposite way. The storm was so bad that there was no way to keep any kind of a sense of direction, not when nothing could be seen but whirling snow and hear the howling wind.

"If this thing wasn't made for snow, we never would have gotten this far," Henry said as he wiped the windshield clean of condensation. The little heater in the buggy was working overtime to keep the window clear, and it was woefully inadequate for the task. "Makes me wish we were back in Nevada, that's for sure."

"It's a long drive back to Nevada," Mary said with the slightest of grins. She, too, was concerned over the storm's intensity.

"That's an understatement."

Mary glanced out the window, trying to see behind them.

"Any signs of the other buggy?" he asked.

She shook her head, her parka rustling. "No, I can't see them at all. We lost them all right."

"It should be fine. They know where to meet up with us. Eventually, we'll all be together again."

Around noontime the storm eased up, the wind barely blowing over fifty miles an hour. The barometer rose as well, signifying the improved weather. The sun peered out through the clouds, the snowy terrain reflecting the rays and making Henry wince as he squinted to protect his eyes. Sunglasses hadn't been something he'd thought to take and now he regretted it immensely.

"Any sign of Jimmy and the others?" Henry asked as he stopped for a moment, to then climb out and stretch.

Mary also got out of the buggy; she used a pair of Bushnell binoculars taken from the bunker to scan her surroundings. "Nothing," she said flatly. Intermittent snow flurries cascaded down, coating her hair with a white coating. Shaking her head, she shook off the snow like a dog after getting wet. The parka she wore was two sizes two big for her, and she resembled a child wearing an adult coat. Henry had joked about it once already, and Mary laughed as well, flapping her loose sleeves, which hung over her hands by a good inch. Now, she'd rolled them up, having to slice each sleeve with her blade to make it feasible. "Maybe they're already there, and passed us in the storm."

"Maybe." Henry gazed out over the stark whiteness of it all, not a footprint to be seen, only the pair of tracks left by their vehicle's tires behind them. He opened his door and prepared to get back in.

"We could call them on the radio, see where they are," she suggested.

"I just tried. No answer. Could be a million reasons why. Might just be out of range or in a depression where the radio waves won't reach." He shrugged. "Who knows? I'm not a radio tech." He began to slide behind the steering wheel, calling out as his head ducked inside, "We should get moving."

"Okay." She lowered the binoculars and gazed out over the frozen tundra one last time without them. She frowned slightly, before biting the corner of her lip in concern, wondering where the others were and hoping they were okay.

Henry revved the engine slightly, as there was no horn on the buggy, and Mary took the hint and got back inside. Her door wasn't even closed before Henry was speeding across the frozen ground, the fresh-fallen snow flying up as the bumper pushed it aside. He was enjoying himself he had to admit, the buggy like a big toy. He'd always wanted to go to the desert and drive a dune buggy around, but it had never happened. This was about as close to doing that as one could get.

"We should be at the valley and those buildings in half an hour or so," he said, handling the steering wheel smoothly. "If they're not waiting when we arrive, we'll double back and do a search. But I bet the radio is being ignored and they're all gathered around a fire in one of those buildings, waiting for us to show up."

Mary didn't reply, as she considered her next words. Finally, she said, "I hope they're okay. I mean, we know there are some really bad people out here somewhere. The evidence was in that small village we just left. If those people found Jimmy and the others..." She trailed off, the meaning clear.

Henry turned away from the windshield to look at her, wanting to reassure her with eye contact. "Hey, I'm sure they're fine. Whoever did that is probably long gone from this area. Besides, Jimmy and Cindy can take care of themselves, and Sue isn't too bad with a gun now either. You know, that reminds me of something that happened when we were on that cruise ship—you remember when we were there, Mary?" He didn't stop for her to answer, the question rhetorical. "So, Jimmy and I were walking along the top deck and this big jerk comes up to us and tells us we have to go scrub dishes, and Jimmy says to him ..."

One moment the world was normal, the sun shining, the buggy gliding across the ground as it made its way to the valley below, Henry telling a funny tale that was amusing Mary.

But then everything changed. Suddenly, there was a loud explosion surrounding the buggy, snow, ice, and rock erupting up from the ground, the force of the mysterious blast enough to cause the vehicle to flip onto its roof. Inside the buggy, the two occupants were thrown around like ragdolls, the powerful concussion sending Henry and Mary instantly into unconsciousness.

Just before Mary fell into oblivion, she had the oddest thought, of how if she was about to die right now, that she wasn't going to get to hear what Jimmy had said to the jerk on the cruise ship.

And how for some strange reason, that bothered her immensely.

Chapter 18

Henry Watson awoke first, his head feeling like it was full of lead; it was difficult to raise it. As he moved, wincing, he felt the dried blood on his scalp cracking, the crust breaking free from his skin. Moaning softly, he opened his eyes to see a blurry form looming over him. From his vantage point on the ground, the figure seemed like a giant.

It was night, which told him he'd been unconscious for quite a while. The figure blocked the overhead moonlight, which allowed Henry's vision to clear more quickly. As it did, he began to make out details about the man, for already he knew it was a man standing over him.

The man wore a long jacket, black, and with the jacket hung open, Henry saw a sword on one hip and a sidearm on the other. In the man's hands was the empty casing to a one-shot LAW rocket, and even as Henry gazed upwards, the man tossed the spent canister aside. So someone had fired a goddamn bazooka at him and Mary, and all signs pointed the man leaning over him, Henry thought.

The oddest aroma floated to him, making his nose tickle. Henry could have sworn he detected the odor of horses, many of them by the pungent smell. He figured he must have rattled his brain a little too much in the explosion, for what would horses be doing in the middle of Alaska?

The man hunched down, crouching, so that he was almost eye to eye with Henry, who had managed to sit up. The instant Henry saw the man's hat, saw the gold military insignia/badge on the center of it, and though he found it hard to believe, he was sure he was looking at some kind of foreign military officer, possibly

Russian. But that made no sense. What would a Russian military officer be doing here in America, and in Alaska of all places?

"I hope I did not hurt you very much," the man said in English with a thick Russian accent, a smile on his thin lips.

Henry said nothing, his musings about the man now confirmed. Out of the corner of his eye, he could see Mary lying still on the ground, after being dragged out of the flipped buggy along with Henry and taken to who knew where. After taking in his surroundings, he saw they appeared to be in a small hollow, which was protected from the brunt of the wind by an incline to the land. Campfires had been made, and around them, many men stood to keep warm.

Looking back to Mary, he saw her breath steaming from her nose in the cold from the fire burning close by. Good, she was alive, though still unconscious. She had a small cut on her forehead but it hadn't bled much even when fresh, and now the bleeding had stopped completely.

Two more men came up and pulled Henry to his feet, so that as the Russian soldier stood up, they were both mostly eye to eye again. The Russian was slightly taller than Henry, but that could have been due to the uneven snow beneath their feet. Henry looked past the man's shoulder to see more than thirty people scattered throughout the hollow, all with horses close by, penned up in a makeshift corral at the rear of the hollow. The bodies of the people and fires were being used as the pretend fence line to keep the horses in one place. By their look, they resembled an army unit more than simple coldhearts or raiders. Maybe they were slavers, but Henry doubted it. Something in the manner of the Russian before him told him so.

Henry had learned a long time ago, back when the dead first began to talk, that when captured by hostiles, he needed to play it close to the vest, to say nothing and act stupid. His father had a saying, one he'd heard countless times growing up. "You can't hear someone when you're doing all the talking." In other words, better to shut up and listen, and in doing so, find that he could learn valuable information when others spoke.

While Henry and Mary had been unconscious, they had been stripped of their weapons. They were helpless, at the mercy of an armed group of raiders or slavers.

Askance of Henry, Mary moaned as she slowly came back to the land of the living.

"It is most wonderful to make your acquaintance. I am Major Ishmael Varakov of the Soviet Armed Forces. Kindly to tell me where I might find the leaders of your country?" the Russian said.

Henry stared at him, wondering if the guy was being serious. To hear such odd words come out of such an imposing figure was off-putting, to say the least.

Unknown but fortunate to Henry and Mary, the leader of the small army had decided to take a different approach to interrogating his two new prisoners. In the past, since arriving in America, he and his men had been rather aggressive in their questioning, which more often than not had resulted in the death of their captors. So now, he'd decided to try a more friendly approach, one where the prisoners weren't tortured—at least not immediately anyway.

Mary stirred and sat up. "What happened?"

"Ah," the Russian said in greeting. "The pretty woman wakes. Good day to you, miss. I am Major Ishm..."

"Yes, yes, I heard you tell Henry. You don't have to repeat it," she said groggily. She took in the armed contingent of men, and Henry was proud to see she barely flinched. She, too, knew how to play it cool when necessary.

Major Varakov blinked in what was an obvious dismissal. He wasn't used to being talked to like that and he felt the anger rising within him. But he forced it back down, wanting to try his new approach right up until he decided it was time for more drastic interrogative measures.

Something told him these two weren't like the others he'd come across since arriving in Alaska. For one thing, they had been driving a motor vehicle outfitted for travel across the frozen land, and their clothes were clean and in good repair. Their weapons were top-notch as well, cleaned, oiled, and in perfect working condition. In the buggy, a stockpile of supplies had been discovered, and when one duffel bag had been opened to find it full of explosives, Varakov had been pleased that the entire buggy hadn't gone up in a blazing fireball. He'd had his men flip it back onto its tires and drive it back to the hollow.

Mary stood up on her own, the soldiers not thinking her a threat, as she was only a woman. She walked over and stood beside Henry, Varakov watching her silently, as did another man who stood slightly behind the Russian Major. The two men began talking together, ignoring the two friends for the moment, although the two soldiers who had lifted Henry to his feet still had their weapons aimed at them.

"Have they said anything worth knowing?" Mary asked Henry, her voice low. "Or who they are?"

Henry shook his head each slightly. "Not really. Only like what you just heard. But I've heard them talking to each other. Sounds like Russian."

"Russian?" Mary asked, perplexed.

"I think they're some kind of invading army, as crazy as that seems. Why else would they be here in America?" He gestured with his chin. "Look, they all ride horses. Like a cavalry or something. They're armed to the teeth, too. I saw Kalashnikovs, Stechkins, and a few Walther PPKs. The leader here has a 9mm

Makarov on his hip. But I'll tell you one thing; they all look like coldhearts to me, or slavers."

"Cannies?"

"Thankfully no. Those are animal carcasses cooking over those campfires."

"What do they want with us?" she asked.

"No idea. But it can't be good."

Varakov had been watching his two prisoners converse out of the corner of his eye, trying to catch what they were saying. He also didn't want to look foolish before his men. While his understanding of the English language was rudimentary at best, his men had no grasp of the language at all. He turned and faced Henry again. "Please direct us to your superior. I have a proposition for him to discuss." He was proud of that last sentence, and it had taken all his mental power to pronounce the words correctly. English was so different from his native Russian, but he felt he was doing a damn good job of it.

"What did you say?" Henry asked. "You're not making any sense." He looked at two Russians standing before him. "Who the hell are you people?"

The man seemed to scrunch his face up, as if in concentration. Finally, he repeated. "Who are you? Ah yes, I understand some. I am Major Ishmael Varakov of the Russian army. This is my second, Sergeant Streltsy." He turned slightly and waved to his men. "This is my army."

Henry took in the Russian once more, now that he knew he was correct about the men speaking Russian. Not seeing the harm and telling Varakov their names, Henry said, "I'm Henry Watson. This is Mary Roberts."

This was all so surreal to Henry. From his knowledge, he knew Russia was very close to America from this region, and given the army traveled by horseback, and though it seemed far-fetched, and given that Alaska was in the midst of a hard winter, the only obvious reason for Russians to be in Alaska was that they had traveled across the ice to invade the United States.

"It is a pleasure to meet you," Varakov said, having trouble with the last part of the sentence.

Henry didn't reply. The words the Russian said seemed to come out of someplace deep down in the man's mind, as if Varakov was dredging up forgotten knowledge in speaking English.

Henry glanced at Mary. "He doesn't know English too well. I don't think he really understands us."

"Is that a good thing or a bad one?" Mary asked. Some of the men around the closest campfire were eyeing her, licking their lips and blowing her kisses. She felt like a cow being sized up for the slaughter, and it wasn't a feeling she wanted to continue. Unconsciously, she moved a few inches closer to Henry.

Varakov pointed to Henry and Mary's weapons on the ground ten feet away, along with the supplies taken from the snow buggy, then he gestured to the buggy itself, which was parked another fifteen feet away. "I want more of this. Where you get them? Where you get auto…automo…." He gave up and pointed to the snow buggy like a hunting dog who'd found a fallen quail his master had shot. "Where you get that?"

Henry debated on what answer to give. He thought perhaps he might come back with a threat of his own, one where he said that he and Mary weren't alone, that even now their friends might be lining up gun muzzles on the Russians. But he decided against it. Even if the others were out there, close by, what could they do to help? The five companions would be woefully outnumbered, and Henry was just glad Sue, Jimmy, and Cindy hadn't been captured as well.

In the end, he made the decision to lie; to admit he and Mary were alone, and deal with whatever the Russian had planned, while all the time hoping for an opportunity to make a break for it. "We have nothing else. We found the buggy."

Varakov hesitated to reply as he digested Henry's statement. Finally, he pointed an index finger at Henry and said, "Nyet. No. You tell me now or die."

Henry stood taller, his chin held high. "Go to Hell."

Varakov cocked his head, not understanding, so Henry made his reply simpler.

"Go screw yourself." He spread his legs to get a better fighting stance, Mary also shifting, ready for what came next. Behind Varakov and to the side a little, Streltsy raised his gun, as did five other soldiers standing further back. The sounds of cocking weapons filled the night, gun muzzles aimed in the direction of Henry and Mary.

Henry knew putting up any form of resistance was tantamount to suicide, but if he was going to die, he would do so on his feet, not tied up like the poor bastard at the small settlement, sliced and diced and left to rot.

Major Varakov raised his hand to stop the others from shooting the prisoners. When he knew order had been restored, he stepped closer so he was only inches from Henry. Glaring at Henry, Varakov reached out and grabbed Mary by the arm. "She die first, then you. Tell me information. Where are, how you say—buggy." He pointed to the companions' weapons. "Where are more guns?"

"Let her go or so help me..." Henry warned, moving so close to Varakov the two men looked like they were about to kiss.

Varakov was furious. Once more he wasn't getting the information he so sorely deserved. He also knew his assumption about these two captives was correct. The two Americans before him weren't like the natives he'd come across previously. The way these two defied him, the way they stood tall, the look in their eyes, the weapons they'd been carrying, all pointed to the two prisoners being from somewhere with resources, and power.

Varakov gestured for two of his men to join him, then pointed to Mary, speaking in Russian. "Tie her hands behind her back and put her on her knees."

"Can we have some fun with her first, Comrade Major?" Piotr asked. "She is pretty. I would like to fuck her, as do the others."

Ivan the Torturer moved up beside Varakov and added, "I would enjoy ten minutes with her, too, Comrade Major. I will get her to talk, and if not that, to scream."

"You will get your chance, Ivan, but not yet," Major Varakov said coldly. "Only when I am through with them; not a second before."

"As you wish, Comrade Major." Ivan turned and went back to join some of the other men by the closest fire.

"It's about to get worse," Henry said to Mary. He couldn't understand what Varakov was saying, or the other men, but by their tone and glances at him and Mary, it wasn't good news.

The two soldiers moved over to Mary, grabbing her, tying her wrists behind her back, then forcing her to her knees in the snow.

"I kind of figured that out for myself," she said as she struggled to get free but was quickly overpowered.

Henry heard the concern in her voice, despite her fighting to remain calm.

Major Varakov pulled a knife from within his coat. Henry braced to attack the man, knowing that the second he moved, he would probably be gunned down. But he'd be damned if who would let Varakov torture Mary while he stood there watching.

Mary, on her knees, held herself upright, her back rigid, defiance on her face. She would show the Russian leader no fear—if she could help it at least.

Looming over Mary, Varakov touched the flat of the knife to her cheek. It was cold on her skin and she fought not to pull away, knowing it would be conceived as her being frightened.

Major Varakov gestured to Henry, and said to his men, "If he moves, shoot him," in Russian.

Henry was about to lunge for Varakov when four soldiers moved into position around him, their rifles aimed at his chest. If he moved a muscle he was dead, the message clear to him by the posture of the soldiers. He didn't need to know what Varakov had told them.

Gritting his teeth, Henry glared fiercely at the Russian soldiers. "You touch her and so help me, I'll kill you slow. You hear me! You're already dead, you bastard; you just don't know it yet!" His fists were clasped by his side, his knuckles white. His fingernails would have bitten into his flesh if not for the gloves he wore.

"What you say?" Varakov asked in English. "I not understand. You are angry, dah?" His English became even more clipped as he wasn't concentrating; only trying to get the words out.

Henry shook his head in disgust. This dialogue was going nowhere. It seemed none of the other soldiers spoke a word of English, and Varakov barely spoke it at all. The sentences he said sounded like something a tourist would read out of a book.

Henry wasn't feeling too positive about the outcome of the situation either. Surrounded by armed men, Mary and himself alone, Jimmy and the others not knowing where they were.

It was pretty obvious what the result of Varakov's interrogation would be a bullet to the head for Henry, and Mary probably raped repeatedly by the men before, she too, received a bullet.

Streltsy moved past Varakov and backhanded Henry across the face. In Russian he shouted, "You will not speak to the major like that!"

Henry was sent falling onto his butt, his head spinning for a moment, dazed. The blow had been powerful. The knuckles of the small man had cut the inside of his mouth from where his teeth had sliced into his cheek. He didn't need to know what the man said, as he didn't know a word of Russian, but it was clear by the gesture.

Getting to his feet, Henry spit a bloody glob of saliva into the snow, a sly grin coming to his lips. "I'll return the favor real soon, asshole; count on it."

"No talk. What not matter," Varakov said in broken English to Henry, the knife never leaving Mary's cheek. "Tell me where you come from. Want bug-gy," he sounded out the word. "Want know where guns come from." He turned the knife so that the edge of the blade was now touching Mary's cheek. If she so much as flinched or even blinked too hard, the razor-sharp blade would slice her cheek open from eye to chin. "You talk now or her face I cut open. Shame I ruin such pretty face. No?"

"Henry," Mary whimpered, her guard dropping with the realization that this was really happening, that she was about to have her face flayed while she was alive.

Henry stared at the soldiers around him, at Varakov, at Mary, who was looking at him with her eyes turned upwards as she knelt on the ground.

There were no options, none at all, so deciding if he was going to die, he would see how many of the bastards he could take with him, he spun around and grabbed the soldier standing just a little too close. The man was young, and his inexperience at guarding a prisoner was his undoing. Henry reached out and grabbed the man's rifle by the barrel, yanking it a few inches before then thrusting it back into the soldier's gut. The air in the young man's lungs left him fast, and he let out a loud "Oomph!" as Henry pulled the rifle to him.

The soldiers were already swiveling their weapons to shoot Henry dead, and he knew he wouldn't be able to so much as get one round off before they did. In the background, behind the soldiers about to fire, silhouetted in the lights from the flickering campfires, five more of Varakov's troops were moving in with guns cocked, seeing Henry resisting.

Henry would have been dead in less than a minute. He knew it, Varakov knew it, and Mary knew it. He would have been riddled with bullets, his body left to rot in the snow, if not for what to him, seemed to be a hell of a coincidence to happen at the exact moment he was about to die.

For simultaneously, just as Henry grabbed the young soldier's rifle, more than a dozen hand grenades rained down into the hollow from above, the explosions blinding those not close enough to be killed instantly, sending snow, ice, and dirt flying off in all directions.

In a matter of a few seconds, the hollow had become a haven of death and screaming chaos.

Chapter 19

As the world exploded into blazing fireballs of ice and snow, Henry used his stolen rifle and fired at the two soldiers about to shoot him. The instant the grenades went off, both soldiers were thrown off guard, not understanding what was happening. They panicked.

Henry didn't.

A veteran of countless unnamed wars with both the living and the walking dead, in a few short years Henry had become a battle-hardened soldier, more than a match for any two or three of the Russian Army.

Both men went down with their chests riddled with bullets, dead before they hit the snow. Spinning, Henry searched for Varakov, wanting to make good on his promise to kill the man, but when he searched for the Russian leader, the Soviet Major was nowhere in sight.

More grenades rained down into the hollow, not close to Henry, but still close enough for ice and debris to pelt him and Mary.

Men were running every which way, trying to escape the devastation. Bloody body parts were everywhere, and a pink mist floated in the cold air thanks to bodies caught at ground zero of a given explosion.

Other than the two soldiers that had been focused on Henry, none of the other men seemed to care about him or Mary, all of them too involved in running for their lives. A few men shot up to the hillsides, hoping to hit whoever was dropping grenades on them, but all they got for their trouble was a small orb tossed directly at them. An instant later the firing ceased with multiple explosions, and more bodies were turned into pink and red paste.

Moving to Mary, Henry helped her stand up, then dragged her more than carried her to where their weapons were piled in the snow. Grabbing his panga, he unsheathed it and cut her bonds, careful not to slice her wrists in the process.

"Thank you," she said gratefully as she rubbed her wrists to get blood circulating. Though only tied for a short time, the man who had tied her wrists together hadn't been kind, and had pulled the knots as tight as possible.

"Thank me when we get out of here in one piece!" he replied while gathering his weapons, Mary doing the same. He had to yell to be heard, thanks to the screaming and yelling of the Russians.

He was still holding the sixteen-inch panga when a burly soldier came out of the darkness, wrapping his arms around Henry and roaring like an animal into Henry's ear.

Henry struggled to break free of the bear-like grip the man had on him, his arms pinned to his sides, but the man was strong, the arms made of pure muscle.

Henry fought back like a trapped animal, however, and with his agility and tenaciousness, was finally able to get his right arm free, the arm with the hand that still gripped the panga. If he hadn't been holding the large blade, things might have gone very different, for hand-to-hand with the monster of man wouldn't have gone in Henry's favor. But fate had intervened once more, and Henry had been holding a weapon, so as he forced his arm free enough to spin his hand around, he managed to jab it behind him, around where he assumed the Russian's stomach should be.

Despite the thick coat the soldier wore, the blade still penetrated, and after a moment of resistance as it pushed through the thick material, it then slid easily into the man's gut.

A grunt of pain filled Henry's left ear as the blade sank deep into the soldier's stomach, and a heartbeat later the grip on him loosened.

Twisting his body clear of his enemy, Henry jumped free, all the while spinning on his heels, the panga coming up in a wide arc.

The blade sliced the man's throat so deep that it scraped spine. Immediately, hot blood gushed forth, spraying Henry full in the face and coating the front of his body crimson. The sudden warmth took him by surprise, after feeling the constant cold on his exposed face.

Spitting blood and tasting copper, he opened his eyes after closing them at the first onslaught of hot liquid, and with the fires burning all around, and only his eyes peering out of a face covered in blood, he took on the resemblance of some sort of demon that had risen from the depths of Hell to seek vengeance on the living.

More than one Russian soldier, running towards Henry and Mary, saw the wraith before them and quickly deviated in their path, not wanting to face the demon warrior.

"Henry!" Mary screamed, seeing the blood covering him. She had barely seen the altercation, it had happened so fast, and she feared the blood was his. She did see the still form prone at his feet, however.

"I'm fine," he said quickly, spitting to clear his mouth of residual blood. "It's all his." He gestured to the corpse with his panga.

More gunshots sounded and a bullet ricocheted off a boulder to their right. Ducking low, Henry led Mary away and out of the hollow.

"Come on, this way," he said.

"What about the buggy?"

"Forget it," he replied. "It's on the other side of those soldiers and there's at least thirty of them. Too much to risk to reach it." The blood was already cooling on his face and neck, and he felt a chill on his cheeks, much more than before. Blood flakes were freezing and falling off his body as he ran. The anorak he wore was waterproof, and the blood hadn't penetrated the material. Soon, it would all be gone, frozen and cracking to be discarded as Henry moved about.

Henry and Mary began climbing an incline to get out of the hollow as fast as possible. Once over the ridge, they would be lost from sight.

Something loomed massive in front of Henry, a darker shape in the night. Acting before thinking, Henry lashed out with the panga, still in his hand, feeling the blade bite into something solid.

Then the light shifted from behind as a fire grew brighter, and Henry realized too late that he'd cut one of the terrified horses that must have run from the hollow when the grenades began to fall.

He'd sliced it good in the shoulder, but it wasn't enough to slow the animal down, and it reared up, its left hoof catching Henry in the chest, sending him sprawling backwards, the breath leaving his lungs. Only the heavy padding of the anorak saved him from cracked ribs. He thought he heard Mary cry out as he was sent flying backwards down the incline, but it happened so fast he didn't know if it was real or imagined.

Rolling head over heels down the low incline that carried him past the hollow and deeper into an impression in the land, a small ravine set off to the side, he reached out to halt his slide, but to no avail. A small boulder struck him in the knee, causing him to yell out in pain.

Ice and snow slid into his mouth, and his face was pelted with ice, as he continued to slide down the low incline. Choking as the snow filled his mouth, he spread out his arms and legs in the hope it might slow him down, while also knowing he might end up breaking a limb on a hidden boulder under the snow. But the risks were worth it to stop his downward momentum.

There were no more shocks of pain after the one with his knee, and he began to slow, eventually coming to rest at the bottom of the incline. He lay still for a full ten seconds, then realized he needed to get moving, but first he needed to take stock of himself and his situation.

He was alive, of course, which given everything that had occurred in the past few minutes, was damn fortunate.

Spitting his mouth clean of ice, he could still taste fresh blood in his mouth from when Streltsy had slapped him, and his anorak was torn up the front from where the horse had kicked him. His chest ached but he didn't think any of his ribs were cracked. Though it pained him to breathe, there was no sharp pain with each intake of breath.

Up above him in the hollow, chaos still ruled the night. He couldn't see Mary, though he did spot shadows running back and forth as the soldiers dealt with the ensuing mess from the exploding grenades. He could only pray she had escaped, knowing there was no way she could go after him when he'd fallen into the ravine.

Wincing with the effort, he got to his feet. He still had his panga and Glock, not letting go of either one when he'd begun his journey downward. He also still had a small hunting knife he kept in his boot. The Russians hadn't found it and he had left it where it was. The knife would have been for later, if there had been a chance to escape, but not when soldiers had their weapons trained on him, watching his every move.

Moving a few feet away from where he'd halted his descent, a few inches of water from snowmelt splashed under his boots; he thanked whatever deity was looking out for him that he hadn't ended up in the water. With no way to make a fire, he would have frozen to death with wet clothes, but as he was mostly dry, he still had a fighting chance to survive the night.

Looking up at the top of the ravine once more, it was a good three hundred feet back to the top. And though coming down had been rather easy, there would be no way to reach to the top without climbing gear and boots made for the task, with ice tips on the footwear to sink into the ice and hold him from slipping.

Plus, the Russian soldiers were everywhere, blundering around the camp as they tried to make sense of the chaos. Shouts and gunfire could still be heard, but not as much as when the barrage of grenades first begun.

Though alone, with no food, water, and no way to stay warm, at least he was free from the soldiers. He could tell that the temperature was dropping, more so with each hour after night had fallen, and it could easily drop to twenty below if not more.

It was going to be tough to stay alive, he had no doubt of it, but he wasn't a man to just give up, and the will to live sometimes was all it took to keep a man alive, despite the circumstances he may be thrown into.

The first thing he needed to do was remain calm. If he began to panic about his situation, then all would be lost before it began. So, as he was safe from attack for the moment, he paused to collect himself and figure out his next plan of action.

More shouting from the Russian soldiers filtered down into the ravine, and soon he could see flashlights from above as the men gathered their senses and began searching for their lost prisoners.

Mary would have gotten out of the camp and made her way to the radar installation, as that was the rendezvous the companions had set up, so that was where Henry needed to go as well. But he had fallen on the wrong side of the Russians, and now he had to loop around them before he could set off after Mary.

She must have escaped, for to think anything different would cause him to tremble in fear for her safety. Varakov would show her no mercy when he found her, Henry as well. He had seen into the man's eyes, and there was no mercy there, only a hardness that would allow Varakov to kill without care. Though Henry had killed and no doubt would do so again, he never killed another soul unless they were threatening harm to himself or his friends.

Before the dead walked, there had been civilization keeping man in check. One human wouldn't kill another for threat of repercussions, whether that was jail or even death row. Though crimes of passion weren't thought through, and the consequences never considered, a person who had a chance to question what would happen if they assaulted or killed another would usually check their actions for fear of the reprisals.

Of course, when society fell, the rule of law and order vanished with it, and only a man or woman's morale code dictated how they acted. Henry had found despite the lack of consequences, most people still acted the same. To kill was wrong, and just because someone could, wouldn't mean they would choose to when the option of not killing was at hand. Of course, there were always people who lived outside the law, and when the world collapsed, their time had come. Cannies, slavers, and coldhearts roamed the land, preying on the weak and innocent. But even before the world shit the bed, these types of people existed, only then they had to stay under the radar, careful when poking their heads up or risk being caught.

Major Ishmael Varakov was one of those men, who given the choice of killing or showing mercy, would choose killing as matter of course, not caring for the moral or legal ramifications. Men like Varakov were the most dangerous of all, men who didn't feel that all life was precious, and did what he wanted, no matter who it hurt. And the man was the leader of more than two dozen soldiers, all who seemed to share the same ideals.

His mouth suddenly felt dry, so dry he could barely move his tongue. Bending over, he scooped some of the snow that was clean, undisturbed, and chewed it slowly. The cut inside his cheek flared up but the cold relieved the pain. When the snow melted in his mouth, he spat it out, a dark red ball striking the white ground, then he ate some more, this time swallowing it.

He had all the water he could drink from the snow around him, but he had no food.

That would be an issue. If he didn't find the others in three days or so, and no food could be found, the situation could prove dire. He could survive for days on water alone, but sooner or later he would require actual sustenance if he wished to continue living.

As he stood at the bottom of the ravine he'd fallen into, he realized the wind was basically zero, the depression shielding him from the worst of it. It would have been a nice place to make camp for the night if he wasn't being hunted. But he knew the Russians would be searching, and from what he'd seen of Varakov, the man didn't seem to be someone who gave up easily.

The sound of automatic rifle fire pierced the night from above, and Henry ducked down, covering his face with the hood of his anorak to hide it from view. His anorak was a deep blue color. Not so good when it came to blending in with his white surroundings, but now that it was night, it allowed him to hide in the darkness better.

He remained crouched low, waiting, but the shooting didn't repeat and he finally stood up.

It was time to get moving.

Chapter 20

In the Midwest, where Henry was originally from, where he called home, winter was difficult even in the best of times. In a place where the temperature easily dropped below zero, there had been times when it was dangerous to be outside for very long, where exposure was a constant threat, despite having civilization to protect him.

At the end of each winter, when the spring thaw finally began, there were always reports of at least a few deaths blamed on the harsh winter, once more proving how deadly the winters truly were.

But compared to Alaska in the heart of winter, the Midwest had been like a warm, sunny day in the Caribbean. In Alaska, it could easily drop to forty below zero during the winter months.

The hard winter still had the land in its iron grip, and it didn't seem like it was going to let go anytime soon. In many places, snow banks ten feet high or more lined once-passable trails, and in others there was nothing but bare rock, the endless wind scouring the ground clean.

It truly was Hell on Earth, that is, if Hell had finally frozen over. Henry knew that native people, called the Inuit, lived in Alaska, and though he'd never met any of them, he had to give a grudging admiration for a people who could live in such harsh conditions, and not only survive, but thrive.

He had two choices at the moment: to find protection from the elements or keep moving to maintain his body heat. With the Russian soldiers so close, he chose option two, and headed out, moving south, where he planned to circle around and double back on his trek to the radar installation.

The storm had begun in earnest once more, a shrieking gale that had him exhausted after only an hour of walking. Hunched over to try and protect his face, each step soon became agony, the wind sending ice particles into his eyes.

No matter how strong the will of a man might be, no matter how determined, after taking such a fierce buffeting for hour after hour, no man could withstand it forever. By the third hour, all he wanted to do was lie down and rest, just close his eyes and sleep for a while. But he didn't, for deep down, he knew if he stopped for even moment, if he succumbed to the gale forces of Mother Nature and surrendered, he would be on the last train west with a direct route to Hell.

He wasn't ready for that trip just yet.

So he forced one foot in front of the other, not thinking about even the second footstep. Only the one he was taking at that exact moment in time was the only one that mattered. Once that footstep was completed, he took the next, once more just focusing on that one. And so it went, one plodding foot after another, as the snow grew deep around him, until he could barely push his legs through the snow.

He did his best not to push himself too hard, for if he exerted too much energy and began to sweat, he would lose body heat, then eventually succumb to hypothermia.

His fingers were slightly numb but there was still sensation there; he knew the signs of frostbite, which were small patches of gray-yellow spots on the skin, complete numbness of the extremities affected, which would later lead to a blackening of the flesh, gangrene, then death.

But he didn't think he would need to worry about that happening to him, for if he didn't find the others by the following night, he would probably be dead from exposure. Not the most comforting thought, of course, but then Henry had known Death was standing at his shoulder for years, just waiting for him to slip up.

To stop his face from freezing, Henry flexed the muscles by smiling, then frowning, grimacing, then looking surprised, complete with open mouth, for a moment.

The night was perpetual where he was, the storm blocking almost all moonlight from penetrating the cloud cover to the ground. Without light, it was even harder going, and after a while he wondered if he was even going the correct way. For all he knew, he'd become turned around in the storm and was even now walking right back into the Soviet's hands.

Thinking about the Russians had all sorts of things floating through his mind. The main one was what the hell were Soviet Forces doing in Alaska? The second was who had been lobbing grenades down into the hollow? Had it been Jimmy, Cindy, and Sue? Or perhaps some villagers who had been searching for the Russians after discovering the carnage they had left in other settlements, and had come looking for vengeance?

None of it mattered at the moment. If his friends had initiated the attack it had worked, and hopefully, Mary had been saved, but he'd become lost in the attack and separated from her.

Gunshots sounded from far off to his right, but it only lasted for a heartbeat and wasn't repeated.

He continued walking, wishing he could be somewhere else, somewhere warm. Suddenly, being back at the empty bunker seemed like a damn good idea.

Making a fire was out of the question where he was. Though he knew how to start a fire by a multitude of ways, such as using an eyeglass lens and the sun, to opening a few bullets and using the gunpowder to ignite some kindling, none of it mattered in the barren land of ice and snow he was trapped in.

He was at the end of his endurance and knew he needed to rest, for if he didn't pick his own place to hole up, he would simply pass out and die right where he was.

An hour later, the storm abated finally, and with it the gray clouds broke up, allowing moonlight to shine down. Before him, was a large snow bank under an overhanging lip of rock shaped roughly like a stone umbrella.

Flexing his fingers and making a fist repeatedly, he got the circulation going enough in his hand to grip the hilt of his panga, from where he'd strapped it back on his leg. When he'd reached the snow bank, he began using the sixteen inches of steel to cut into it, making one-foot square cubes, which he then began to stack on top of one another. He worked soundlessly, stacking them so that he made a small tunnel, which when finished, he crawled into. The top was open to the night, and if he'd had tools other than just his panga, he would have tried to also make a roof, but at least with a wall on both sides and the rock overhang above, he was mostly out of the wind.

With the wind not affecting him, he suddenly found that his face wasn't as cold, and the rest of his body felt slightly better also. He sat still, breathing into his anorak, which had been pulled up as far as it would go, the hood pressed tightly to his head, and simply breathed slowly.

Every five minutes he stood up and swung his arms and kicked out with his legs, knowing he needed to keep moving, keep his circulation from slowing or risk death.

God, he wanted to sleep, but he forced himself to stay awake, to get up every five minutes and exercise. He ate some of the snow, chewing it until it melted in his mouth and slid down his throat.

Just before dawn he finally succumbed to sleep, but this time it was because he chose to, not because his body forced him to.

Feeling relatively warm enough to risk it, he dozed for over an hour, still getting up every ten minutes or so, sluggishly moving his body, only to sit back down again and doze off. He made sure to push the anorak under his butt so he wasn't sitting on the snow, for it to then seep into his pants.

He napped until the sun had halfway risen, then set out once more. He forced as much snow into his stomach as he could, and for the moment, hunger wasn't an issue, but by afternoon he knew it would become more prevalent as only water as sustenance would take its toll, especially due to the amount of energy he was expelling just to walk through the heavy snow. Once more, in many areas, it was more than three feet high, while in other places there was virtually nothing, the wind having blown the snow away, where it gathered in ten foot or higher snow drifts.

In the places where the snow was heaviest, he simply slogged through it, raising his feet as high as he could before lowering them. If there were any crevasses hidden in the snow, he wouldn't know about them until he was falling through one. He tried not to think about that, for if he fell into an opening in the ground, he would never be able to climb out and would be lost forever. Mary, Sue and the rest would never even know what had become of him, his frozen tomb sealing him in ice forever.

He began to move north, hoping to meet up with the others eventually. His toes were starting to hurt as well, and even inside his gloves, his hands were becoming tender, so that making a fist was now difficult.

By midday he paused to rest, standing on a high slope in the land, as more snowfall fell across the land. Through the constantly falling snow he could have sworn he spotted the tallest radar dish of the installation miles away in the distance, but then the snow coalesced, obscuring his vision. He had to wonder if he'd seen the installation at all, that it hadn't simply been a mirage, an image his frozen brain had conjured up in desperation.

Either way, from how far away it appeared, it would be impossible to reach before nightfall, when once more the temperature would drop low enough to possibly kill him.

If he didn't find decent shelter and food, he wasn't looking too fondly on his chances of surviving another night alone in the desolate and frozen wilderness of Alaska.

But he still wasn't ready to die, not even close, so he began moving again, fighting for each minute, more on auto-pilot than through conscious thought.

As the hours passed, he quickly fell into a lull, where he was barely aware of his surroundings, so exhausted from hunger that it came as no surprise to him when he suddenly found himself facing a large gray wolf, which had come loping out of the descending fog, its huge paws allowing it easy movement over the fallen snow. The wolf hadn't expected to come across Henry either and it stopped, unsure of what to do next, whether to attack or retreat.

If Henry hadn't been so fatigued, he might have noticed the black streak going down the center of the wolf's skull, or how the fur was matted and missing in places, where scars were visible. He might have come to the realization that this was the same wolf that had saved him from the bear when he'd ventured out alone from the complex.

Not that it would have mattered one iota. For the wolf wasn't there to save him, it was there to make him dinner, much as it had the bear after finishing it off.

If the wolf hadn't been hunting alone, and the pack it traveled with had been right behind it, it would have been a guarantee that Henry Watson would have died that day. Though he would have gone down fighting, in the end, he would have been overwhelmed by the wolf pack.

But the alpha wolf was hunting alone, and so man and beast stood before one another, each taking in the other, as if one was waiting for the other to act first, both surprised to find the other out alone this cold day.

Fumbling under his anorak, Henry managed to pull his Glock, gritting his teeth as he forced his frozen fingers to wrap around the grip, his index finger to slide into the trigger guard and put pressure on the trigger, but not pull it—not yet anyway.

"What the hell do you want?" he snarled at the wolf, the Glock leveled at the animal, the gun shaking slightly as Henry fought to keep it level with the wolf's head.

From twenty or so paces from one another, the wolf bared its teeth and snarled in return, its right front paw scraping at the snow in warning. Hot breath plumed from its mouth in thick clouds of steam that were caught by the wind to be blown away.

"Get out of here, damn it," Henry hissed. "I don't want to waste bullets on you. Just go away."

The wolf lowered its head in reply, or seemed to, as Henry watched it, its eyes never leaving Henry. He tried to watch its hind legs, for if they twitched even slightly, it was a good chance the wolf was going to lunge at him. It was the toughest thing he'd ever done. His concentration was at an all-time low, and it was all he could do to stay focused on the animal and hold the Glock steady in case he had to shoot. Truth was, deep down inside, he didn't even know if he could get his finger to bend enough to squeeze the trigger. He didn't know who he was trying to fool more; himself or the wolf.

There was a tensing in the wolf's shoulders that caused Henry to decide it was as good a hint of a coming charge as he was going to get. Knowing he needed to act fast, he squeezed the trigger, wanting to end the threat with extreme prejudice and be damned the wasted bullets.

Though it took all he had, he was relieved when his finger did as it was told and the trigger was squeezed on the Glock, a double tap exploding out of the barrel, two 9mm rounds of death sent straight at the wolf's head.

But his aim was off due to his fatigue and the bullets barely grazed the wolf's skull, but each still did hit their mark if only slightly, and the wolf didn't like it one bit.

Not understanding how it could be hurt when the prey wasn't before it, somehow it understood that the pain it felt was from the man before it. Yelping in surprise and pain, it decided there were easier targets to kill that day; it turned tail and loped off the way it had come. Henry watched it go, the gray tail swishing once behind the wolf before it was gone.

"Yeah, you better run," he whispered, not wanting to waste the energy of speaking aloud. He looked warily around, turning in a slow circle, waiting to see if he would see any signs of a Russian patrol coming upon him. The brief report of the Glock would have echoed across the land, but it would have happened so fast that he was pretty sure there was no danger.

Satisfied he was safe from discovery, he began to walk once more.

Chapter 21

Henry spotted the small bear cub just before night had fully fallen. Only the fading light had allowed him to see it against the terrain where the snow had mostly been blown away from the ground, thanks to the gusting wind. The dark brown fur coat enticed Henry, and the rolls of fat the bear had accrued to survive the winter called to him. He was so hungry he could hardly focus. No matter how much snow he ate, it never seemed to fill him, and only dulled the aching in his gut for a short time.

With panga in hand, he began to stalk the cub, wanting to kill it for both its meat and the fur covering its body. Whatever slim, inner guilt he might have felt for killing a bear cub was quickly washed away with the knowledge that if he didn't commit the act, it would probably mean his death.

He was in a barren area, with nowhere to hole up for the night, which was why he'd still been moving and not huddling under some overhang of rock or scrub. But it seemed his luck was holding, and while not dead yet, the cub gave him a chance to not only live, but continue living for days to come.

Moving to within twelve yards of the cub, he crouched low, his eyes locked on the animal. It was small for a bear cub, and couldn't have been more than a year or two old, but he knew though basically a baby, the cub still had claws that could slice and dice him as if he were made of paper.

The only advantage Henry had was that the cub, when standing on its hind legs, was barely as tall as him, so at least Henry wasn't outclassed in the weight department. Also, though the cub had fearsome claws, Henry's panga was more than a match for the cub, and if he didn't screw it up, in a matter of moments the sixteen inches of honed steel would be buried in the cub's skull.

The cub still hadn't noticed Henry, its snout buried in the snow, where it was trying to dig up something in the frozen ground. Raising the panga high over his head, Henry prepared to lunge forward and slash down.

He was only a few feet from the cub when a loud roar came from behind, causing him to stop in his tracks and spin around.

The largest brown bear he'd ever seen was charging directly at him, and unlike the last bear he'd come afoul, this one wasn't going to do anything but gut him like a fish.

The bear's head was low to the ground, the mama bear running at him like a bull, its teeth bared, claws so long they caught the moonlight, reflecting the wan light like thick icicles. Powerful muscles roiled under the thick fur, and the eyes that were locked on Henry showed no mercy.

Dropping the panga, Henry froze in terror momentarily. Exhausted to the point of death, even his iron will was shocked by the advancing behemoth, knowing it would tear into him, slicing, cutting, biting.

But that hesitation lasted for barely a second, then his instincts kicked in, and though slower than normal, were still faster than most men thanks to the hard life he'd been living for years.

With the panga having barely landed in the snow, he was already pulling his Glock free of its holster, his hand wrapping around the grip. His gloved finger slid into the trigger guard and he lined up the bear's head, the same as he had with the wolf.

But this time he didn't wait to see what the bear would do, giving it a chance to flee, for he already knew. The cub forgotten, Henry began to fire, one round after another, forcing himself to shoot slowly, carefully. He desperately wanted to squeeze the trigger as fast as he could, to send as many bullets into the charging monster as possible, but he held back, knowing if the rounds didn't hit something vital, the bear would only end up killing him anyway, and whether it survived its wounds wouldn't matter as Henry would've been dead.

In the back of his mind, he realized the mother bear before him was even larger than the one he'd fought before, not that it mattered of course. A foot extra in height, larger claws, none of it mattered when even the smallest of the litter could kill him easily if he was unarmed when attacked.

The bear galloped like a horse, its head swinging from side to side so that Henry couldn't get a good bead on it when he fired. His rounds only struck the shoulders or chest of the animal, and though spots of red appeared in the rippling fur, the bullets didn't seem to be slowing the bear down in the least. Compared to the size of the animal, the 9mm rounds weren't enough stopping power unless the beast's head or something extra vital was hit, and even then it would be a matter of volume for the bullets to take their toll.

The distance between them was closing fast; Henry had seconds before the bear was upon him.

He only had a few more bullets left in the clip and there was no time to switch out the spent one when it happened for a new one.

Knowing he needed to make the last shots count, he went down on one knee, using every remaining bit of strength to keep the gun level and not shaking.

He forced himself to relax, to let peace wash over him, all sound being blocked out, as he lined up the bear in his sights.

While the world went quiet to Henry, outwardly, the mama bear was roaring, its heavy footfalls echoing across the snow-covered ground, its teeth gnashing together with loud clicks. It was enraged, wanting only to protect its offspring.

Henry heard none of it, his inward Zen concentrating on shooting the creature coming for his blood.

He fired one of the five remaining bullets, but it missed the head and struck a shoulder.

"Shit," he hissed, staying focused. The bear was only a dozen yards away and getting closer with each breath he took.

Firing again, he shifted his aim, going for the legs. The bullet struck a knee, sending the bear staggering, but through sheer will it righted itself and kept on coming.

The third round sank into its broad chest, just below the head, and it might have been Henry's imagination, but it seemed the bear slowed slightly.

Two bullets left and the bear was looking strong as ever, if a little wobbly from being shot in the leg. It was so close he swore he could smell it, as he fired the second to last round in the Glock.

The bullet clipped an ear, then struck the shoulder, almost exactly where another had hit previously.

The bear slowed a little more, but kept on coming.

With one bullet remaining, he knew he had to make it count, so he held off, waiting for the bear to get as close as he possibly dared. He thought back to the British invasion of Boston, how the saying "Don't shoot till you see the whites of their eyes!" was yelled across the battlefield. Whether that truly was said or not was irrelevant, for at this moment in time, in this private battle between man and beast, the saying was as apt as ever before.

The bear was within fifteen feet, twelve feet, ten feet,

At nine feet, Henry fired, which by the time he squeezed the trigger, the bear was no more than six feet from him. At point blank range he couldn't miss, and just before he threw himself to the left to avoid being trampled, he could have sworn he saw the bullet penetrate the bear's right eye, the large orb exploding outward, a pinkish-white ooze spraying off in all directions.

But then he was lunging to the side as the bear tore past him, his quick reaction enough to allow him to escape being crushed, but not so fast that the bear didn't actually still clip him with its body, sending him sprawling face-first into the snow.

He felt the ground tremble as the bear collapsed a few feet beyond him, but he knew he needed to be sure before he even thought of resting. A bear the size of the one attacking him needed to be killed with extreme prejudice, and as fast as possible. He would only get one chance at it, and that chance might have already come and gone.

His eyes caught the glint of steel in the snow. He reached out and gripped the hilt of the panga, then rolled onto his butt. The bear was down but it was still moving. Henry got to his feet, swaying slightly, feeling light-headed. He shook it off and stumbled towards the bear, the panga held out before him, ready to hack or slash.

The bear was lying on its side, its fur rising and falling steadily, its labored breathing loud in the quiet night.

Henry never slowed his pace as he came at the animal, his eyes taking it all in instantly. The bear was down, yes, but that didn't mean it wasn't about to get up any second and renew its attack.

Moving to its head, he saw the gaping eye socket where his bullet had hit, but it didn't matter to him whether it would eventually be a killing shot, for he brought the panga down in a chopping motion, directly onto the bear's forehead, all the force he could produce put into the downward swing.

The blade bit deeply, going in so far that when he tried to remove it, he discovered that the panga was stuck in the skull, the metal gripped tightly as if he'd been cutting wood that had sagged inward onto the blade. It didn't matter, for the bear was dead, its skull cleaved almost in half.

It let out a loud *woof* and went still, the last gasp of breath warm on Henry's face. He slumped to his knees before his kill, his mind still lost in the battle, to wired to relax, to accept that the fight was over.

A low mewling came from behind and he spun around to see the bear cub standing there, watching. It saw its mother dead before Henry, could smell her blood in the snow; it wailed in grief.

"Sorry, kid," Henry called to the cub, his voice hoarse and barely more than a whisper. "It was either her or me." He waved it away, throwing a snowball at it. "Go on, get outta here. It was gonna be you here not her. She gave her life so you could live." He tossed another snowball at the cub. "And don't do anything to change that, either," he warned. By the third snowball, which hit the cub right on the nose, it finally turned and ran off into the night, wailing the entire time.

Henry watched it go, and when satisfied it was truly gone and wouldn't be returning, he turned his attention to the mother bear. First, he placed a foot on the skull and began wiggling the panga, knowing he needed to slide it out rather than just pull it. With a little wiggling and twisting, not to mention almost falling on his butt when he slipped on the ice under the snow, the blade soon came free. Hot blood gushed out of the gaping skull wound, followed by a generous helping of bear brains.

He stopped what he was doing and gazed around the area, making sure nothing, neither human nor animal, was approaching. The gunshots had been brief, and he doubted if anyone, such as the Russians, who might have heard the sound, would have been able to get his location, but he hadn't survived as long as he had by making a foolish mistake now. Listening to the wind, and detecting nothing out of the ordinary, he went back to work, satisfied he was alone.

He took a quick moment to reload his Glock, popping out the spent clip and pocketing it to re-use later; he slid in his only replacement clip. After ejecting the first round and reloading it, satisfied the spring mechanism was functioning well, he slid it back into its holster.

He reached out and touched the side of the bear, feeling the warmth underneath the fur. It called to him, and he wasted no time. Using the panga, he sliced into the side of the bear, warm blood gushing out of the wound to steam in the night. He took off his gloves and shoved them in his anorak pockets, and after sliding up the sleeves of his jacket as high as they would go, he pushed his hands into the open wound up to his elbows, careful not to scratch his hands on any broken ribs.

Instantly, his hands and wrists became so hot that he thought they were on fire, as if he'd shoved them into an oven and they were being cooked. But as his hands thawed even more, normal sensation returned, and soon his hands were feeling comfortable, the burning sensation having ceased.

He considered for a moment taking off his clothes and climbing into the bear's carcass, allowing its fading warmth to fill his entire body. Then he reconsidered, knowing it would be foolish. As the temperature dropped and the blood turned cold, he would only end up being encased inside the frozen carcass, trapped forever.

No, though tempting for the instant heat, in the end it would only end in his death. He'd settle for just his hands and arms within the warm carcass.

As he stood there warming his arms, he bent over and lapped at the dribbling blood, gagging at the salty taste filling his mouth. Closing his eyes, he fought the urge to vomit, and as soon as he felt able, drank some more. The blood would nourish him far more than snow ever could.

When he began to feel the warmth fading from the bear, he removed his arms, and quickly wiped them dry on the already matted fur. When he had them as clean as he was able, he put his gloves back on and rolled the sleeves of the anorak down. His circulation was back to normal, his hands at last feeling excellent. He wished there was time to shove his feet into the carcass but knew there wasn't.

Using the panga, he carved some thin pieces of meat off the bear and ate it raw, chewing with concentration, and forcing himself to swallow it when he wanted to spit it out. When he finished, he sliced some more and went through the same actions, knowing if he didn't take it slow, and not eat too much, too fast, he would risk throwing it all up. His stomach wasn't used to food after days without, and he needed to take it slow and careful.

The bear was large enough to use as a wall, a natural windbreak, and once more he began to create snow blocks, as well as any large rocks he could find and break free of the earth, having to chip away at them to free each one of ice. Only a few trees were in the area, but he was able to cut the lower branches down and use them as a half-ass roof. He gazed down at the little home and shook his head in shame. It was terrible, and needed much more work, but he knew he was at the end of his endurance. With some of his body warmed up, and food in his belly, which also warmed him up as it was digested, he couldn't even stand up, let alone continue working on the small hut. So he crawled into his shabby home, pressed his head against the still partially warm bear's fur, and instantly falling into a light sleep.

In the middle of the night he awoke, shivering in the biting cold. Sure enough, the hut hadn't been solid enough and the cold had been seeping into it from the moment he'd climbed in and fallen asleep. He tried to stand but the hut was too small, and he didn't want to venture outside. Though cold inside the shelter, it was even colder without it. So he got to his knees and tried to exercise, the effort difficult, given he wanted to sleep some more.

But his hands and feet were numb and he knew he needed to begin moving, to fight off the cold.

But as he moved, swinging his arms, bending and unbending his legs, drowsiness fought to reclaim him. But this time it was more insidious, a temptation of warmth and rest; that he'd tried his best, and should feel no shame in giving up. All he had to do was lay down and close his eyes, and all his suffering would be over.

Just close his eyes; that's all. Rest, warmth. He deserved it. It was time to stop now.

Just give in.

That's all, just give in.

Just…give…in.

He'd stopped moving and was only sitting on the ground, eyes glazed over, seeing nothing.

He was almost under, his eyelids drooping, his breathing slow-ing.

All he had to do was let go of that little bit keeping him awake.

So close.

So close.

"No, damn it. No!" he suddenly shouted, and pushed up, standing, knocking the half-ass roof of the shelter asunder. "I won't go out like that!"

A wolf howled from nearby, but not so close he needed to fear it. But soon, the wolves and other scavengers would be coming, wanting to feed on the fallen bear. Looking around, all he saw was darkness, and overhead a blanket of stars, as if the universe had rolled them out just for him.

Kicking the shelter aside, he moved out into the snow, leaving the bear carcass behind. He needed to be moving, walking, not just trying to exercise. Only full movement would allow him to stay awake until sunrise.

He pulled the hood closer around his head but then decided it was a mistake. If he was going to travel blind in the dark, at least he should be able to hear his surroundings. Being practically blind was bad enough, but adding being deaf as well and it was a combination rife with danger.

He stamped his feet a few times to get the circulation going a little more, the exercise waking him up, and started walking. His only option was to reach the radar installation he'd seen before, where he hoped the others were holed up, waiting for him to arrive. Even if they weren't waiting for him, at least there would be solid walls and a ceiling to keep out the cold. Hell, maybe there would be some old furniture he could use as kindling for a fire. As he walked, just the idea of a fire made him want to move faster, but he held off, knowing he needed to pace himself.

The moon came out every ten minutes or so, breaking past the clouds, bathing the land in a pallid glow. It helped push back the indigo night.

He walked for more than an hour, thankful that there was no storm for a change. It seemed the snow never stopped falling in Alaska, or at least since he'd arrived.

Reaching the top of an incline in the land, he spotted the radar dish about three to four miles away. He watched it for a full twenty seconds, and it never wavered, the image never dissolved. It wasn't some kind of snow mirage, it was real. He was close. Or at least, closer than he'd been thus far.

Hoping that his suffering was almost over, he trudged onward, figuring in two hours or less he'd be there.

Only he didn't compensate for his exhaustion, and though he'd eaten, he had still pushed his mind and body to their extremes.

Soon, he began to hallucinate.

Long-dead comrades floated in the air before him.

Jeffrey Robbins was there, only his head wasn't on his shoulders, but was being held in his hands. The mouth was moving, and though no sound was uttered, Henry knew the words were full of accusation, the man blaming Henry for his death back at the shopping mall outside of Boston.

Henry walked right up to the vision, and even waved a hand through Jeffrey's midsection, and when nothing stopped his arm, he pushed onward, ignoring the ghost from his past.

Scott Peterson was there also, waiting patiently as Henry reached the top of a parallel ridge. Scott's throat was torn out, blood dripping down his body, which was skeletal. The arms were spread wide, the face looking forlorn, a pleading look in the ghostly eyes.

Henry ignored the shade, knowing he had no guilt in his heart for Scott's death, or Jeffrey's. But then, if he didn't feel responsible for their deaths, why would the apparition of both men have been placed before him?

Blinking his eyes to clear them of any further visions, he only found another before him. A handsome black Labrador retriever sat on its haunches, mouth open with tongue hanging out, tail wagging happily. Which was an even odder sight as the dog was riddled with bullets, blood seeping from each gaping wound to pool on the ground, though it didn't spread out and seep into the snow, as it wasn't truly there.

Guilt welled up within him as he walked past the dog, which never moved as Henry trudged onward.

"I'm sorry, boy," he whispered, but said nothing more, for there wasn't anything else he could say. The dog had been shot to death when it was left behind, the companions having needed to use an A/C duct in a ceiling to hide in, and at the time, there was nothing Henry could have done to change the way events had played out.

After taking ten steps, Henry couldn't help but glance over his shoulder to see if the dog was still there. It wasn't. Another ghost of his past had faded into the night, once more nothing but a lost memory.

Reflectively he looked down at the ground, almost expecting to see it saturated with crimson blood, but there was nothing but ice and snow.

He began to move on, and mercifully, no more visions plagued his beleaguered mind.

Sometime later, he thought he spotted a pack of wolves on a nearby rise, moving parallel with him. One wolf was huge, with gray fur and a black streak going down the center of its head, but when he closed his eyes to clear them from tearing up from the cold, the pack vanished. He waited for them to reappear, but they never did, and in that time he began to question if they'd been there at all. Perhaps the pack was nothing but another vision, his exhausted brain playing even more tricks on him.

Dawn came before he reached the installation, the bright reds and oranges of the coming sunrise filling the sky, beautiful, the growing light of dawn finally pushing back the night. Henry barely noticed it, his mind focused on moving forward, much like before, one step at a time, and only one step.

His eyes were blurry from constantly freezing, and unfreezing, as Henry blinked and blinked again. His eye protection had been in the snow buggy, and with each passing hour, his vision had deteriorated.

But finally he was there, looking down on the valley that contained the radar installation. Off to the left, in the distance, the massive dam dominated the valley and land around it, seeming to dwarf all that lay beneath it.

He began descending the ridge, but it didn't go as smooth as he would have liked. Cold beyond cold, his hands numb, his feet frozen, he stumbled and fell countless times, entirely using whatever remaining reserves of energy he'd acquired after eating the bear meat. He lost one of his gloves in a fall, and cut his right hand on his palm when he reached out to halt his fall, only to end up grabbing a sharp rock or piece of jagged ice. His other wounds began to ache as well; the gunshot wound on his arm, the cut between his shoulder blades, all burned with renewed fire thanks to the bitter cold. He whacked his knee so hard when he fell once that he wanted to cry, but fought off the feeling as a waste of energy. He began to walk with a limp after that.

He descended into a depression in the land, and for a few minutes there was no installation to see, and he began to wonder if he'd seen it at all, or if it had all been a cruel joke.

But when he reached the top of the shallow depression, and once more the installation loomed before him, barely a quarter of a mile off, if not closer, he knew he was okay. Gauging distance in his condition was all but impossible. The land was mostly level, with no more dips in the ground that would cause him to slow down.

As he began to walk across the open plain, he knew right then that he was going to reach the installation; he was going to live. The sun was still rising in the sky, but the night was gone, the prospect of a new day shining down on the land.

As he shuffled forward, he thought he saw people coming towards him, and though his vision was corrupted, he was pretty sure he recognized the shapes, the way they moved. But then, it all could have been a dream formed by his fractured mind, and in truth, the radar installation was nowhere before him, and that there were no people at all. Reality had faded away to him, where he didn't truly know what was real or imagined.

He was perhaps all alone, out on the tundra, miles upon miles from anything, and that he was slowly dying, freezing to death, with no one to see or hear him.

With reality a blur, he had no way of knowing what was real and what was fake, but he knew that either way, he was at his end.

Either the buildings before him were real, as were the people calling to him, though he couldn't hear them, or else it was all a creation of his mind and he was about to die.

Either way, he'd done his best; he could finally rest with that knowledge. Dropping to his knees, relieved to be so close to salvation but unable to continue, he wearily sat down and rested. Closing his eyes, he slumped to the ground, the snow accepting him like a warm blanket. Even if he wanted to go on he couldn't. Not one more step. He'd reached the end of his endurance and he knew that no man could have done better.

He waited for either the people running towards him to reach him, or if not that, he waited for Death to take him.

It didn't matter which way the die was cast, for his ordeal was over.

He could finally sleep.

Chapter 22

Henry Watson opened his eyes, unsure where he was or if he was alive or dead. And if he was dead, where had his soul ended up?

He could hear singing, which was odd, a melodic voice that floated in the air, seeming to caress him. Was he in Heaven? For most of his adult life he'd debated his faith, both his beliefs as a child about Heaven and Hell and his intelligence as a man, warring with one another.

His head hurt, as did the rest of his body. Feeling weary, his mind fuzzy, he took in the room he was in. If this was Heaven, then there had been a lot of hype for nothing. Moving his head slightly, he felt a twinge of pain. That settled it for him. He was most definitely alive. Everything he learned about Heaven told him he shouldn't feel pain there.

So then where on Earth was he? For the life of him, Henry couldn't focus his mind enough to figure that one out.

Glancing down at his prone body, there were no shackles on his hands or legs, so he knew he wasn't a prisoner, and the door to the room was half open as well, which confirmed his assumption.

Footsteps sounded in the corridor, the clicking noise making his head hurt even more. He had to close his eyes and ride it out as the sound grew louder.

Then the door parted wider and Sue appeared, holding a bowl of soup and a bottle of aspirin. Upon seeing Henry's eyes open, she gave him a wide smile.

"About time you woke up," she said and crossed the room, sitting on the bed beside him. Taking in the room one more time, he saw five other beds. A dorm room of some kind, similar to the one at Area 51.

"How long?" he asked, his voice cracking. Sue handed him some water, and he drank half the bottle. The plastic of the bottle was battered and worn from constant usage. Canteens had their place but a good, old-fashioned, bad-for-the-environment water bottle always did the trick. He popped a few aspirin she handed him and he took another drink to wash the pills down. She took the bottle from him.

Sue instantly knew what he meant and replied, "Over sixteen hours." She leaned over and rubbed his chest gently. "I was beginning to get worried." Her hand crept up to his face, caressing his jaw with a thumb and index finger. "You need a shave, badly."

He grunted in response. He had several days of facial hair on him, true, but the last thing he was concerned about at the moment was shaving. He tried to sit up, but gave it up after the first try. He felt weak as a new-born kitten.

"I was pretty much done for," he said in a low voice. Then he thought of Mary. "We got separated," he explained. "Is she..?"

"She's fine, if that's what you mean," Sue said. "It was us that caused the mayhem, when you were both captured by those soldiers. Jimmy had the idea to throw grenades down, cause a distraction for you two to escape. Of course, no one expected you to fall down into that ravine. Mary killed two soldiers and managed to get away, where we met up with her. I wanted to go after you, to search, Mary too, but Jimmy overrode us. He said it was too risky."

Henry nodded at that, proud of Jimmy for making the correct decision. "He was right. It would have been far too dangerous to come after me." He paused and added, "I would have left him too if the situation had been reversed."

A shadow fell across the open doorway and Henry was pleased to see it was Mary.

Seeing he was awake, she went to him and gave him a hug. "I thought I heard voices, and it didn't sound like Sue was talking to you alone." She grinned. "She's been doing that, you know. Like you were in a coma or something."

Sue nodded. "It's true. I was hoping you'd hear me and wake up."

"I never heard a word of it, honey, sorry," he said.

Mary stood back a bit, crossing her arms over her chest. Her hair fell across her shoulders, a few strands over her face. She brushed them aside and behind an ear.

"Where're the others?" he asked. "Are they here, too?"

Sue answered first. "Jimmy and Cindy went to the dam to check it out in the remaining snow buggy. He radioed back there's a small town at the base of it. Looks deserted, he said. At his last check-in, they were going to investigate further."

"They need to be careful," Henry said. "Those Russians are still out there and I bet they'll be looking for me and Mary."

Sue suddenly looked concerned and she even glanced at the door, as if the Soviet Army would come exploding into the room with guns blazing.

"I think we should be all right for another day or so," Henry explained. "Their horses were scattered when Jimmy started throwing grenades. It'll take them time to round them up, but their leader, Varakov, well, he isn't the type of man to just give up and go away. He came here looking for something and don't ask me why, but I think he found it in Mary and me."

"I hated leaving you," Mary said, moving closer to the bed again. "I wanted to follow you into the ravine but I knew I shouldn't. Still, it was all I could do not to jump after you down that hill."

"I'm glad you didn't. It was hard out there for those two nights. I didn't think I was gonna make it a few times either. I'm glad you didn't have to go through that with me."

"Why?" Sue asked. "What happened out there?" She was worried. What had Henry experienced out in the frozen wilderness alone? What hardships had he endured? He'd been covered in frozen blood. Had it been human or animal?

Smelling the soup, he took it from off the small table next to the bed, where Sue had placed it. Ignoring her questions, he began to eat. "Wow, that's good. I can't believe how hungry I am." It was then he realized he was wearing new clothing, his boots against the far wall, near a small fire. An old vent for cooking or laundry was over the fire, sucking out most of the smoke. "My clothes?"

"I took off your old ones. They were covered in blood. I thought it was yours at first, but then saw it wasn't," Sue said in relief. "We can't wash them so I threw them away."

"You cleaned me up good," he said, seeing his hand was bandaged where he'd cut it on the rocks during his descent. His bullet wound also had a fresh bandage. "Thank you."

"Of course." She leaned forward and kissed him, softly at first, then more deeply. He had to put the bowl of soup down or risk spilling what little remained.

Mary stood by and watched awkwardly, suddenly feeling like a third wheel. "Uh, maybe I should go?"

"No, don't go. We have more to discuss." He gently pushed Sue away and threw off the blanket covering him, then slid his legs off the bed. Standing unsteadily, he ignored the help from the women as he struggled to gain his balance. A bolt of pain from where he'd whacked his knee caused him discomfort; he ignored it. "I'm fine. Let me do it."

Mary and Sue shared a glance that said, 'Men, always having to act so macho,' but neither offered to help Henry again.

Walking, or rather, limping, slowly around the room, Henry fought off the wave of dizziness pulling at him, and soon was feeling like his old self, if a little bone-weary. Stretching his arms and bending from side to side, he got out the kinks from sleeping for so long. "So, did you find anything of worth around here?"

Mary replied to his question, Sue sitting on the bed and listening.

"Nothing was here other than the empty buildings," she explained. "It looked like others had stayed here recently. It's a guess but I think the Russians were here. One of the buildings smelled of horses and there was horse crap everywhere."

Henry considered the information. "Hmm, they must have used a building as a stable. Makes sense." He walked over to his weapons on a far table and began donning them. "Maybe that means we'll have some more time. If they'd been here already, maybe they won't come back here immediately searching for us."

"What's our next move?" Mary asked.

Suddenly his bladder demanded attention and he grinned. "Well, my next move is to use the bathroom."

"Of course, here," Sue said, handing him a makeshift chamber pot. "We'll give you a minute to yourself."

Henry nodded as both women left the room and Henry opened his zipper. A sudden feeling of contentment filled him as he emptied his bladder. He began to get worried the bowl he was using would overflow, but just before it became a concern, his flow slowed down and then stopped. Careful not to spill any of it, he placed it on the floor in the corner to be disposed of later.

"Okay, all set. You can come back in," he called as he fixed his pants and once more donned his weapons.

He crossed the room and stood before Sue, taking her hands when she held them out to him. He felt better with his weapons on his person again. While holding her hands, he turned to look at

Mary. "We're going to have to fight those soldiers whether we like it or not. Those men are some type of invading army, and I'll be damned if I'll let foreign invaders come to America and do as they please. There might not be much of the United States left, but hell, guys, I'll defend what's left with my life. Are you with me?"

Mary weighed his words and then nodded. "Hell yes, I'm with you. My grandfather fought in WW 2, and he used to tell me stories of what it was like, and why he felt proud to fight. This might not be as grand as that war, but in many ways, it's the same thing." She flashed a wide grin. "Let's get those commie bastards and send them back to Russia."

Henry looked at Sue, his eyes prompting her to reply.

She let his hands go and made a fist in one of hers. "They attacked you and Mary for nothing, and would have killed you if you hadn't escaped. I say we kill them all before they do it to all of us."

"Well said." Henry went to his anorak and began shrugging back into it. There was blood splatter on most of it but it was his only jacket, so Sue hadn't discarded it, despite the stains. "Gather all our stuff; we're leaving here. We need to join Cindy and Jimmy. If we're going to fight, it's better if we're all together."

"We don't even know if they're going to agree with us," Mary said.

Henry considered her words before adding, "If they don't want to fight then we'll discuss it, but I think we know them well enough to assume what they'll say when we ask them. Right?"

Both women nodded. Each of the group knew the others as well as themselves. It was highly unlikely either Jimmy or Cindy wouldn't want to fight, especially not if the others were onboard.

Moving quickly, they gathered their gear and prepared to set off to the abandoned town. It was barely more than two miles away, with flat walking on a slight downgrade to reach the base of the dam, and from there they would have to walk up a path only made for horses or hiking. Jimmy had explained all this to Sue earlier upon his and Cindy's arrival at the path.

The remaining snow buggy was parked there now, left by Jimmy and Cindy when they hiked up to the town.

Soon, Henry, Mary, and Sue were passing the vehicle as they began to trudge up the path. Henry felt revitalized despite his past ordeal. After being a prisoner, it felt good to be taking the fight to the enemy, feeling as if he was in control again. He looked forward to seeing Jimmy, too.

He knew that once the companions were all together, they could plan their next move.

Chapter 23

"Are you fucking crazy?" Jimmy yelled in abject shock at what he'd been told, his initial reaction of pleasure at seeing Henry alive all but forgotten. "I'm not fighting a bunch of crazy Russians and possibly getting me or Cindy killed for the sake of some antiquated patriotic bullshit."

"But, Jimmy, you don't under stan…" Henry rebutted but was quickly cut off.

"No, old man, I understand just fine." Jimmy jabbed his finger accusingly at Henry. "All of you are fucking insane."

"But Jimmy," Mary tried. "Hear Henry out, he's just trying to…"

Jimmy stuck a hand in Mary's face, palm out. "I don't give a goddamn what he's trying to do. All I know is if those assholes are coming to look for us, then it's time we got the hell outta here."

"Jimmy, please," Sue said, also adding her input.

"No, Sue, don't please me nothing." Jimmy turned to face Henry once more. "What the fuck is wrong with you? Huh? We've been surviving by the skin of our asses for years, never taking unnecessary risks. Me and Cindy just barely got you and Mary free from those peckerheads, and what do you want to go and do now? You wanna go find and fight them? Like some movie hero charging to chase off the invading Russians."

Henry had stopped talking, and despite his gung-ho attitude, had to admit Jimmy was making sense. "Well, when you put it that way."

"When I put it what way?" He glared at all of them, with the exception of Cindy, who agreed with Jimmy that taking on the Russians was foolish. He paused for a second, gathering his thoughts a little more coherently. He tried not to think that in this particular moment in time, that it was actually Jimmy Cooper who was the one being the voice of reason. Normally, he would be the first person to volunteer to go and kick some ass, but after Henry had laid out what he, Sue, and Mary had discussed, he simply couldn't go along with it. There was no benefit to fighting the Russians. If they wanted Alaska, or half the damn country, they could have it. Until they actually got in Jimmy's face, he figured live and let live. Especially, when the companions were outnumbered at least five to one, if not more.

"Look, Henry," Jimmy began, this time his voice calm, the younger man in control. "There's too many of them to take on with just us. We've already lost one buggy, and all the supplies that were in it. They almost killed you and Mary, and if not for my brilliant strategizing…"

"Oh please," Mary said, rolling her eyes.

"And if not for my brilliant strategizing!" he continued louder, unperturbed by the interruption. "Both you and Mary might be dead right now. So if me and Cindy get a vote, we say let's hightail it back to that bunker or whatever it is and try our luck with the matter transfer thingy one more time."

Henry locked gazes with Jimmy for a full ten seconds after the younger man had finished, then he turned and looked at both Sue and Mary, who seemed to be pulling back from their first decision.

When Jimmy had seen Henry arrive with the women, his eyes had lit up and he had given Henry a big hug, relieved to see his friend in one piece. But that happiness had quickly changed to annoyance upon hearing Henry's plan for the Russian soldiers.

He felt slightly guilty at his outburst and at yelling at Henry, but damn it, he knew he was right. Henry, being older, still had a way of looking at some things that Jimmy thought was crazy, which was probably why the two of them had butted heads so much over the years.

The five of them were standing inside an old building with half its roof missing. It had once been a small museum with four separate rooms, and was filled with many different novelties and artifacts. Most of the items had been destroyed from exposure to the weather over the years, but one item that was interesting in its own right was still intact and in good condition. It was a genuine fake rocket with a launcher; no motor or explosives, just a dummy. It had been part of an exhibit about the Cold War and the Cuban Missile Crisis.

The museum was located in the center of a little mining town that had been all but destroyed from avalanches, most of the structures now nothing more than roofless shacks and fallen-in buildings.

The museum seemed terribly out of place in the abandoned town, but then, who was to say what the small town had looked like when it was booming. Evidently, some town leader had wanted a little culture in their tiny town in the middle of nowhere, and so had managed to get a museum built.

"Well, Mary, given this new information, what do you two think we should do?" Henry asked her.

Mary let out a heavy sigh and shook her head in defeat. "I hate to say it, but Jimmy makes some good points," she replied. "It sounded great at first, us fighting off the invading Russians, but in reality, it's pretty stupid to even try it. Not if there's nothing to gain but our pride."

Jimmy clapped his hands happily and threw his head back while looking up at the roof, as if he was talking to God. "Halleluiah, she gets it. That's exactly what I was trying to say!"

Henry looked to Sue for her answer. Though he was the unrequited leader, it wasn't a dictatorship. He valued the others' opinions and made his final choices on what they wanted.

"I'll go along with whatever you want to do, Henry," Sue said. "Jimmy has some points, and so do you. I know I get a vote but it would be foolish of me to act like I know the best thing to do."

"That's not why you get a vote, Sue," Mary said.

Sue turned to face Mary. "I know that, dear, and I thank you all for allowing me to vote like you do. But let's be honest. I'm not like the rest of you. Sure, I'm learning, but in a way I'm still a liability. So you all make up your mind and I'll go along with whatever you decide." She hesitated before adding, "But I will say this, if I can. To fight for nothing seems silly to me. Henry had me going with being loyal to America but Jimmy's changed my mind. America might be dead or it might not, but whether we live or die here won't matter a damn. We need to worry about ourselves, like we've always done. To hell with the Russians or what's left of this country. If it means even one of you might die, it's not worth it."

"Well, folks, that seals it for me," Henry said. "Jimmy's changed my mind. Let's just hole up here till tomorrow morning, then we'll all get back in the last snow buggy—yes, I know it'll be a tight squeeze—and we'll haul ass back to the bunker and try our luck with the matter transfer unit and beam out of here, or whatever the proper term is." He looked at each of them quickly. "Any objections?" No one said a word, nor gave any inclination they didn't agree. "Okay then." He brought his hand down in a cutting motion. "The meeting's over. We leave here and to hell with the Russians. They want this place, they can have it."

Chapter 24

With night having fallen over the small town, the companions made camp in one of the small shacks in the center of town. Henry decided the museum was too large to defend, and so wanted a smaller structure to hole up in.

Cindy was on sentry duty, having taken over for Jimmy an hour ago.

The moon was more than half full and high in the sky, bathing the land in its pallid glow, the pristine white of the snow glistening like diamonds wherever it was touched by the wan light. Patches of ground where the wind had blown the land clean were devoid of snow, and here and there greenery could be seen. Spring would come to this frozen land eventually, and no matter how cold it was now, one day soon it would be a more temperate climate.

But not this night.

Cindy pulled her jacket closer around her as she made her rounds, walking high up on a narrow ridge overlooking the valley and town below. From her vantage point, she had a clear view of every side, with the exception of behind her, where the dam sat ominously, a thin stream of water spilling from a small crack at its lip.

Moving carefully among the large boulders that made up the ridge, she could hear the small river running as it made its way past the adult-sized stones at the foot of the dam's spillway. The sound was soothing to her and she hummed to herself, as if the noise was music.

Turning around, she gazed up at the majestic dam, with its pumping stations and high towers. Though the moonlight helped to push away the darkness, it barely illuminated the trail leading up to the town, the path covered with ice and snow, so that the earlier trek had been difficult and fraught with danger.

As she peered over the ridge, she could just barely make out the spot where the snow buggy was parked at the base of the trail, camouflaged with branches and snow so that it wouldn't be found. Turning her attention to the small town, she could easily make out the orange-ruby glow in one of the windows of the home where her friends slept, huddled together for warmth. A fire had been built, the smoke escaping out a hole in the roof, one that had been there before the group had arrived. Using an old metal barrel, a warm fire had quickly been made. She had felt that warmth only an hour ago, all of her friends sleeping around the barrel, comfy in their bedclothes, the army-issued sleeping bags found in the bunker were getting good use this night. She was already looking forward to returning to her sleeping bag in another two hours, when Mary was supposed to relieve her. Shivering in the cold, she continued moving; knowing to stop and stand still would only make her colder.

The frigid wind tugged at her blonde ponytail, and she pulled her hat down lower on her head to cover her ears a little more. But before she did, she could have sworn she heard something.

Spinning on her heels, her eyes took in the area before her, and far off where the dam was. The sound she'd detected was that of earth falling, as if some stones had been dislodged before tumbling down the hill.

Gripping her M16 tighter, her eyes raked the land, trying to pull out anything amiss amidst the deepening shadows.

She stood perfectly still, eyes shifting from side to side, using her peripheral vision to detect movement that her normal vision might miss. Not realizing it, she held her breath, and like a statue, faced forward, watching, listening.

She was about to give up and resume her normal patrol when the sound repeated itself, louder this time. It came from her right this time, and she swiveled slightly, her eyes focusing on that one spot. There was an old concrete sluice hanging precariously over the side of the valley, more than ten feet protruding out into space, the end lost in the darkness.

If it ever let go, the entire collection of stone, concrete, and metal would go tumbling down to the town below, perhaps crushing the shack Henry and the others were now sleeping in.

Cindy began to walk, heel to toe, moving as slow as possible, so as not to call attention to herself if someone was searching for her as she was for them. The sound she heard might have just been a stone falling, perhaps jostled by the strong wind, but if it wasn't, then she damn sure wanted to check and make sure. As she shuffled across the ridge onto an open area, she felt exposed, and she tried not to think if there was someone out there, who had night goggles, what an easy target she must be making. She knew if that was so, she wouldn't know she was shot until after she was lying on the ground, her life's blood leaking out of her. Gritting her teeth at the thought, Cindy continued moving a little faster, wanting to reach a large crop of boulders where she could take cover and be blocked from view from below.

When getting closer to where she thought the noise had come from, she in fact, did detect the most unnatural, but softer sound of metal scraping on metal.

Her eyes glossed over the deserted town below, until locking onto the sluice once more. Now that she was closer, she stared at the spot, and after a full minute, spotted actual movement. Sucking in an intake of breath, as if to gasp in surprise, she stopped herself.

As she watched, three shapes became more distinguished out of the darkness. But then one moved more than the others and to the side, and she realized there were four shapes, all dressed in dark colors to blend in with the environment of shadows.

One of the shapes was doing something at the main support for the sluice, while the three other shapes stood around it, looking out over the valley, as if on watch.

Cindy had a decision to make, one she loathed to come to without having all the information she needed. The shapes weren't clear enough to discern exactly who the people were, and if she opened fire, she might be killing innocent civilians, perhaps just out hunting on the mountain.

But though that was a consideration, she highly doubted she was watching natives out on a hunting trip. After all, there were far more easily accessible areas to hunt than the side of the ridge, directly at a sluice that if taken out, would rain debris onto the town below, a town now containing her friends.

Her decision was pretty much made up right there and then. Though it would be terrible if she killed innocent people, the risk of not firing at them was simply too great. There was no time to get down the ridge and rouse her friends from slumber, and perhaps they could all run for it, so it was up to her to act now and deal with the consequences later, if there were any.

Not wanting to take any longer to act, knowing each second could be the one that allowed the shapes to do their nefarious work if they were up to no good, she yelled out a warning, hoping it would stop all work on the sluice supports upon finding out they were discovered. But no sooner was she yelling out than she was squeezing the trigger on her M16, spraying the darkness with rounds, the 5.56mm bullets ricocheting off the rocks and steel of the girders, giving off sparks that lit up the night around the shapes, as well as striking some of them head on.

Two of the shapes went down without so much as a grunt, riddled with bullets before they even knew what was happening. The other two were quicker to react, and began to return fire, their Kalashnikovs stuttering a steady staccato, the 7.62mm bullets zipping past Cindy as she dived for cover. Splinters of ice and rock flew up around her as the ground was sprayed only a few feet from where she was hiding.

Coming up and raising the M16, she fired in the general direction of the targets again, then rolled to the side to end up crouched behind a boulder roughly the size of a small car. Peering over the edge, she could see the two shapes were still there. One shape was busy again, while the other was looking out for where Cindy was.

The shape that wasn't trying to shoot her was her real target, she quickly realized. The shape was that of a man, she could tell. Both of them were actually, and the one hunched over the girders must have been setting some kind of explosives to send the whole thing tumbling down into the valley. Why else would they be there and even now defending their position with their lives?

It had to be the Soviet soldiers, and she cursed inwardly that she and her friends had been found so quickly. If they hadn't been found by morning, the group could have driven out of the valley, returned to the complex, and with luck, would have left Alaska and the soldiers behind forever.

But the Russians had found their hiding place far too quickly than Henry, Jimmy, or any of the others had foreseen, and now they were under attack. If only they had known, perhaps the companions could have set out immediately when it was decided they weren't going to fight the Russians. But then hindsight was easy when it came, and what could have been didn't matter at the moment. Now, all that mattered was to stop the two men trying to blow up the sluice and kill her sleeping friends.

The man protecting the one hunched over stood taller as he began to shoot at her. Cindy dropped down to the ground and returned fire as bullets ricocheted all around her, one zipping past her face so close that she could have sworn she felt its passage on her cheek. Her aim was true and she shot the man three times, sending the body falling down the slope, hands and legs splayed out before each was broken and shattered from the fall. If the bullets that hit him hadn't killed him outright, the fall surely would. The man screamed out in Russian as he fell, reaffirming her idea that her targets were Russian soldiers.

The fourth man gave up his machinations and receded into the shadows, trying to escape.

The cold wasn't a factor to her now, her body filled with adrenaline, her heart pumping faster as she fought for her life and for the lives of her friends—no, scratch that: her family.

Footsteps sounded from behind her and she rolled onto her back, her M16 coming up and around to shoot the approaching attackers. But no sooner did she prepare to fire when she saw it was Henry, followed by Jimmy and the others. Lowering the rifle, she waved for them to get down and seek cover. What had she been thinking? Of course, once the gun battle began, with the reports of the rifles echoing off the valley walls, Henry and the others would have been alerted to the gunfight and come running, awoken suddenly from their slumber.

"What's the situation?" Henry asked as he crawled up beside Cindy, Jimmy right behind him. Mary and Sue were following close behind the men. Henry was feeling much better after a few more hours' of rest, and other than a few new aches and pains, was back to normal.

"Four men were over there, or there were four," Cindy explained, pointing out to the iron supports for the sluice. "There's only one left, but I think he's the most dangerous. I heard one of them yell out in Russian, or I think it was Russian. It wasn't English, that's for damn sure." She began to get up. "You and Jimmy cover me, I know which way he went."

"Got it, whenever you're ready," Henry said, Jimmy agreeing.

"Okay, do it now," Cindy said and jumped up to begin the hunt. She began to jog in the direction the last man had disappeared, while Henry and Jimmy sprayed the hillside around the iron supports, firing over Cindy's head as she moved, while she did her best to stay as close to the ground as possible. Their bullets spanged off the metal and ricocheted off the rocks, the sound echoing out into the valley below.

But the four-man team hadn't been alone, and soon sporadic gunfire was coming from the trail below, but due to the gunmen's location, the shots went wide of their chosen targets. Mary and Sue began returning fire, not so much to hit anyone but to keep the gunmen honest.

The fourth man, who had escaped being killed by Cindy, was called Karamatsov. He was the explosive expert in the troop of Russian soldiers. The first time he'd seen the dam he'd wanted a crack at it, but Varakov had shut him down fast. Later, when the Americans had escaped, and were tracked to the small mining town, he had been given the chance to show his skills. The plan was a simple one: to blow the supports of the sluice and bring half the hillside down onto the sleeping Americans. Karamatsov had first wanted to blow the dam, but Major Varakov had given him a direct command not to do so. If the dam went, not only would the town be destroyed, but so would anything else in the valley; the Russians would be swept away in the deluge as well.

Karamatsov was deaf in one ear; this thanks to an ill-timed exploded bomb he'd been setting some years ago. So when his three protectors suddenly began taking fire and shooting back at someone, it took him some time to figure out he was under attack. By the time he realized what was happening, he was the only man still left alive.

His skill was explosives, not firearms—he didn't even carry a gun—so he quickly retreated down the hillside, knowing the plan had fallen apart before it could be enacted. He still held the block of C-4 that he'd planned to attach to the sluice. It had a timer on it but there was also a manual override. Gunshots began to pelt all around him and he realized he was trapped. And to add to this, one of the Americans was running straight for him, a rifle leveled and ready to kill him, while other Americans sent covering fire to keep him pinned down.

He might be trapped, but he was far from helpless. If he was going to be killed, at least he could take the Americans with him, for the shock of the blast would be more than enough to kill them all, or at least disable them, which would then allow Varakov to attack unhindered. He knew to return to Varakov as a failure would be far more dangerous to his health than if he died on his own terms. Major Ishmael Varakov was not a man to disappoint.

One of the Americans that had arrived after the initial gunfight, threw a phosphorous grenade at the hillside, the entire area around Karamatsov becoming illuminated in stark white light. He was now exposed, with not even the darkness to help hide him.

With nowhere to hide or run he began to climb down the hillside, heedless of his footing, slipping and falling in the snow and ice, only blind luck allowing him to maintain enough balance not to pitch face first down the slope.

The C-4 was held tightly in his arms, cradled against his chest like a newborn babe to its mother. Cindy spotted the man and opened fire, bullets spraying all around him, but once more, Karamatsov's luck held and not one bullet struck him, though he did slip and fall onto his butt, nearly dropping the plastic explosive.

Cindy saw none of this, and kept running at the man, who was in plain view on the hillside. But she slipped and the M16 fell from her hands as she fought to keep her balance and not go tumbling head over heels down the hillside herself. The rifle bounced down the steep incline a few feet and stopped when it became wedged between two rocks. Cursing, she knew to try and get it would waste precious time. With no other option, she pulled her hunting knife and renewed her chase of the last man.

Knowing his time was up, Karamatsov began to fumble with the bomb, his fingers numb from the cold, trying to work the manual override.

"Jesus Christ!" Henry screamed, seeing the bomb when a flickering shaft of light from the phosphorous grenade illuminated the man's body clearly. "He's got a bomb! Cindy, get back! Cindy!"

But the blonde woman couldn't hear Henry, too focused on the man before her, as well as the reports of the gunfire coming from above and below.

Jimmy, seeing what was going to happen, tried to get up and go after his woman, but he put too much pressure on his bad leg and it gave out on him, not able to take the strain. Though he'd been healing, he still needed to take it easy, and he'd pushed himself hard to get up the trail from the town when gunfire had woken him and the others. Now he was paying the price, his own body betraying him when he needed it most. "Shit, my leg!" he screamed, then added, "Cindy, stop, come back!"

"I'll get her," Henry said and was about to begin the mad dash to catch her when suddenly there was someone running past him, blonde hair floating out behind her, almost glowing in the light from the phos grenade.

"Sue, what the hell are you doing?" Henry yelled, seeing her racing off after Cindy.

"Saving you!" she called over her shoulder. She knew Henry wasn't up to a run down the hillside, not after the ordeal he'd suffered. He might say he was feeling better but she knew him too well to believe him. He would always brush off his own suffering, not wanting to be a bother to the others.

Henry wasn't about to let her go alone, however, and he jumped up, ready to chase after her, but a barrage of gunfire from below forced him back down to the ground to find cover. "Sue, get back here goddammit!" he shouted, but she wasn't listening, her attention focused solely on Cindy, who was twenty feet away and getting nearer with each step she took.

Karamatsov had found the trigger to the bomb with his shaking fingers and was only waiting for Cindy to get closer, so that there was no way she would escape the blast of the C-4. He licked his lips, knowing he had only moments to live, but despite this, he found himself oddly at peace with it.

Cindy was only fifteen feet away, the blade in her hand gleaming in the light of the grenade. Karamatsov's finger hovered over the switch that would ignite the bomb, ready to flick it in another heartbeat.

Suddenly, from behind the young blonde woman, another woman appeared, grabbing the younger one and throwing her backwards by the collar of her jacket.

Karamatsov's eyes went wide as his intended target was forced to a halt and then thrown to the ground. Not about to let his suicide go to waste, he jumped up and began to run at the two women, who were entangled together on the ground.

Sue, seeing the man running at her and Cindy, and the bomb he held before him, acted without thinking, only wanting to save Cindy from the impending explosion.

With Cindy yelping in surprise, and angry at being stopped, Sue shoved her away, Cindy sliding further down the hill and out of the blast radius. Sue still didn't understand the man had a bomb, and even if she did, she might not have stopped, as she was seeing red and only wanted to kill the Russian soldier.

Sue pulled her .22 and got to her feet, then spread her legs wide so that she had full control of herself as she began to shoot.

The small .22 rounds struck Karamatsov, but didn't stop him, though the man grunted with each round that hit him. He wasn't worried about the wounds; he only needed to live for a few more seconds; he continued to move closer to the woman who stood before him. The younger female was down the hill and out of reach, but this new woman would suffice. As long as an American died when he did, he would go to Heaven a happy man.

Many things happened simultaneously in those frantic seconds. To many of the people who witnessed the moment, it was like time froze for a few heartbeats, so that the last moments could play out in full, and no one would miss even an instant of it.

Farther up the hill, still crouched down due to gunfire from below, Henry watched Sue begin to fire at the Russian, all the while the Russian bomber continued to move closer to her, somehow shrugging off the bullets she pumped into him as if he was a God who knew no pain. Henry called out to Sue but his voice was lost amidst the din of gunfire, and he reached a hand out to her, as if by his will alone he could pull her back to him, to keep her safe.

Further down the hillside, Cindy regained herself and tried to climb back up, and it was just as she began to stand that she saw the Russian and Sue come together, her eyes wide when she realized what the man held and what was inevitably going to happen.

Both Jimmy and Mary stood immobile together, their mouths hanging open, as they watched the tableaux play out on the hillside in terror.

Far below, at the foot of the trail leading up to the mountain town, Varakov also bore witness to the drama happening above. Seeing the two small figures moving closer together, and recognizing one as Karamatsov, and having a pretty good idea what was going to happen, he smiled slightly, looking forward to the show. His men stopped firing, also realizing what was about to happen in the space of a heartbeat, and wanting to see it all.

Karamatsov made it all the way to Sue, her gun clicking on an empty round. The man was riddled with bullets, one even having struck him in the head, only to rebound off his skull and leave a bloody head wound, and it was all he could do to stand upright. He was only seconds from death, but still, he stumbled forward, never slipping on the uneven and frozen ground, never falling to his death.

So many things could have saved Sue at that moment; so many things could have gone differently.

But for some reason only the Universe knew, none did.

Karamatsov reached out and grabbed Sue by her jacket, as if he was an old friend who was just pulling her in close for a kiss in greeting. Sue, reacting to the attack, pulled her small hunting knife and jabbed it into Karamatsov's throat, the entire blade sliding in one side until the tip protruded out the other side. With the man spitting blood, she saw his eyes begin to glaze over in death as she struggled to free herself. Deep down, she felt pride, knowing when she had needed to act, without thought she had done so. Finally, she could stand tall with the others, knowing she could take care of herself. She wasn't just a meek little lamb anymore, she was a warrior, a fighter, who knew that if the chips were down, she could be there to help her friends.

That was when the C-4 exploded, Karamatsov last moment in life used to flick the switch to the bomb with his thumb. He died with a smile on his bloody lips.

Just before the bomb exploded, and the millisecond the gunfire from below ceased, Henry jumped up and prepared to run after Sue, heedless of the danger he knew he was racing to.

He had barely gotten to his feet, his eyes never leaving the two figures, when he saw Karamatsov pull Sue close, and even from the distance separating him from the Russian, Henry saw the smile appear on the dying man's lips in the dying light of the phos grenade.

For some reason, Henry knew what that meant. He didn't know how, or in no way should he, but for some reason he felt deep in his gut that seeing the man smile like that, he knew the jig was up…and he'd failed to save Sue.

The noise of the powerful explosion was muffled only slightly by the two bodies, and rock and dirt flew off in all directions as a large chunk of the hillside was blown outward.

Henry was thrown backwards from the shockwave of the explosion, and Cindy dropped to the ground. She quickly pressed her body close to the hillside, which prevented her from tumbling down to the bottom, as rocks and debris rolled around her, threatening to push her down anyway.

The sound of the explosion echoed across the valley, rebounding off the dam to come back once more.

As Henry lay on his back, staring up at the night sky, he suddenly felt a wet mist land on his face. When he held up his hands, he realized it wasn't rain, it was blood, a red mist that was floating out over the hillside. Blinking his eyes clear, he sat up, his eyes immediately going to the hillside. Of Sue and the Russian, there was no sign, both bodies having been vaporized at ground zero of the explosion.

Movement from farther down the hillside caused him to turn his head, and he hoped that by some miracle it would be Sue. Instead, he spotted Cindy getting uneasily to her feet, and beginning the trek back up the hill to the trail, where she could then reach the others, who were waiting for her. The Russian bomber had been far enough away from the sluice that the explosion did no damage other than to send a large amount of rocks, ice and gravel rolling down the hillside, where it piled up at the top of the trail, none of the debris going into the town proper.

Henry didn't move, didn't breathe, as he gazed out across the hillside, the smoke already clearing, the debris that hadn't tumbled down the side beginning to settle, and what had melted in the heat of the blast already refreezing to hold it all together

Henry felt sick to his stomach as he wiped his face with the sleeve of his anorak. As he wiped away the blood of the woman he loved from his warm flesh.

"No, she can't be gone," he said softly, too far into shock to yell out her name in grief, so that it echoed out into the valley.

Standing slowly, Mary and Jimmy came up behind him, no one speaking, everyone in utter shock at the loss of one of their own. Jimmy suddenly let out a loud sigh of relief when he spotted Cindy climbing upwards, and he hobbled over to her as she joined them. He hugged her close, squeezing her so hard she began to slap him on the back to release her. He realized he had come far too close to losing her as well.

Henry couldn't move, couldn't speak, as he watched the wind blow the red mist away from the hillside, taking it out across the plateau to be lost forever in the night. Taking with it the last trace of the woman he loved.

Varakov signaled for his men to retreat, to move away from the bottom of the trail. With four more of his men killed, and those added to the ones he'd lost from the attack when the two Americans had escaped his grasp, he barely had thirty men left.

But at least the Americans had lost one of their own for the four men Varakov had just lost. Still, he didn't know how many more were up above. For all he knew, there were dozens of Americans waiting to attack him, or perhaps there were only a handful. He didn't know, and due to this uncertainty, didn't want to risk a frontal assault now, especially when the element of surprise was gone. But the thrill of a true fight flooded his veins. Finally, he had found real soldiers in America, men and women who were true warriors and knew how to fight, and would provide him a challenge.

After falling back, he had his men make camp along the river that was fed from the opening in the dam, the water running down it to create the river that meandered across the valley. It was barely twenty feet wide, with a thin crust of ice along its edges. The trail that led up to the abandoned town was close by as well, easily guarded from where the soldiers' camp was, which is why Varakov had chosen that precise spot to make camp. The companions' last snow buggy was hidden only fifty feet away, but so good was the camouflage job that it remained unnoticed. Even in daylight it might stay hidden from discovery.

"What do we do now, Comrade Major?" Streltsy asked, as he joined Varakov at the river's edge, the commander staring into the moving water. Darkness had descended once more, only the half moon and stars illuminating the area. Men were beginning to get fires going, and soon Varakov knew he would be warm.

"Now, we wait."

Streltsy looked like he would protest the decision but Varakov held up a hand to stop his second-in-command from speaking.

"They can go nowhere right now. They are trapped. There is only one trail leading down from there and we can guard it easily from this location. We have them right where we want them, my friend. If we wait long enough we can starve them out, and then they will beg us for mercy not to kill them. Then they will tell us anything we want to know." Varakov smiled, though the gesture didn't reach his eyes. "We have already won the battle, Streltsy, even if the enemy does not know it yet."

Chapter 25

For the first hour after retreating back to the safety of the boulders, no one did anything but deal with the loss of Sue. Mary and Cindy sobbed softly, holding one another as they consoled each other. Cindy felt terrible and believed it was her fault that Sue had died, but when Henry told her that was the farthest thing from the truth, and had locked gazes with her until she relented, the blonde woman had accepted his findings, despite still being wracked with guilt.

Secretly, though Jimmy also felt terrible, he was relieved that it had been Sue and not Cindy who had perished. Though he cared for Sue as much as the others, he loved Cindy deeply, and though he would never tell Henry nor anyone else this hidden thought, he felt blessed Cindy wasn't dead. Of course, his heart went out to Henry, and he did all he could to console his trusted friend.

The last time they'd lost a team member, Raven, it was a devastating blow to the group, but eventually, they'd overcome it. Death was a part of life nowadays, and to not accept it when it happened would be foolish.

Henry was hit the hardest from Sue's passing, and was still in shock, and it was all he could do not to go charging down the trail, blasting away as he went.

Filled with equal parts grief and anger, he was a conflicting mass of emotions that the others found hard to deal with. One moment he looked to be on the verge of tears, and a second later looked as if he would tear the mountain down with his bare hands if it meant he could bury his enemies beneath the rubble.

In the end, it was Mary who got him under control, letting him vent his frustration and loss at her until finally he just couldn't do it anymore; he fell to the ground, head held low, on the edge of sobbing but never crossing that threshold. Henry wasn't a man ashamed of his emotions, and if he'd wanted to, he would have felt no shame in crying for Sue before the others. But at the moment all he wanted was revenge, all he wanted was to kill Varakov and his men.

Oddly enough, once more it was Jimmy who stopped Henry from charging off on some suicide attack.

"They got us by the balls, Henry." Jimmy pointed down to the bottom of the valley, where the pinpoints of fires from the Russian camp could be seen. "There's only one way in or out of this dump up here. We try and make a run for it and they pick us off like fish in a barrel. We go attacking them and the same thing happens."

"You're right on that point," Henry growled, regaining some of his composure. Thinking of vengeance allowed him to focus on something other than Sue being gone, so for now, he had something to keep him sharp, let him avoid grieving, which would come in the middle of the night, when he reached out to touch the side of the bed or bedroll she would have occupied, only to find it empty. At those times, he wondered how he would deal with it, and though he knew after the loss of both Emily and Gwen, there was a time when life could be appreciated once more, at the moment, all he saw was death through his eyes, all he saw was murder. "But there's another option you may not have thought of."

"Jesus Christ, Henry," Jimmy said, amazed that Henry could actually come up with an idea on how to get them out of their predicament, especially while dealing with the loss of the woman he loved. "Are you saying you've come up with a plan? How?"

Henry turned and gazed out over the valley to the massive concrete wall of the dam, his eyes taking in the cracks in the surface thanks to the moonlight. Each crack was a weakness to be exploited, and he knew it was the best way to settle his score with the Russian soldiers. Pointing to the dam, his jaw taut, his face masked in shadows as the moon went behind a cloud, he said softly, "With that."

"The dam?" Mary asked before anyone else could speak.

"Yes, the dam. Come on, there's work to do. At first light I want to be ready." Without waiting for a reply, he began moving across the ridge, to where their gear was stacked in a neat pile. He needed a rope to scale the side of the dam. Henry knew if he finished his plan early, he would be tempted to enact it while it still remained dark, and he hoped he would be able to hold off until morning. When his plan came together, he wanted it to be light out so he could watch it all come to pass, so he could bear witness to the deaths of Varakov and his men. He needed to see it all, needed to watch them die.

He felt it would be the only way he would ever truly know peace again.

Hours later, with the first orange and red lines of light caressing the sky along the eastern side of the dam, Henry joined Mary and the others as they gathered at the ridge overlooking the valley, and the dying pinpricks of campfires far below. Off to the right, high up, the deserted town sat silently.

Henry was covered in dirt and grime from his long hours of work. Jimmy, too, was filthy, the two men having worked all through the night, with the help of Cindy and Mary, who were also filthy, but not as bad as the men.

Henry had worked tirelessly, never so much as stopping for a drink of water. Mary had forced him once or twice to take a break, with the promise that the work would continue while he rested.

Finally, as the false dawn lightened the sky, the work was finished, and now Henry anxiously waited for a few more minutes, wanting to ensure it was bright enough for him to see his handi-work.

Beside him, taken from the museum, sat the dummy missile on its false launcher, the body painted red, white and blue, with ASAF painted on its side. It was aimed right at the camp far below, which seemed odd, for without an engine, there was no way to launch it. The missile was about seven feet long, with four angled fins on its back. It looked every bit as deadly as an armed one, only this one lacked the true punch of the weapon, the lack of a warhead making it useless for war. But Henry had another use for it this morning; one that he knew would add just a little poetic license to his plan.

Stenciled on the side of the missile's sleek body, there was one new word he'd added, four letters long and painted in blood— Henry's blood. But beside it, in smaller letters, two more words were there as well. It was all a message for Varakov, one he was looking forward to giving to the man.

Jimmy hobbled up to Henry, wiping his hands on his jacket to clean them, before sliding his gloves back on. The work had been delicate and most of the time gloves hadn't been used, despite the cold night air.

For Henry, the work had been cathartic, and though he was still filled with grief and rage, since his plan began, he'd been able to focus on something other than losing Sue. He almost didn't want the night to end, for in the morning, his vengeance would take shape, and if it worked out like he wanted, the target of his hatred would be gone and he would have nothing else left but his grief.

But one thing at a time.

"How we looking?" he asked Jimmy as he gazed out across the valley with his Bushell binoculars.

"All set, Henry, just give the word."

He nodded, never taking his eyes away from the small fires far below. "Soon."

Major Varakov was awake a little before dawn, not having slept much that night. He walked to the river and relieved himself, his urine steaming in the cold air. Finished, he zipped up and walked back to one of the fires, his hands held out before him to warm them. All around the camp, he could see the shapes of sentries; double what he usually would have on guard. With enemies so close, he wasn't taking any chances, and if the Americans were foolish enough to try something, he wanted his men ready to fight.

A horse whinnied in the darkness and he turned to where they all stood together, tied to a gnarled tree. If not for the steep trail, he might have considered taking his men up to the town he'd spotted with his binoculars, where the Americans were holing up he assumed, and attack them head on, but the trail was too steep for horses, and without their use and that advantage, attacking on foot was suicide.

He had no choice. He had to wait out the Americans, and when they were weak from hunger, he could stage an attack and take them down easily. He was optimistic he would take a few of them alive. He hoped the one called Henry was taken alive at least. It warmed him to think of the lesson he would teach the American when he had the man under his knife. That western bravado would evaporate once Varakov began flaying the man alive; he had no doubt of it.

Once more, he wondered just who had attacked him and his men the previous night, and had rained down what seemed like hundreds of hand grenades but in fact was less than a dozen. Had it been friends of the two Americans he'd captured? Or perhaps it was some other band of fighters. Since arriving in Alaska, the pickings had been slim for enemies to fight, and with the exception of the two Americans he'd found, no others had given even token resistance.

He was confident this would be the case in much of America.

Once he destroyed this small pocket of resistance, there would be no stopping the Russian invasion of Alaska, and then later, when he returned to Mother Russia with his full report, the rest of the country.

Twenty minutes later, the sun was beginning to rise, bright and strong, despite its lack of heat. Satisfied it was as light as it was going to get, and out of patience, Henry went over and tapped Jimmy on the shoulder, where the younger man was talking to Cindy and Mary.

"Okay, Jimmy, it's time. Let's do this thing."

With the night fully gone and the land bathed in light, Varakov walked over to where the slope began to become steep, to then lead upwards to the trail that would reach the deserted town.

On the ground before him, four men slept fitfully, wrapped in their bedclothes and sleeping bags: Streltsy, Piotr, Ivan, and Petroff, the last man seeming none the worst for wear after losing three toes from frostbite. All four men slept with their weapons either at arm's length, or actually inside their sleeping bags with them. One of them snored loudly, but with their faces buried in the bedrolls, he didn't know who it was.

Major Ishmael Varakov of the Russian army clapped his hands together for warmth, as well as to rouse his men for the coming day, but before he could open his mouth to shout at them to get the hell up, a strange sound came from above.

Looking up, he was surprised but not scared to see something long and cylindrical barreling down the mountain, directly to where he was standing.

The object was alone; there was no rush of rocks, snow and ice joining it. Whatever it was, it bounced and jounced across the uneven hillside, sometimes rolling, and sometimes sliding. If it was a weapon, it didn't seem to be a very good one. But he was no fool, and anything coming down the slope could be dangerous.

Yelling a warning, he kicked the sleeping men to wake them, as the entire camp went into action, fearing they were under attack.

That was when Varakov realized the object was some kind of missile or rocket, and with his eyes going wide in terror, he raised his hands before him out of reflex to ward off the coming danger.

Chapter 26

Henry watched as the fake missile rolled and bounced down the slope until it finally reached the camp, almost coming to a stop directly before Major Varakov, who was yelling at some of his men to attention, that they were under attack.

Henry watched it all with his binoculars, Jimmy, Mary, and Cindy standing behind him, only their naked eyes letting them see what was happening.

At any other time, Jimmy would have been acting like a spoiled child, demanding Henry share the binocs with him; but not this time.

As Jimmy shifted his gaze from the camp below to Henry, he watched the older man's face, the way the jaw was taut, the mouth tight, teeth grating across one another slowly, as if Henry was grinding his teeth. He knew his friend needed to see what happened personally, to let Henry see his plan play out in its entirety; it would be the only way he would ever heal over losing Sue.

So Jimmy stood quietly with the others, all of them off to the side, the dam over to their left; close enough to see what would come next, but not too close to be in any danger.

Through the binocs, Henry watched the first part of his two-part plan play out. The dummy missile remained intact all the way down, which was what he'd wanted to happen, and as it came to a halt before Varakov, he watched the Russian leader duck down and raise his hands before him, as if that alone could protect him from an explosion.

Other men did the same, expecting the missile to blow them into a bloody paste, but after ten seconds passed and nothing happened, everyone near the missile began to relax.

Henry watched Varakov walk over to the missile and prod it slightly with his foot, the cylinder rolling a little before coming back to its original position. Through the binocs, Henry saw there was a large crack in the housing, and he knew what the Russian Major would see.

Nothing.

An empty casing.

"Now?" Jimmy asked, anxious to see the next half of the plan enacted.

"Not yet, just a little more," Henry said, never removing his eyes from the binocs. He watched Varakov closely, studying the man's face through the lenses, wishing he could put a bullet in that same face. But his plan would have to do, so he calmed himself and continued to watch. "Don't worry, Jimmy, the show's about to begin. And when it does, it's gonna be a doozy."

After cautiously peering into the crack in the missile's housing, expecting to see the innards of a bomb, Varakov barked out with laughter. "It is a dummy! The Americans are trying to scare us with toys!" He turned to his men, who were all watching him. "Relax! The missile is empty. It is a fake. All of you get back to setting up. They may try to attack why we stand around foolishly, gawking like newborn babes." He pointed to three men. "You three, see to the horses."

"Yes, Comrade Major, one man said, followed by another.

Streltsy stood slightly behind Varakov, the two men gazing down at the missile.

"What does this mean, Comrade Major?" Streltsy asked, confused by this strange act from the Americans.

"I don't know, Comrade," Varakov replied. "Perhaps they are trying to frighten us. It will not work of course."

Streltsy was also studying the missile and he noticed something that didn't appear to be part of the original paintjob. He pointed this out to Varakov, who knelt down to inspect it.

"It appears to be written in English," Major Varakov explained as he tried to read the word. There were two other words there as well, but they were partially hidden in the snow — the words were colored a reddish-brown color.

Streltsy gestured to the letters of the larger word in plain sight. "The color of it looks weird for some reason, Comrade Major? Is that paint?"

Varakov pulled off his glove and rubbed some of the 'paint' that the word had been drawn in, then with it sticking to his naked fingers after the paint had warmed to his touch, he sniffed it. Coppery, with a hint of metal. "No, Comrade. Not paint. Blood."

"What does it say?"

Varakov wiped his fingers clean on his jacket and donned his glove once more. With his breath steaming from his nose, he concentrated on the word. He had learned to write English in school decades ago, as well as speak it, but he barely remembered any of the writings now. Having only the bare rudimentary in speaking it, his reading of the language was abysmal. But he tried to remember what the headmaster had taught him anyway, and did his best to sound out the word.

"B…B…OO…" He began, stumbling over the simple word.

"Boo?" Streltsy repeated, not understanding. "I do not understand. What does 'boo' mean?"

"Quiet, I am not done yet," Varakov said and once more began to sound out the word. "B…B…O…O…." And then it clicked in his mind and he figured out the last letter, sounding out the word once more. "Ah, M is the last part of the word. 'BOOM!' it says."

"BOOM?" Streltsy repeated. "That does not make sense. The missile is a dummy, you said so." He pointed to the other two words, obscured by snow. "There are two smaller words below the larger one. What do they say, Comrade Major? Can you read them as well?"

"Let me see." Varakov knelt down and rubbed snow away to expose the two words, before rolling the missile slightly so he had a better view. These words were much easier to read and he did it on the first try; he was proud of himself actually. "The words say, 'For Sue.'" He looked up at Streltsy, who shrugged at the reading of the words. "Who is this 'Sue'?" Varakov asked, confused. "Is she their leader perhaps?"

"I do not know, Comrade Major. Perhaps she is some kind of…" But his words were cut off when there was a loud popping sound from above, followed by two more. Pop, pop, pop, like firecrackers only louder.

As the two men stopped what they were doing, as did the rest of the Russian soldiers, all eyes focused upwards, to peer up at the massive dam looming over them.

The dam that was beginning to show massive cracks in its facade, cracks that were even now, as the men watched, getting wider, allowing millions of tons of water to pour out and flood the valley.

Only seconds before the loud popping began, Henry stood on the ridge, holding a small black box with a red button in its center; the radio antenna was pulled out so there would be maximum reception and broadcast. His left hand still held the binoculars to his eyes.

He stood motionless, studying Varakov through the binocs as the man crouched down at the missile. He watched the man's lips move, and though not able to read lips, as the man sounded out the three words Henry had written on the missile in English, even a novice like Henry could see what the man was saying. He waited for Varakov to say the words "For Sue," then he grinned widely. But it wasn't a grin of pleasure, it was one of malice.

"Got you, asshole," he hissed under his breath as he pressed the button on the box. "Boom."

No sooner was the button pressed than the pops began to sound off behind him, at the dam, where the four companions had worked tirelessly all night setting up plastic explosives, Henry having them use every last brick and grenade they had managed to take with them from Area 51. Luckily, those munitions had been in Jimmy's snow buggy and had been carried up to the town when they had made camp there the previous day.

Henry felt the rumble under his feet as the explosives erupted, cracking the dam beyond its capacity to withhold the millions of tons of pressure, opening it up to allow the deluge of water that had been pent up on the opposite side to pour out into the valley below.

Henry didn't see the dam go; he never took his eyes off Varakov, but Jimmy and the others did. First, there was only the sound of the popping, and from so far off, the noise of the explosions wasn't that intimidating.

There were large puffs of smoke in three places; one in the center of the dam, right between the two towers, and the other two on both sides, where there had been large cracks already. Though the dam had those cracks and was holding back the water at the time, those areas were ripe for exploitation.

For a few brief moments, nothing seemed to happen, as if the explosions had been for naught and the mighty structure of concrete and steel wasn't going to budge, but then, second by second, the cracks in the facade began to grow, spreading across the massive wall like when a person would step on thin ice.

As the cracks grew, so did they begin to spread, and though slowly at first, water began to spray out, cascading down like a hundred tiny waterfalls. But as the cracks widened, the water rushed out, and soon the cracks became so large that there was no more structure left to withstand the pressure, and in one mighty push, the dam failed, the entire center collapsing in on itself, water pouring out to be measured in tons; thousands upon thousands of gallons.

From high on the ridge above the town, where the companions stood safely, the collapse of the dam was a spectacular sight to behold, but from on the ground, at the bottom of the valley, as Varakov and his men gazed up at the approaching tsunami, the view was downright paralyzing.

Henry never took his eyes off Varakov, wanting to burn the images of the man's last moments in his mind forever. When he was lost in his grief, these would be the images that would keep him sane, would allow him to move on as time passed.

The water poured out and surged across the valley, washing away everything in its path. The small deserted town was caught up in the flood as well, and only where the companions stood remained untouched, too high on the slope to be reached.

What was left of the town was washed away as the water gushed out of the destroyed dam, massive waves pulling up what trees there were, pushing massive boulders before it as if they were tiny rocks caught in the surf.

Jimmy, Cindy, and Mary all watched with mouths agape, amazed at the awesome destruction they were witnessing.

Henry, saw none of it, his eyes always locked on Varakov, as the man broke free of his paralyzed state and began yelling at his men to move, to run, to gather the horses, to do something, even when there was nothing they could do but die.

For a few seconds, Jimmy began to get nervous as the flood waters continued to rise to where he was, only sixty feet away but seeming to be getting closer with each passing second. He wondered if the plan was about to go wrong, and that they too, were going to be swept away in the flood. But the reservoir emptied quickly, and as the water began to recede as fast as it rose, Jimmy's panic subsided.

The noise of the water rushing through the valley was deafening, like a thousand airplanes were taking off simultaneously, their jet engines blasting at the same time. It became so loud Mary had to hold her hands over her ears, wincing from the pain.

Some of the Russians, including Varakov, began to climb the slope, hoping to escape the rushing water beating down on them.

Half of the men managed to get off the ground, and to avoid the massive wave as well as the debris being pushed with it. The other half were bowled over, crushed to a pulp by the churning water, boulders and trees swirling around within like a giant blender, mashing and pureeing the bodies until there was nothing left but bits and pieces that were spread out across the flood, bobbing around until the deluge ran out of energy and began to slow, the water receding as fast as it arrived.

The Russian camp disappeared in a flash, swallowed up by the flood. Horses screamed as they were swept away, buried under thousands of gallons of water, drowning along with their masters.

Any corpses not destroyed in the initial waves were taken down the river, which swelled to a dozen times its normal size. Any bodies that didn't become snagged on outcrops of rocks or were washed ashore on the river banks, continued on for miles before finally coming to a stop, where they then meandered calmly in the normal current of the river. Fish quickly began picking at the bloody bodies, sensing a new food source.

Eventually, the river would end, and once more the water would freeze, any body parts becoming stuck in the ice, a hand sticking out here, a leg there, half a face over there.

Ivan the torturer went farther than all the other Russians. He floated on his back, his legs broken, one arm gone, broken clean off, the other nothing but a twisted, sagging limb that was worthless. But he continued to float, though unable to move, to stop himself. When he reached the end of his journey, and the ice began to form around him, he still lived. He lived for the entire day and long into the night, before finally succumbing to hypothermia and dying. His eyes remained open, even in death, as he stared up at the sky.

Though his death was rather gruesome on the suffering meter, compared to almost all of his victims, he really died pretty easy, the cold taking away most of the pain as he slowly froze to death. For a man who should have died screaming in the most painful way possible if there was any justice in the world, after dishing out so much pain and suffering, he died silently, never uttering a sound.

Major Varakov survived the flood, managing to get high enough on the slope that though the water struck him, he held on tight to an outcropping of stones, and though the water tugged at his legs, trying to tear him from his perch, he fought to hang on and won.

Two other men lived as well. Streltsy, his loyal second-in-command, who had joined Varakov on the slope, and the third was, of all people to survive, Rhzhdestvensky, his large bulk soaked all the way through, and though he'd been shot in the shoulder, the fat man had used all his strength to climb higher than the others, and by doing so, live through the flood.

The rest of Varakov's remaining army was gone, washed away by the flood waters. Horses, provisions, ammunition and guns, all destroyed.

The water receded fast, and as he began to climb down, Varakov saw that there was absolutely nothing left. The land had been scoured clean, leaving only the bare ground beneath the snow and ice.

Lowering the binoculars, Henry pulled his Glock and checked to make sure his panga was on his hip. "There's three of them left alive. One of them is Varakov."

"And?" Jimmy asked, speaking for the women as well.

"And we finish this now." Henry began to walk, reaching the edge of the ridge and climbing down. He was careful he didn't slip and fall in the snow and ice covering the rocks. Now would not be the time to turn an ankle; that would be the epitome of irony. Below him, he could see the three men who had survived as they lay on the slope, the water having receded, leaving them on the hillside like landed fish. Glancing over his shoulder, he was pleased to see Jimmy, Mary, and Cindy following. For just a moment he expected to see Sue, trailing last in line, but then he came back to reality and knew that could never be. He felt the grief overwhelming him and with his iron will alone, forced it back down, burying it deep inside. Later, he would let it out, but not now.

Now there was only death for his enemies.

"Don't get lazy," he called out in warning. "They're more dangerous than ever, now that they know we've got 'em cold."

"Are we taking them prisoner?" Mary called as she began picking her way down the slope, moving to what was left of the trail leading from the town to the ground below.

"What do you think?" Henry called in return.

At the bottom of the incline, Varakov and the two men were getting to their feet. Seeing the Americans coming for them, they knew they needed to move as well. One at a time, Varakov and his two remaining men began their descent, all the while moving towards the swollen river.

With his Glock gripped firmly in his right hand, Henry picked up his pace, wanting to catch the men before they reached the river.

It was almost over, and when he finally caught up to the three Russians, it was going to be quick. No talk, no chatter about who killed who and is going to pay in blood. The instant Henry had Varakov in his gun sights, he was going to shoot the man dead, then his two lackeys.

Major Varakov was moving well over the terrain, though his pace was slowed due to his clothing being soaking wet. His feet were already numb, the water inside his boots chilling him to the bone. His gloves were useless so he tossed them away. He didn't even know where he was going; only that the Americans wanted blood and he didn't want to assist them in their quest.

"Hurry, comrades, we must reach the river," Varakov told Streltsy and Rhzhdestvensky, who was laboring to keep up, his massive bulk a hindrance.

"We need to stand and fight," the fat soldier said. "We still have our sidearms; we can hold them off, perhaps kill them."

"That would be a mistake, soldier," Varakov replied, and when he turned to glance over his shoulder at the fat man, who was opening his mouth for a rebuttal, suddenly the rotund face exploded outwards as a bullet penetrated the skull from behind.

Rhzhdestvensky took three more steps forward, not seeming to understand he was dead, before the massive bulk of fat and blubber toppled face first onto the water-logged ground, a large splash of water flying out in all directions as the body displaced the liquid in a deep puddle. The chubby legs and arms of the Russian twitched and flailed for another moment, then the nerve receptors gave their last, ceased firing, and all movement stopped. The distinctive odor of feces filled the cold air, the dead man's bowels having released in death.

Cursing in his Native tongue, Varakov began shooting at Henry, who never slowed his pace, never even tried to drop down and seek cover to avoid being shot. He was a man on a mission, and though perhaps later he would regret his actions as foolish, for a dead man couldn't exact revenge, at that precise moment in time, all he saw was red; all he wanted to do was kill the man who had caused Sue to die.

Streltsy joined his commander in returning fire, but soon Mary, Cindy, and Jimmy were shooting as well. The two remaining Russians, being outnumbered, began to run towards the river, knowing it was their only escape.

Varakov wasn't relishing jumping into the frigid water, and no doubt he would either drown or die of hypothermia, but it was still a chance to survive and in Mother Russia, he'd learned that sometimes a chance is all a man needed.

"Varakov!" Henry shouted, hoping to cause the man to delay, or hopefully, to make him even stop and try to shoot again, but the Russian soldier knew survival didn't lead in that direction. Even if he managed to shoot Henry or one of the others, perhaps even kill them, there would still be more of the companions to deal with. For Varakov, it wasn't about revenge; all he wanted to do was escape to fight another day.

Bullets pinged off the rocks and ground around the two Russian men, and when they were no more than twenty feet from the river, Varakov let out a grunt of pain and went down, his left leg having been hit in the back of the thigh. His 9mm Makarov PM went sliding across the ice, out of reach.

"Major!" Streltsy yelled and ran back to help his commander, who took the assistance with a grunt of thanks. With Varakov leaning on Streltsy, barely able to put weight on the wounded leg, the two Russians continued their dash to the river.

Henry had made it off the slope and was running, eating up the distance separating him from the two men. He had stopped firing, not wanting to waste ammunition as he ran, though the Glock was still held firmly in his right hand, ready to use if either of the Russians tried to turn around and shoot him.

Henry quickly outdistanced Jimmy and the others, his attention locked on the backs of the two escaping men.

When he was no more than fifty feet from them, he fired the Glock again, two times in a quick double tap, the bullets hitting Streltsy in the center of the back. The smaller man let go of Varakov and cried out, before dropping heavily into the mud, which was already beginning to refreeze.

Major Varakov only had time for one glance at his fallen friend, and when he did, he saw Streltsy's face, and in that brief glimpse, watched the life go out of the man's eyes.

Streltsy exhaled a soft, "Run," before going still. But then the body started to twitch, and Varakov realized it wasn't life that did this but that more bullets were striking the dead man's body. Varakov knew he needed to keep moving, or he would join his friend in oblivion.

To punctuate his thoughts, a bullet zipped by his head. Leaving the corpse of his friend behind, he began to run once more, though it was more of a pathetic shuffle due to his bleeding leg.

But he was close when Streltsy had gone down, and he reached the river's edge in a few moments; he stopped and turned around to face the American named Watson, who was running at him, pistol held up and ready, prepared to shoot him. Varakov knew he had to make a decision there and then, and deep down, he accepted that there was only one true option left for him. But when he reached the river, and saw its churning, frigid waters, he began to have second thoughts. He'd always had a fear of drowning, even as a young boy and now, seeing the rushing water before him, he didn't want to plunge into the icy coldness. But he knew there was little choice, and there was an upside to his going in, for even if he died in the rushing water, at least he would deny the American the joy of killing him. At least he could cheat the man of that. It was nothing compared to what he had wanted to do of course, for the Americans had ruined his plans to invade America. It had all been for nothing. Though most of the people he met were worthless scum, it appeared that even a few with courage were strong enough to cause Mother Russia some difficulty if they tried to invade.

Locking eyes with Henry for one brief moment, he turned and prepared to jump into the river, just as Henry fired two more times, but Varakov, not stable in his standing position, instead of leaping straight on into the water, slipped on the ice beneath his feet.

But the slip actually saved his life, for Henry was spot on with his shots. The first one barely clipped Varakov in the right shoulder, nothing more than a graze really, and the second bullet, which would have struck the man directly in the center of the face, only ended up becoming a glancing blow to the temple. The Soviet Major, his body going horizontal to the ground, his feet going out from under him in a comical fashion, landed hard on his back.

But by pure luck his body, which had gone limp thanks to the concussion he'd just received from the bullet that glanced his temple, landed so that his upper torso ended up in the water, his legs remaining on dry land, and no sooner did this happen, than the current caught him and pulled him out into the rushing tide.

Unconscious, Varakov floated down the river, only his head bobbing up and down.

Running to the river's edge, Henry let out a loud yell of frustration as Varakov floated away. He raised his Glock, wanting to shoot, but the Russian's head was a constantly moving object, and he knew there was no way to hit it. In only seconds, the small target was too far downriver to even be seen.

"Shit!" Henry yelled again, standing at the water's edge, watching the head disappear from sight. It looked like he was weighing the decision to jump in as well, to then swim after the man. He might have done it, too, if not for the others coming up to join him, Jimmy watching the river intently, seeing nothing.

"Where'd he go?" Jimmy asked.

"Gone," was all Henry said.

"Yeah, but you shot him a bunch of times, right? I saw him get hit in the leg first, then the shoulder. He's dead, Henry, you killed the bastard."

Henry didn't look at Jimmy for a full minute, only the sound of the rushing river filling the silence, but finally, he turned and locked gazes with the younger man. "Did I?" He shook his head. "I want to know for sure, damn it. I want to see the man's bloated corpse before me. Only then will I know he's dead."

Mary moved up and touched Henry on the arm. "But surely no man could survive three bullet wounds, then a dunking in that cold river. That water must be twenty degrees if not worse. He has no supplies, no reinforcements." She sighed. "Henry, it's over. He's either dead or will be. No one could survive that."

Henry studied his Glock for a few seconds, as the four friends stood silently at the river's edge, while all around them, the water left over from the flood continued to freeze, covering the entire valley in a sheet of ice. Mixed in with the ice was all sorts of items, everything from dead animals, to bits of wood, to fractured pieces from a civilization that no longer existed, items such as license plates, old tires, and shopping carts; whatever had been at the bottom of the reservoir before the dam had burst.

The sun was high in the sky, which was devoid of clouds, and despite the brightness, there was no heat.

Henry felt cheated of his vengeance. But Mary was right, there was no way Varakov could survive with all the abuse he'd just received, but Henry wanted to see the body for himself, needed to see it. He gazed out across the swirling maelstrom of the bloated river, his eyes locked on the far side, though he didn't really see it or anything else.

Finally, Henry sighed. Turning, he looked at the others and said, "I want to follow the river, see if the body turns up." He faced Mary only. "I need to do this, Mary. I have to." He then looked at the others altogether. "I'll go alone if I have to."

"Okay, Henry, okay," Mary said. "We understand; you don't have to go alone. Besides, that way is the same way we need to go if we're going back to the bunker. So, it's not like we're going out of our way. But can you wait till we get our gear together?"

"It shouldn't matter anyway," Jimmy said. "Another hour won't make much of a difference."

"No. No, I suppose it won't. Okay, one hour. Then I go. With or without all of you."

Chapter 27

Amazingly, the last snow buggy was where they'd left it. When the flood had cascaded through the valley, the rear axle of the buggy had become hung up on a section of sharp boulders. So the vehicle hadn't been washed away with everything else in the valley.

Though all the supplies were soaked, more than half of it was salvageable, including food and ammunition.

Henry and Jimmy fiddled with the engine, and on the fifth try, it even started. After blowing out a thick cloud of black smoke, the engine idled roughly for a bit before evening out; it was like it had never been caught in the flood at all.

Cindy drove once more, as she had been driving that buggy all along. Henry sat in the passenger seat, and Mary and Jimmy sat in the rear. It was a tight fit for them both but they made due.

The drive along the river was silent, no one speaking, the mood solemn. Everyone missed Sue, and the fact that they would never see her again was an ever-present shadow, looming over all of them.

Sometimes there was no way for the buggy to follow the river's path, and when this happened, Henry would get out and continue on foot, to then meet up with the buggy once it drove around the obstacle, when the way was clear to use the vehicle again.

He found no sign of Varakov, though he did find more than his fair share of bodies and parts of them. Horse carcasses were prevalent as well, where they'd been caught by the crags of rock lining the river, which had receded to half the size as when the group had set out. By midday, the river was back to normal, and though it took some cajoling, Henry finally gave in and they abandoned the search for Varakov's corpse.

Setting off across the tundra, they began to backtrack to the complex, and two hours later, as they made no more stops, the snow buggy was idling before the large outer door leading into the underground complex.

Henry was the one to get out and go to the panel for the outer door, and after he'd punched in the code, the door slowly began to open.

Cindy drove the buggy inside and Henry closed the door with the code, walking in after the vehicle was fully inside. He waited until the door was once more sealed before climbing into the buggy again. Cindy went to the motor pool.

Inside the large complex, the temperature had dropped slightly, but as soon as they entered, the heat began to flow in through the ventilation, warming the interior.

Henry didn't plan on staying long enough for that to matter.

Once the snow buggy was parked and they were gathered in the motor pool, where they would all then walk to the dormitory for the night, Henry instructed, "Let's stay the night, get some rest, and tomorrow after breakfast, if we can figure out how to work it from here, we use the matter transfer thing and jump out of here." He glanced at the other faces before him. "Sound good?"

No one objected, all on board with Henry's thoughts.

The buggy had been unpacked and anything they were taking with them when they left was being carried. The complex had nothing they could use other than a safe roof over their heads, so there was no reason to stay longer than a day. They'd all been through a hell of a lot over the past two days, and at least one good night's sleep should do wonders for their mental health.

"You said 'jump' out of here," Jimmy said as they prepared to leave the motor pool. "You just come up with that?"

Henry shrugged. "Sure. Seems appropriate given what happens. Why? You don't like it?"

"No. No, it's fine with me. Just wanted to get our terminology correct."

Henry only grunted in response and Mary and Jimmy began to walk out of the motor pool and into the hallway leading to the dormitories. Cindy held back when she saw Henry hadn't moved yet. Mary and Jimmy were talking together, or more likely, arguing, and neither noticed the other two weren't right behind them.

When Cindy was alone with Henry, she moved close to him, so close she could hear him breathing. "Henry, I know I already said I'm sorry, but…well I… If I'd heard you call out to me…maybe she wouldn't have gone and…"

"No, Cindy, stop right there," he cut her off. "You have nothing to feel guilty for. I told you this earlier. Sue did what she did because it was who she was. She was brave, and she'd told me a few days earlier that she wanted to pull her weight more with all of us. We've learned to fight and kill to survive. That wasn't her, but she was learning. Not because she wanted to kill, but because she knew that in killing, she might save one of us from dying. So don't ever blame yourself for what happened. We lost Raven, which was hard on all of us, and I won't lie and tell you this isn't even harder for me, but she died saving you, and though it sucks not to have her with us, I can kinda take a little solace in knowing that."

Cindy was crying, despite Henry's comforting words, still feeling guilty.

He pulled her close, hugging her. "So never think you don't deserve to be alive, that it was either you or her. Besides, Sue wouldn't want you to be all mopey because she saved you. She'd want you to go out there and live life to its fullest." He placed an index finger under her chin and raised her face so she could look up into his eyes. "You understand what I'm saying? I mean it, all of it."

She sniffed and wiped her eyes with the back of her jacket, then sniffed a second time. "Yes, I hear you. But it's…"

"I know; you don't have to say it." He turned and began to walk after Jimmy and Mary. "Come on, let's catch up to the others. Oh, and you know what?"

"What?" she asked softly.

"It was bad enough we lost Sue, but at least we didn't lose you, too."

She managed a brief smile. "Thanks, Henry. I really mean it."

"I know you do."

Carrying their bundles of gear, they began walking side by side, while ahead of them, Mary and Jimmy's voice filtered back as they continued to bicker.

Later that day, when everyone was relaxing and gathering their thoughts, Henry snuck off to be alone.

Realizing how dirty he was, he decided to take a shower, but he wasn't under the hot spray for more than a minute before he felt his mental guard slip and grief well up inside him. His thoughts went back to the last time he'd been in the showers, Sue with him, the two making love.

Without realizing, and unable to control it, he began to shake, and though he didn't want to let go, he found it was hopeless.

Like a tidal wave of emotion was consuming him, Henry began to cry, deep, hitching sobs that shook him to his core.

The water cascaded over his face, washing away the tears, so that it was almost as if they were never there to begin with.

When he couldn't remain standing any longer, feeling weak, he turned and pressed his back against the wall, the hot spray now missing him entirely as it splattered onto the floor to swirl down the drain.

Without even knowing he was doing it, he dropped to the floor, his back sliding across the wall until he was sitting with legs spread out before him, hands limp in his lap. His head remained low, and his naked body still shook from his suffering.

He stayed that way for a very long time, sitting on the floor, until there were no more tears left to shed. He was there for so long that eventually, all the hot water was gone from the almost endless water tanks, only cold water spraying out of the shower nozzles.

The next morning, after eating a quick meal taken from their supplies, the four companions gathered on the center dais in the matter transfer room, their gear piled up alongside them. Once more, Mary had read through the manuals, and she had found that the controls were pretty much the same as at Area 51. She'd learned that where there were more of the matter transfer units throughout America, they were all operated the same way. Of course, it was all supposition on her part. For all she knew, there had only been two units made operable, one in Nevada and the one in Alaska. No matter how many manuals she searched through, there had been no list of other units that might have been active.

"What'll happen if we're sent back to Area 51 and there's nothing there but a radioactive hole in the ground from the meltdown?" Jimmy asked, always the positive one in the group. "We might end up materializing in the middle of a nuclear inferno or some shit."

Mary bit her lip in thought on that one and had finally replied, "I would think there's some kind of redundancy that would send us right back here, that is, if this is the only unit left working."

Cindy had spoken up then. "So we have no idea where we're going to end up?"

Henry had nodded. "Yes, that's pretty much the gist of it. It's either that or try and figure out how to make our way back to the mainland on our own." He was feeling better after letting out his grief the previous night. There was still a deep hole in his heart, but his emotions were under control again.

"Oh, hell no," Jimmy said. "I've had enough cold weather to last me a lifetime. I say let's go for it."

Henry looked at his three friends, one at a time. "Well, are we still all on board with this?"

No one changed their mind, despite broaching some reservations.

Henry nodded to Mary, who was standing by the consoles for the unit. "Okay, Mary, whenever you're ready, let's go."

Nodding, she looked down at the buttons and knobs, and while biting her lip again, unsure even though she'd read the manual more than once, she pressed the buttons that should activate the sequence.

Not waiting to see if she did it correctly, she jogged over to the dais and joined the others. Everyone was sitting down, and she also dropped down.

For a few tense moments nothing happened, only a soft humming from within the machinery hidden behind the wall of the room.

Jimmy was about to open his mouth and say something sarcastic when a thick mist began to form across the floor, and everyone's hair began to rise up on its own, a clear sign of a static electricity charge filling the room. Jimmy quickly shut up.

Henry reached out instinctively to his side, his hand going out to find Sue's hand, so that they could hold each other as they jumped, but he pulled it back as fast as he began to move it, realizing there was no one there to touch. A pang of grief flooded his body as he once more realized she was gone forever.

It was going to take him a long time to fully recover from her loss, a long time of expecting to turn around and see her standing there, smiling at him, waves of love literally coming off her whenever he saw her.

But he'd gotten past his late wife Emily's death, and if he could do that, he knew he could one day be okay with Sue being gone. He would never be one hundred percent, he knew that, and accepted that the pain of her loss would always be with him, but he also knew he'd be better than he was now. All he could do was take one day at a time. But Christ, it was going to be hard right now, when the pain was so fresh, the loss so palpable.

"Okay, here we go again," Mary said from beside Jimmy. Electrical lightning began to shoot up all around them, and everyone had looks of fear on their faces.

"We can do this," Henry said. "Just stay calm."

"Stay calm, the old man tells us," Jimmy muttered. "Easy for him, when more than half his life is already over. I'm still young. I've got a shit load of time left."

"Shut up, Jimmy," Cindy said, annoyed.

"What? Why?"

"Jimmy," Mary added, "Please, for just once, will you shut up?"

"Oh great, not you, too." Jimmy frowned, then began to pout. "Everyone's against me."

Cindy took his hand in hers and smiled. She kissed the back of his hand. "Now, lover, you know that's not true at all. We all love you."

Jimmy's face turned beet red as he lowered his head in an 'Aw shucks, I didn't mean nothin'' look.

Henry watched the women banter with Jimmy, and despite his sadness over Sue, he actually smiled. Mary saw him smile when she glanced over at him. She reached out her hand for him to take.

He did, the two holding hands. Jimmy and Cindy were holding hands as well, and Mary reached out and took Jimmy's free hand with her other, then Cindy took Henry's free hand, so that they sat together in a circle, each holding on to the other.

The way families would do, giving comfort and support to the ones they loved.

The mist grew thicker, the electrical lightning more powerful, and as the humming of the machinery grew even louder, Henry felt his consciousness slipping away.

His last image before he fell into an oblivion that he didn't know he would ever wake up from, was the faces of his friends, no, take that back, he thought. The faces of his family.

Though Sue was gone, he wasn't alone, he still had people who loved him, who would do anything for him, even die, and he would do the same in return.

And sometimes, even when the entire world was shit, and each day was a battle to survive, sometimes, that was all a man needed to keep going.

With those last comforting thoughts floating through his mind, Henry Watson's head slumped down to his chest, and he closed his eyes.

Epilogue

Major Ishmael Varakov had always been a survivor.

Ever since he was born, he had fought against the odds.

One time, when he was five, he'd become lost in the forest of Katyn, twelve miles from where he lived in the small village of Smolensk. His family had gone to visit relatives and had stopped to take a break on a dirt road that led through the forest.

Ishmael had always been a curious boy and had sat by the road, playing with his toys; the carved, wooden shapes of soldiers his father had made for his birthday.

Though told to stay close, he had seen something in the woods, and like any small child, had become fascinated by it. Wandering off, he'd been lost for more than two days before he was found.

What was odd was that when the family found the boy, after getting other volunteers to join in the search as well, Ishmael had been healthy, not starving at all, which one would expect when finding a small child after two days lost in a harsh forest. But the boy had eaten when he'd become hungry, and the front of his shirt, covered in dried blood, was a testament to his resourcefulness.

Weeks before, when his father had brought home game to clean for supper after hunting, Ishmael had watched how his father had stripped the carcass, and what to eat and what to toss away, so when the boy had become hungry to the point he wanted to cry, he had stalked a rabbit and caught it in its own warren. Ishmael had eaten the rabbit raw, as he had no weapons but his teeth. He'd been the talk of the entire village after that.

Major Ishmael Varakov hadn't changed that much from the small boy he once was when he grew to adulthood, and as he floated down the rushing river, barely conscious, the water having snapped him back to wakefulness, he fought with the same determination that he had back when he was a child.

Though his arms felt like lead weights, he forced them to do his bidding. Reaching out, he pulled a stray, floating leather pack from one of the lost horses to him. Thus remaining afloat, he began to kick until he overcame the current and reached the side of the river. By the time he managed to catch onto something that stopped his momentum with failing strength, he was more than two miles away from where he'd fallen into the water. With one hand on an outcropping of rock, and one on the pack, he slowly pulled himself halfway out of the water, and then once he'd done that, he finished the job, until only his feet were submerged.

Exhausted to the point of collapse, bleeding from multiple wounds, he swung his legs out of the water and onto dry land. He laid there for more than an hour, just concentrating on breathing. He thought he heard a vehicle motor once over the rushing water, but it came and went so fast he assumed he'd imagined it.

Struggling with the pack's buckles, he finally opened it, and though no weapons were inside, there were other supplies he could use, including two pyrotabs to start a fire. Once he was warm and his clothes were drying, he could see about his wounds.

His leg was causing him great agony, and even as he lay on the ground, blood was seeping into the ice bordering the river, making a dark red circle under him. His shoulder bled as well but not as much, and now that he was out of the water, the wound had begun clotting on its own. His head wound was the least of his worries. Though he had a massive headache, after an inspection he was relieved to feel that the bullet had only grazed his skull, and out of all his wounds, that one was the mildest.

Shivering, he knew he needed to get moving or else he would die of hypothermia.

He was already making plans in his mind as he grabbed the pack and began to crawl away from the river.

How he would patch his wounds and then steal a horse or a vehicle, to then go back to the frozen Bering Strait and make the crossing alone. He knew he could do it, for the fire of hatred in his belly for the Americans who had caused him to fall so low needed to be quenched. Henry Watson and his people would be hunted all across America, and Major Ishmael Varakov would not stop until the man was weeping at his feet, nothing but a bloody mass of bleeding wounds and sores. Only then would Varakov kill Watson, slicing his throat from ear to ear, and then still only after he'd killed each of the man's friends before Henry's eyes. Oh yes, Varakov would create new ways of torture for Henry Watson and his people, ones where death never came, only more suffering and pain.

He began walking slowly, limping heavily, leaving small drops of blood in the snow behind him, a clear trail if anyone was following him. There was nothing he could do about it. He needed to get out of the valley, where the land and its surroundings hadn't been soaked in water; only then could he find kindling to make a fire.

It took more than four hours of walking before he made it out of the valley, only his lust for vengeance keeping him moving, and he knew even that fire of rage burning within couldn't help him go on for much longer. He would need to make a fire before nightfall or he would certainly die.

Ahead was a rock face that would shield him from the wind on one side. That would be where he would make his camp. For also near the rocks were small trees and shrubs, the area around them on the ground covered with sticks and branches that had broken off in past storms. This he could use to make his fire. Closing his eyes, he imagined sitting by the flickering flames, the heat coming off the fire suffusing his body, healing him, wrapping him in its warm embrace.

He trudged onward for a few minutes with his eyes closed, for he knew where he was going and there was nothing in his path to trip him, only the wide-open tundra on all sides, the valley far behind him.

A low growl came from up ahead, and it caused him to snap open his eyes. He stopped walking the moment he saw what was waiting for him.

Unknown to him as he'd moved towards the rock face, a pack of five wolves had come from around it, seeing the lone man, and sniffing the blood leaking from his leg wound on the wind.

Before Varakov could do anything to defend himself, which wasn't much, the wolves surrounded him, their heads low to the ground, their mouths dripping saliva.

Many things happened simultaneously in that moment; all occurring so fast they were like one incident, blended together in time.

Varakov, seeing he was about to be attacked, reached down and pulled out his only remaining weapon; his sword. But he was slow and weak, and his drawing of the blade was clumsy. In fact, his fingers were so numb he barely managed to pull the sword from its sheathe before it fell from numb fingers to stick point down in the dirt. He looked at the sword stupidly, knowing he needed to grab it, for it was his only chance of survival. If he could kill one or two of the beasts, perhaps the others would decide he wasn't worth the fight and retreat. And then he would have fresh meat, and the hide of the killed wolf could be dressed and cleaned so that he would have a new coat. Once more, the tricks he'd learned as a boy, watching his father clean a kill, would be his salvation.

But as the sword fell to the snow to become stuck, one of the wolves was already lunging at him, and Varakov's outstretched arm suddenly found that it had a wolf attached to it. Ishmael Varakov yelled long and loud, the teeth of the wolf gripping so tight that they cracked the bones in his arm.

His training as a soldier came to the front of his mind, and no sooner did he yell than he clamped his mouth shut. Remaining stoic. A Russian soldier showed no fear to the enemy. Be it man or beast.

Still amazingly on his feet, he tried to punch the wolf, but to no avail. As he went to swing his fist, a second wolf attached itself to that arm, teeth clamping down like a vise. Varakov, unable to support himself with two adult wolves on his arms, went to his knees, his leg bleeding even harder now that he was putting more pressure on it. Smelling the fresh blood from his bleeding arms and leg wound, the wolves went mad with hunger, for though they'd been eating well, they were almost always hungry, and had acquired a taste for human flesh over the past week.

On his knees, helpless, as the two wolves chewed on his arms, the alpha of the pack moved closer, so close that Varakov could smell the carrion on its breath.

The remaining two wolves circled him as well, looking for their chance to dart in and begin to feed.

Varakov wasn't giving up just yet, and as he knelt before the alpha wolf, his mind was whirling with how he would escape, to live on to seek his revenge on the Americans. A Russian soldier of the Soviet Party never gave up, never surrendered.

The alpha wolf was much larger than the others. Gray, with a black streak going down the center of its skull, the fur matted and missing in places, where scars were visible, one ear missing, the wound looking new, though Varakov saw none of this. All he saw were the sharp teeth as the alpha opened its jaws wide, saw the gleam of no mercy in its dark eyes.

"Come on, you bastard. I am not afraid of you. What are you waiting for?" Varakov hissed in Russian, defiant to the end.

As if the words were the cue for the alpha to attack, the wolf snapped its head forward, its sharp teeth locking onto Varakov's throat, tearing and rending at his neck.

Varakov refused to scream at first, holding to his stoicism to him like a shield, but no matter what he might think he was, in the end, he was still human, and even a Russian soldier could only take so much pain.

The last two wolves darted in, knowing once the alpha began to feed, that they too, could now join in. Each one picked a leg, teeth tearing into the warm flesh, until all the wolves were ripping the limbs from the human torso.

Major Ishmael Varakov of the Soviet Army, born in the small village of Smolensk in Russia, finally began to scream.

If another living soul had been on the tundra to hear, they would have found that the screams lasted much longer than anyone would have expected, but then, what else would one expect from a stoic Russian soldier?

But eventually, the screams stopped, to be replaced with the sounds of feeding.